'This first novel of a planned trilogy is stylish, taut and compelling and a film adaptation is in the pipeline. With characters you can't help sympathising with against your better judgement, Sigurðardóttir takes the reader on a breathtaking ride' *Daily Express*

'The seamy side of Iceland is uncovered in this lively and original debut as divorcee Sonja finds herself coerced into drug trafficking while her banker girlfriend Agla fends off a criminal investigation in the aftermath of the financial crash. Tense, edgy and delivering more than a few unexpected twists and turns' *The Times* Crime Club Star Pick

'A tense thriller with a highly unusual plot and interesting characters' *The Times*

'The Nordic crime wave just keeps coming ... The eponymous "snare" here is a hydra-headed monster ... Sigurðardóttir avoids inviting easy sympathy for any of her characters, even the beleaguered Sonia, but she keeps us reading' *Guardian*

'The intricate plot is breathtakingly original, with many twists and turns you never see coming. Thriller of the year' *New York Journal of Books*

'This rattlingly good read could only be improved if this were the first in a trilogy. And it is!' *Strong Words*

'Terrific and original stuff, with some keen-sighted and depressing reflections on Iceland's place in the world' European Literature Network

'The Icelandic author and playwright Lilja Sigurðardóttir delivers a sparkling firework of a novel, tightly plotted, fast-paced, and crackling with tension, surprises and vibrancy ... If the first glamorous instalment of the Reykjavík trilogy is just a starter, then I cannot wait for the rest of feast to be finally available in English, to be devoured by English readers' Crime Review

'Fast-paced and pulse-racing, *Snare* is a novel that will capture your attention completely as you race to the finish' Swirl and Thread

'This novel is full of tension and a brilliant cast of characters full of fiendish malice' Chillers, Killers & Thrillers

'*Snare* by Lilja Sigurðardóttir is a fast-paced, heart-pounding ride that takes you into the depths of Reykjavík's underbelly' Bloomin' Brilliant Books

'Written in fairly short chapters, *Snare* is an incredibly pacey book, in which the translation effortlessly carries you from one person's perspective to another. Highly recommended' Live and Deadly

'Full of suspense and intrigue, this crime story about love and revenge had me hooked from start to finish' Novel Deelights

'Sigurðardóttir perfectly balances the darkness of the crime world against the lightness of love and loyalty, and I was engrossed in the layers of storytelling that she perfectly weaves' Beverley Has Read

'A sharp-edged suspense thriller with a healthy dose of Scandinavian Noir to take it to another level' Always Trust in Books

'I felt her fears, her longings, her love, her desperation... none of which could have happened without Lilja Sigurðardóttir's prodigious writing style' Rambling Lisa's Book Blog

'Astounding writing!! An excellent addition to the Scandi Noir genre, packed with tension, suspense and a crime story that gets under your skin!' The Quiet Knitter

'There is risk on every page and DANGER lurks around every corner and screamed out at me ... If you are looking for a stunning crime novel that delivers on many levels, then *Snare* is a five-star read' The Last Word Book Review

'*Snare* is an exceptionally good thriller translated into pacey and urgent English language by Quentin Bates ... edge-of-the-seat stuff' Words Shortlist

'*Snare* was a highly original and tense read that I flew through. It gripped me immediately and caught me in its own unique snare. I read it in one breathless sitting ... it's outstanding' Novel Gossip

'It has you sitting there literally on the edge of your seat, uncertain if you're brave enough to turn the next page ... Superb writing, storytelling and a bright new star in Lilja Sigurðardóttir' Books Are my Cwtches

'It's unique, chilling, tense and full of suspense. A real page-turner' It's All About the Books

'It is daring storytelling with a fresh feel to it. Reading this book is a risk worth taking' Nordic Noir

'This book would make a fantastic film/TV series and I love the cover. Go dip your toes in the icy waters of Nordic Noir – you won't be disappointed!' Bibliophile Book Club

'Sigurðardóttir's prose is truly a treat and gave life to the text ... I loved how the author was able to take a regular occurrence and make it thrilling, especially having Sonja handle the situation like a boss!' Clues and Reviews

'On finishing the all-important last sentence on the last page, I was left with two overriding feelings; firstly, I must know what happens next, and secondly, this book is absolutely screaming to be made into a movie' Nic Perrins

Trap

ABOUT THE AUTHOR

Icelandic crime writer Lilja Sigurðardóttir was born in the town of Akranes in 1972 and was raised in Mexico, Sweden, Spain and Iceland. An award-winning playwright and a screenwriter for TV, Lilja has written six crime novels, with *Snare*, the first in a new series, hitting bestseller lists worldwide. The film rights have been bought by Palomar Pictures in California. She lives in Reykjavík with her partner.

Follow Lilja on Twitter *@lilja1972* and on her website: *www. liljawriter.com*.

ABOUT THE TRANSLATOR

Quentin Bates escaped English suburbia as a teenager, jumping at the chance of a gap year working in Iceland. For a variety of reasons, the gap year stretched to become a gap decade, during which time he went native in the north of Iceland, acquiring a new language, a new profession as a seaman and a family, before decamping en masse for England. He worked as a truck driver, teacher, netmaker and trawlerman at various times before falling into journalism largely by accident. He is the author of a series of crime novels set in present-day Iceland (*Frozen Out, Cold Steal, Chilled to the Bone, Winterlude, Cold Comfort* and *Thin Ice*), which have been published worldwide. He is the translator of Ragnar Jónasson's Dark Iceland series, available from Orenda Books. Visit him at *www.graskeggur.com* or on Twitter *@graskeggur*.

Trap

Lilja Sigurðardóttir

Translated by Quentin Bates

**ORENDA
BOOKS**

Orenda Books
16 Carson Road
West Dulwich
London SE21 8HU
www.orendabooks.co.uk

First published in Icelandic as *Netið* by Forlagid in 2016
First published in English by Orenda Books in 2018
Copyright © Lilja Sigurðardóttir, 2016
English translation copyright © Quentin Bates, 2018
Map copyright © Martin Lubikowski

ISBN 978-1-912374-35-9
eISBN 978-1-912374-36-6

The publication of this translation has been made
possible through the financial support of

📖 ICELANDIC LITERATURE CENTER

Typeset in Garamond by MacGuru Ltd

For sales and distribution, please contact
info@orendabooks.co.uk or visit *www.orendabooks.co.uk.*

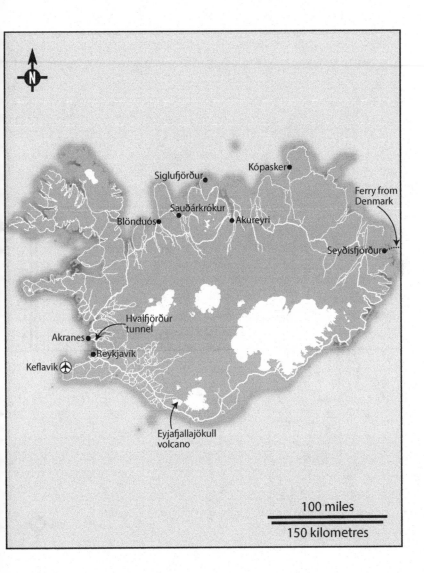

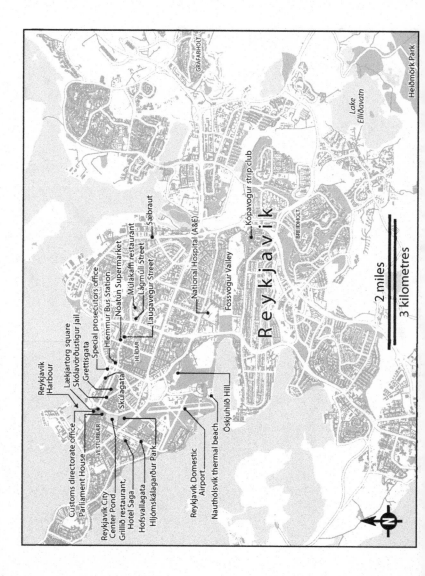

Reykjavik Harbour
Lækjartorg square
Skólavörðustígur jail
Grettisgata
Special prosecutor's office
Hlemmur Bus Station
Nóatún Supermarket
Múlakaffi restaurant
Lágmúli Street
Laugavegur Street
Sæbraut

Customs directorate office
Parliament House
Reykjavik City Center Pond
Grilið restaurant, Hotel Saga
Hofsvallagata
Hljómskálagarður Park

VESTURBÆR

HLÍÐAR

National Hospital (A&E)

Fossvogur Valley

Kópavogur strip club

Reykjavik

BREIÐHOLT

GRAFARHOLT

Lake Elliðavatn

Heiðmörk Park

Reykjavik Domestic Airport
Nauthólsvík thermal beach
Öskjuhlíð Hill

2 miles

3 kilometres

N

Pronunciation guide

Atli Thór – Atli Thor
Austurvöllur – Oyst-uur-voet-luur
Bragi – Bra-gi
Breiðholt – Breith-holt
Davíð – Dav-ith
Dísa – Dee-sa
Eyjafjallajökull – Ey-ya-fyat-la-jeok-utl
Finnur – Fin-noor
Guðrún – Guth-ruun
Gunnarsdóttir – Gunnar-s-dottir
Hallgrímur – Hatl-griem-oor
Hljómskálagarður – Hl-yowm-scowl-a gar-thur
Húni Thór Gunnarsson – Hueni Thor Gunnar-son
Iðnó – Ith-no
Illugi Ævarsson – It-lugi Eye-var-son
Ingimar Magnússon – Ingi-marr Mag-noos-son
Jóhann – Yo-hann
Jói – Yo-ee
Jón Jónsson – Joen Joen-son
Jón Sigurðsson – Joen Sig-urth-son
José – As in Spanish
Kauphöllin – Koyp-hoet-lin
Keflavík – Kepla- viek
Kópasker – Keop-a-sker
Krummahólar – Krumma-hoel-ar
Lágmúli – Low-muel-ee
Laugardalur – Loy-gar-da-lur

Laugavegur – Loy-ga-vay-gur
Libbý – Libb-ee
Listhús – List-huus
Margeirsdóttir – Mar-gayr-s-dottir
María – Maria
Marteinn – Mar-tay-tn
Mjódd – Mjow-dd
Múlakaffi – Moola-café
Ólafur – Ow-laf-oor
Öskjuhlíð – Usk-yu-hlith
Reykjanesbraut – Reyk-ya-nes-broyt
Reykjavík – Reyk-ya-viek
Ríkharður Rúnarsson – Riek-harth-uur Ruenar-son
Thorgeir – Thor-geyr
Tómas – Teo-mas
Valdís – Val-dees

Icelandic has a couple of letters that don't exist in other European languages and that are not always easy to replicate. The letter ð is generally replaced with a d in English, but we have decided to use the Icelandic letter to remain closer to the original names. Its sound is closest to the hard *th* in English, as found in *th*us and ba*th*e.

Icelandic's letter þ is reproduced as *th*, as in *Th*orgeir, and is equivalent to a soft *th* in English, as in *th*ing or *th*ump.

The letter *r* is generally rolled hard with the tongue against the roof of the mouth.

In pronouncing Icelandic personal and place names, the emphasis is placed on the first syllable.

April 2011

1

Sonja was wrenched, shivering, from a deep sleep. She sat up in bed and looked at the thermometer on the air-conditioning unit; it was thirty degrees in the trailer. She had closed her eyes for an afternoon nap and fallen fast asleep while Tómas had gone to play with Duncan – a boy of a similar age who was staying in the next trailer. While she'd been snoozing, the sun had raised the temperature in their little space to thirty degrees, at which point the air-con had rumbled into action, blasting out ice-cold air.

Her dreams had been of pack ice drifting up to the shore alongside the trailer park, and however ridiculous the idea of sea ice off the coast of Florida might be, the dream had been so vivid that it took Sonja a few moments to shake off the image of grinding icebergs approaching the beach. While she knew the dream had been a fantasy and that the chill of the ice had in fact been the air-conditioning, it still left her uneasy. A dream of sea ice wasn't something that could bode well.

Sonja got off the bed, and as soon as she stepped on the floor, she stubbed a big toe on the loose board. This trailer was really starting to get on her nerves. But it didn't matter, because it was really time to move on. They had been here for three weeks, and that was already a dangerously long time. Tomorrow she would discreetly pack everything up and in the evening, without saying goodbye to any of the neighbours, and under cover of darkness, they would drive away in the old rattletrap she had paid for in cash. She had coughed up a month's rent in advance, so the trailer's owner wouldn't lose out.

This time, she and Tómas would travel northwards to Georgia and find a place there to rent for a week or two; and then they'd move on again – to some other location, where they would stay, but then depart before they'd put down any roots. They would leave before they could be noticed, before Adam could track them down. Adam who was Tómas's father; Adam who was her former husband; Adam the drug dealer. Adam the slave driver.

One day, once they had travelled far enough and hidden their tracks well enough for Sonja finally to feel secure, they would settle down. It would be in a quiet spot, maybe in the US, or maybe somewhere else. In fact, it didn't particularly matter where the place was, as long as it was somewhere they could disappear into the crowd, where she wouldn't constantly have to glance over her shoulder.

Sonja peered into the microwave – something that had become a habit. Inside, giving her a sense of security by being where it should be, was the sandwich box full of cash. It was a white box with a blue lid, and was stuffed with the dollars and euros she had scraped together during the year that she had been caught in Adam's trap. This bundle of cash was her lifeline, in this new existence where she dared trust nobody. She had got herself a prepaid Walmart MoneyCard and had loaded it with enough to keep them afloat for a few months, but she had not dared apply for a normal credit card; she didn't want to risk Agla, with her access to the banking system, using it to track her movements.

Her heart lurched at the thought of Agla. The memory of the scent of her hair and the warmth of her skin under the bedclothes brought a lump to Sonja's throat that refused to be swallowed. The more time that passed since their parting, the harder she had to work to stop herself from calling her. Iceland was behind her, and that was the way it was. This was her and Tómas's new life, and she was fully aware that to begin with it would be a lonely one. But loneliness wasn't her biggest problem; a much weightier concern was their safety –Tómas's in particular. If she allowed herself the luxury of contacting Agla, there was every chance that Adam would sniff out their communication and use it to track her down.

Sonja opened the trailer door and sat down on the step. The air outside was hotter than inside the trailer and the afternoon sun cast long shadows from the trees across the bare earth at the centre of the cluster of trailers. Sonja took a deep breath of the outdoor air and tried to throw off the discomfort the dream had left her with. The old, toothless guy opposite stood over his barbecue, which sent up plumes of smoke as the fire took; Duncan's mother sat in a camp chair outside the trailer next door, listening to the radio. There was a peace to the place, but it would soon come to an end, broken by the noise of traffic and horns on the freeway as people began the commute home from work.

Duncan came out of his trailer at a run, along with the basketball that he dribbled everywhere. He half crouched over the ball, and Sonja smiled to herself. She and Tómas had seen that his weird dribbling technique didn't affect his accuracy when he shot for the basket. His skill at basketball was unbelievable, and after a few days playing together, his interest had infected Tómas as well.

Tómas...

'Duncan! Where's Tómas?' she called, and the boy twisted in the air, dropped the ball through the basket fixed to the trunk of a palm tree and, when his feet were back on the ground, shrugged.

'Where is Tómas?' she repeated.

'I don't know,' Duncan said, still dribbling the ball. 'He went down to the beach just now, but then some guys came looking for him.'

'Guys? What guys?' In one bound Sonja was at Duncan's side.

He finally let the ball drop from his hands. 'Just guys,' Duncan said. 'Just some guys.'

'Tell me, Duncan. Where did they go?'

Duncan pointed towards the woods that lay between the trailer park and the beach.

'What's up?' Duncan's mother called from her camp chair, but Sonja didn't give herself time to reply.

She sprinted towards the beach, her mind racing. The vision of ice on the shore, the groaning of the floes as the waves grounded them on the beach and the chill that the white layer brought with it clouded her thoughts as if the dream were becoming a reality. She cursed herself for not having bought the gun she had seen in the flea market at the weekend.

It's never good for an Icelander to dream of sea ice, she thought. That means a hard spring to come, and ice brings bears.

2

Tómas jumped from stone to half-buried stone at the edge of the woods, where they formed steps rising up a slope and finishing in the sand at the top of the beach. He was barefoot as he had left his sandals at Duncan's place. But that didn't matter; the sand on the beach was soft underfoot, and he could collect his sandals on the way back, before his mother could find out that he had taken them off.

He was only going to pick up a few shells – preferably the black ones, which were the rarest and also the best. Most of the shells on this beach were yellow, brown or a rust red, but there were the occasional black shells and those were the ones he needed for what he was making. It was a suggestion his mother had made. She said it was something she had done as a child, and by the time the cigar box was almost covered, Tómas could see that it was going to be impressive. The box had come from the old guy who lived opposite and Tómas was going to use it to store football pictures. And then his mother had suggested that he should cover it with shells, so Tómas had spent three evenings gluing them in a pattern to the outside of the box. Now he needed just one more row of black shells to finish the job. There was no doubt in his mind that this was going to be the finest box in the entire world in which to keep football pictures.

The tide was high, leaving the beach so narrow that it would be difficult to find any shells now. He would have to come back once the sea had receded. Tómas dug his toes into the sand, his attention now on the entrance to an ants' nest. There were no ants in Iceland, so this was something new to him, something he found fascinating. The ants' nest was nothing more than a hole in the ground, but dozens of ants marched to and fro in perfectly ordered single file. They were so intent on what they were doing that it had to be something very special – some kind of ant construction project, perhaps. Tómas picked up a stick and pushed it into the hole, in the hope of reaching all the way down to the nest, but it seemed to be deeper down than he had thought. The ants were alarmed, and for a few moments rushed around in all directions. But they were unbelievably quick to regain their usual discipline, and set about repairing the damage done to the entrance to their nest.

'Tómas!'

He glanced up from the ants' nest, looking for whoever had called his name from the other set of steps down to the beach, on the car park side. There were two men waving happily to him. What did they want? He walked hesitatingly towards them, stopping a good way short of where they stood. They looked like they could be Mexicans, and Duncan said those were people you had to be careful of. Tómas didn't know why – there were no Mexicans in Iceland and nobody had told him just why they were so dubious.

'What?' he called to the men, who both smiled amiably. They didn't look dangerous. One of them sat down on a rock and the other walked away towards a car.

'You want to buy a puppy?' the man sitting on the rock asked. So they were salesmen. Florida was full of people selling stuff, and a lot of them were Mexicans.

'I already have a dog,' Tómas replied, his curiosity piqued.

'Where is it, then?' The man asked, raising one eyebrow.

Tómas shook his head. 'He's at home in Iceland,' he said. 'But one dog is enough. My mother wouldn't let me have another one. We're just here for a long holiday.'

At least, that was what he hoped he was saying. His English was pretty good by now, but he still occasionally used the wrong words, which made Duncan laugh.

But this man didn't laugh. 'Well,' he said and sighed, 'I don't know what to do with the puppy back there in the car. I guess I'll just have to drown him.'

'No!' Tómas yelped, stepping closer.

'What do you think I should do with him?' The man asked. 'Do you know anyone who would take him?'

'Is he big?' Tómas asked.

'No. Tiny. Pretty much new-born.'

Tómas's heart ached. Maybe he could take the puppy and he and his mother could look after it for a few days while they looked for a home for it. Surely she wouldn't be angry if he came home with a new-born puppy he had saved from drowning?

'Won't you take a look at him?' The man said, getting to his feet. 'He's over here in the car.'

The man walked away and Tómas followed him over the sand dune and into the car park, even though he was already starting to feel guilty because Teddy the dog had been left behind in Iceland and he hadn't seen him for such a long time. The other man was sitting in the driver's seat, smoking. Tómas was furious that he should be smoking near a new-born puppy. Everyone knew that smoke was unhealthy.

But as the first man opened the car's rear door, he froze as the realisation dawned on him.

'You called me Tómas,' he said, looking at the man. 'How do you know my name?'

3

Agla woke up with such a sharp pain in her chest, she was convinced she was having a heart attack.

She rolled onto her front, fighting for breath, and realised that she was in the middle of the living-room floor. By her side was a rum bottle that had tipped over, leaking dark liquid into the silk Turkish carpet. She took some deep breaths, but the pain did not relent – it was now spreading in waves to her belly. This wasn't a heart attack – this was pure sorrow. She had dreamed of Sonja.

Agla crawled on all fours to the sofa and hauled herself onto it. Could it really all be over? Could Sonja have genuinely vanished from the face of the earth? Could it really be true that she would never touch her naked skin again, fold her arms around her, see the spark of life that appeared in her eyes every time she smiled?

Agla looked around the living room. The curtains were drawn and the room was in semi-darkness, even though, according to the clock, it was past midday. She remembered practically nothing of the previous evening, except that she had sat in the car outside Sonja's place for a long while, in a bizarre attempt to feel closer to her. The rest of the evening was lost in a haze. Her eyes stopped at the bag of coke on the table. Next to it were two lines that were ready to be snorted, and the glass tabletop was scattered with more, so she must have spent a few hours there. She should get those two lines inside her, take a shower and get on with doing something useful. Two lines would give her the energy for that. She would be cheerful and optimistic, bursting with self-confidence, and maybe in the right frame of mind to meet her defence lawyer; perhaps even to buy some groceries and have a proper meal. That was the joy of coke – it changed not just the way you felt, but your general outlook, making you believe that everything would work out for the best. Agla leaned forwards, rolled a five-thousand-krónur note into a tube and snorted the first line.

But as the hot buzz flowed through her veins, disappointment flooded through her body. The pain in her heart didn't give way, instead it grew as her heartbeat galloped, and she suddenly felt as if she had already been locked in a cell, alone and isolated, and she began to sweat. There was no point talking to the lawyer – new ideas now would change nothing. It was too late. Her heart was threatening to burst out of her chest, and she longed to howl; to scream and yell and break things.

But she did none of these things. Exhaustion overwhelmed her, so complete that she could no longer move. Then she began to feel nauseous and despite being bathed in sweat, shivered as if she were chilled. That damned cocaine had just made things worse; she had clearly been overdoing it recently.

Agla felt herself rise out of her body, up to the living-room ceiling, from where she looked down on herself, sitting in a singlet and ripped tights, with mascara smudged down both cheeks and her hair like a badly made haystack. It seemed so unreal, so unlikely that this wretched vision of a person could be her, that for a moment she felt she had travelled back in time, was once again a hopeful young woman, and was looking at her future self, asking in fear and astonishment just what had gone so badly wrong.

As Agla returned to herself, the pain in her heart took over. She was petrified: the reality was that it was all over – she was on her way to prison, convicted of market manipulation, and Sonja had fled the country. There was every chance she would never see her again. She had lost the only thing that had made her life bearable since the financial crisis. Although she had known from the moment of that very first kiss that this sweet, burning passion of theirs was something temporary, the fact that it was over was more painful than she could ever have imagined. The tears streamed down her cheeks and her heart seemed ready either to burst out of her chest once more, or to break inside her.

4

This time the beach seemed unbelievably long, and the sand was soft beneath her feet, so that she sank into it with every step. The effort to move was painful when she wasn't making the progress she wanted. It was almost like her recurring nightmare, in which she ran and ran but stayed in the same spot.

The beach was deserted, or at least this section of it, between the rocks, was empty, but in the car park on the other side there was a car – she could just see its roof over the dune. But while instinct told her that was where Tómas was, something else insisted that wasn't the way she should be going. She pumped her feet against the soft sand and pushed forwards until she finally reached the steps up to the car park that overlooked the dune, her lungs now burning with exertion. She lost her footing in the sand, but instead of slowing down she used her hands as well and scrambled up the steps on all fours until she got to the top and rose again to her feet. She jogged, panting, to the car. As she approached, a door opened and a man stepped out.

'Is my son here?' she called, just as she saw Tómas sitting in the car.

She didn't hesitate; she went straight for the man. Although she was petite and had no hope of overpowering such a heavily built guy, she had to try; every nerve in her body demanded it. She crashed into him with all her strength, shoulder first, and managed to knock him off balance for a moment. He teetered and stepped back to regain his balance, at the same moment holding Sonja fast in his grip. Then he turned her nimbly around without letting go of her wrists. As she was spun it felt like a dance. But this dance, in a car park in Florida, was deadly serious – lethal even – and she knew it had to be linked to her past in Iceland.

The man, who had a Mexican look about him, tied her hands behind her back with tape, placed a hand on her head, just like a policeman, and then pushed her into the car. Wanting to show some resistance, Sonja struggled, but she really wanted to be there in the car where Tómas was – she *needed* to be with him. She dropped into the seat next to her weeping boy. His arms were taped behind his back, just like hers, and a piece of tape had been put over his mouth, but Sonja could still see his lips moving to form the word *Mum*.

Mum, his lips said through the tape and the tears streamed down his cheeks.

Sonja leaned over to him, put her head by his and shushed quietly. 'I'm with you, sweetheart. Mum's with you.'

She wanted to take him in her arms, but this would have to do, her head next to his for a moment, before the man reached into the car and hauled her back. He tore a strip of tape from a roll and made to tape her mouth shut.

'Please, don't...' was all she managed to say before the grey tape covered her mouth and all she could do was breathe through her nose.

5

The two men in the front of the car spoke to each other in Spanish, so Sonja couldn't understand their conversation. They seemed calm, which was good, she supposed. They weren't behaving as if they were crazy, but as if they were running an errand. The driver took a left turn down the track and parked across the entrance to the trailer park, then the one in the passenger seat jumped out. Sonja stretched to see where he was going. He jogged straight towards her trailer, slipped through the door and closed it behind him. What was he doing? Was he looking for cash? Was there something else he was searching for? And how had he known which was their trailer? She shuddered at the thought that these two men must certainly have been watching her and Tómas for some time.

Sonja mumbled into the tape, trying to get across the message that she had something to say. Maybe the driver would pull the tape off to find out what it was. She could tell them about the cash in the microwave, in return for letting her and Tómas go. But the driver half turned in his seat and hissed at her to be silent. The panic grew in Tómas's eyes and the tears began to flow down his cheeks again, so Sonja decided it was better to try and stay calm.

A moment later the other man loped out of the trailer and ran over to the car, stuffing something into his pocket. In his other hand was a white box with a blue lid: the money box. Maybe the microwave hadn't been the ideal hiding place after all.

'*Vamonos*,' the man said the moment he was in the passenger seat, and the tyres squealed as the driver spun the car around and took off towards the freeway.

Sonja leaned to one side and laid her cheek on Tómas's head. He was shaking with fear and she longed to wrap her arms around him and whisper comforting words in his ear, but the only thing she could do was be close to him so that he would get some comfort from her warmth, just as he had when he was a baby. Back then the place he wanted to sleep was on her belly, feeling her body heat and hearing her heartbeat.

Sonja did some breathing exercises. She filled her lungs with air, counted to four and exhaled. It relaxed her body and made it easier for her to take in enough oxygen through her nose alone. She would be of no use to Tómas if she were to have a panic attack and use up all her strength by thrashing about. She had to stay calm for his sake. All this was terrifying enough without him having to deal with her fear as well.

At the next junction they took the freeway, heading south. Sonja watched the signs as they passed them, trying to work out where they were heading. The whole thing was so unreal that if it hadn't been for the pain in her constricted arms she would have thought it was a dream, that it was just another lousy nightmare.

The men in the front stayed silent as the car hurtled along the freeway, past the endless woodland that covered the landscape like a thick suit of clothes, making the view monotonous. Compared to this, Iceland seemed almost naked, with no trees to be seen, and all its secrets unprotected. The only things that changed here were the signs; Sonja read them carefully without taking her cheek from Tómas's head. He seemed calmer now, if his breathing was anything to go by.

Then she saw the sign for Orlando International Airport and her heart lurched. If they were heading there, then they were being flown somewhere. Could someone be sending them back to Iceland? She watched anxiously as the airport signs became increasingly frequent, and when the car turned off the freeway at the last one, she sighed and felt a wave of disappointment mingled with relief.

All the worst things she had imagined throughout this bizarre journey left her: the insane serial killers, organ thieves and kidnappers all became less likely as the airport approached and reality came closer. Her old, miserable reality. When the car rolled into the airport car park and the door was wrenched open, all her suspicions were confirmed.

6

By the time Agla regained some normality, it was almost midnight and her face was swollen with grief. It had been years since she had cried like that. In fact, she couldn't remember how long ago it had been since she had last shed a tear. The strange combination of sorrow and the effects of the coke had stayed with her all afternoon, and she had alternated rambling through the apartment like a ghost with throwing herself onto the bed and howling into the pillow. Now, after a shower, she finally felt a little better and her thoughts were straightening themselves out. She applied some make-up, loosely brushed her hair, pulled on some trousers and a shirt, pushed her feet into some shoes, without bothering with socks, and put on her coat. The evening air outside was bitterly cold and the frost stung her skin, which was still tender from the shower. She wrapped her coat tightly around her. It was just as well the hotel was only a short walk away. A proper meal would cheer her up.

'The kitchen's closed,' the young man at reception said coldly. Agla had interrupted his computer game – she could see it was now paused on the screen in front of him.

'Don't you do room service?' she asked. 'Can't I order a meal from room service and eat it here?'

She waved a hand towards the sofa that occupied a corner of the lobby, but the young man shook his head.

'Room service is for guests in their rooms,' he said and grinned. 'That's why it's called room service.'

'Then I want a room,' Agla said, taking her wallet from her coat pocket.

'What?'

'Get me a room,' she repeated, fishing a credit card from her wallet and sliding it across the desk in front of the young man. 'If that's what it takes to get something to eat here.'

He took the card with a doubtful expression on his face. 'You're sure? You're going to take a room just so you can order room service?'

'That's right,' Agla confirmed. 'And you might as well take my order as well, since you're booking me in. I want the steak, medium rare, chips and a beer.'

She had hardly closed the room door behind her when the food arrived. She sat happily at the table, inhaling the scent as the waiter lifted the cover off the tray. The steak was overcooked, but she didn't feel like complaining. She was too hungry for that. She cut it into pieces and dipped each one in the cocktail sauce that had come with the chips, which made up for it being overdone. She reached for the remote and switched on the TV, not so much because she wanted to watch anything in particular, but more to get something out of having paid for a room to get a fairly average dinner.

On the way back down in the lift she took a five-thousand-krónur note from her wallet and, once she was downstairs, she slapped it on the reception desk. 'That was fine, thanks very much.'

The young man stood up behind his computer and watched as she walked out of the building. Agla was sure that there must be something sheepish about the expression on his face. It would have been easy enough for him to bend the rules, let her order room service and eat it in the corner of the lobby, but that would have taken him away from his computer game. He ought to be ashamed of himself, and she didn't make a habit of letting men get in her way with their little rules.

Back home, she felt more her usual self. Taking a deep breath, she summoned up the energy she needed to check out how things stood. She sat at the kitchen table with her laptop and logged into the AGK-Cayman statement page. Her lawyer, Elvar, had told her that now that the investigation was complete the special prosecutor's office would no longer be monitoring her phone and computer. With the long delays between the investigation, the court proceedings and when a sentence would eventually be handed down, she had in fact been free to work on her investments for a few weeks; she'd simply not had the energy to face the situation. Now it was time to take the Caymans money in hand. That crap never seemed to do anything but lose value, though. Letting it drop endlessly wasn't really an option, although it wasn't easy to see what other choice she had. Realistically, it was little short of a miracle these days if you let your money look after itself and didn't lose any of it. But that was far from good enough for her. She would have to get busy and find a way to make more. But the whole process with the special prosecutor had given her self-confidence a beating. All the same, she couldn't deny that things had turned out better than she could have expected. Of course she would be spending time in prison – Elvar's guess was that she would get more than a year inside – and then, of course, there were the legal costs and all that stuff. But in truth the prosecutor's office had hardly even scratched the surface. They were sure they had scored a goal, but had actually never managed to ask the right questions. If they had they would have seen the real state of affairs. And that was bad. She owed a lot of money and needed the investments to do much, much better.

Agla scowled as she scanned the statement. If AGK-Cayman looked bad, then there was every chance the other funds would be much the same. She had the feeling that this was like walking into a burned-out house. These were ruins, charred junk that hadn't been moved for months, and she didn't even have the spark of an idea as to how she could turn these funds around. This was going to be a battle. She was regretting looking at this now, so late in the evening; it would certainly keep her awake.

She closed the laptop, and as soon as she stood up she felt it. She had heard no sound; she had noticed no movement from the corner of her eye. Instead she sensed it as if the cells of her skin knew: she was not alone in the flat.

7

Adam opened the car door for Sonja as if she were a film star arriving at a premiere. But the smile playing across his face vanished when he saw that Tómas was tied up and that his mouth was taped over.

'You didn't have to tie up the boy!' he snapped at the two Mexicans, who immediately started to explain that he had fought like a tiger and there had been no choice.

Adam began to pick at the tape over Tómas's mouth, but the driver reached in front of him and pulled the tape off with a jerk. Tómas yelled at the sudden pain and Adam glared at the man, who laughed as if it was funny. Then he took out a pocket knife and crouched behind Tómas to cut the tape holding his wrists together. Tómas was still crying, but as soon as his hands were free he threw himself at his father and held on to him tightly.

The driver then cut the tape around Sonja's arms and went to help her with the tape over her mouth. She swatted him away and picked at the tape herself; it seemed to have taken root. As she pulled at it, the thought occurred to her to take to her heels, run from this car park and search for someone who might help her and take her to the police, where she could have these men charged with kidnapping. But that was an idea that was best forgotten. Adam would be out of the country before long and when all was said and done, legally he still had custody of Tómas. She was the one who was in the wrong. She was the one who was the real kidnapper. As she struggled to remove the tape from her face, the Mexican who had been in the passenger seat took two little blue books from his pocket and handed them to Adam: he had taken their passports from the trailer. Her stash of money was just a bonus. Adam shook the two men's hands as they left, and asked them to give Mr José his kindest regards. With that, Sonja understood. She had met Mr José in London a few months before – an encounter she would have preferred to forget. As far as Sonja could make out, Adam was working for Mr José, who had eyes and ears in the States, of course, just as he undoubtedly had his hooks in people all over the world.

As the Mexicans drove away, Adam sighed and smiled. 'Sonja, Sonja, Sonja,' he said, shaking his head. 'Who's been acting the fool, then?'

He stroked Tómas's head, and Tómas looked up at him in confusion. Reality seemed to be gradually catching up with him. Sonja could almost see his mind trying to understand the mess that the day's turmoil had created.

'You have a choice,' Adam said. 'The first option is that you come home to Iceland with me and Tómas, and we start again where we left off. The other is that you say goodbye to both of us here and now. For good.'

8

Agla tiptoed towards the living-room door. The light had been bright in the kitchen, which made it difficult to make out anything in the dark living room; she stopped in the doorway and felt for the light switch. Now she was sure she could hear breathing, but then she told herself that it had to be her imagination and overstretched nerves playing games with her after all the coke and booze she'd consumed recently. But still, there was something that stopped her walking straight into the room; all her senses were screaming that there was someone there in the darkness; someone waiting for her.

She found the switch, expecting the room to be filled with a sudden brightness, but instead it was bathed in a faint, almost yellow glow. The dimmer was turned right down. But this half-light was enough for her to see him by – Ingimar. He sat in the armchair facing the door, relaxed, his legs spread wide and his hands resting on the arms of the chair. Agla ran a whole series of choice epithets through her mind; she had to exercise massive self-control in order not to let them all come tumbling out. She would far rather be meeting some anonymous burglar or a violent criminal than Ingimar.

'Good evening, Agla,' he said without moving, and without taking his eyes off her. She sighed and dropped onto the sofa facing him. It had to happen. She should have known that once the special prosecutor's investigation was over, there would be a knock at the door, a reminder of the debt; the big debt.

'How did you get in?' she said, shifting on the sofa and pulling out the cushion she had sat on. As she did so, she upset a beer bottle, which clattered over on the tabletop. It wasn't the most dignified response, but that didn't matter. What was essential was to look him in the eye and not flinch. She had to stop her gaze from flitting this way and that, not let him see the nervousness his appearance had triggered.

'I have my ways. It's unfortunate that when I knock on a door like any other visitor, people aren't inclined to let me in.' He paused, then said. 'We both know why I'm here.'

Agla nodded. She was completely aware of why, but she had expected that the reminder would be channelled through Jóhann. The last thing she had expected was that Ingimar would come straight to her.

'Your timing is spookily accurate,' she said. 'I was just this minute taking a look at how things stand.'

Ingimar smiled. He had a benevolent smile, but it vanished as quickly as it had appeared, and his face turned serious. Without a smile, he looked far from benevolent.

'I can imagine things look grim,' he said.

Agla agreed. 'Times are hard right now,' she said, 'as everyone knows. So patience is the key.'

'That's it: patience.' Ingimar smiled again.

Agla squirmed in her seat. The possibilities were flashing through her mind, as she tried to work out at lightning speed what the worst outcome could be and searched desperately for some kind of strategy.

'Couldn't we say that, with the situation as it is, there is no other option but to be patient?' she replied.

Ingimar shrugged his shoulders. 'You could say that,' he said. Then he leaned forwards in the chair, an intense look on his face. 'You're good at covering it up, Agla, but you know as well as I do that even if you three were to sell everything you have, it wouldn't cover the debt. All the stocks, the tangles of debt, everything you have is junk. And it'll be a long time before it'll be anything other than junk. Am I right?' As he dropped the question, he nodded as if agreeing with himself.

There was no point in arguing. Of course he could see what the situation was – Ingimar was no fool. He was probably as far from being a fool as any man could be.

'And although you're pretty sharp,' he continued, 'you'll need some kind of miracle to get these assets to produce any dividends.'

Agla didn't reply. He was right. She understood that, and now he knew that she did.

'But now you're free of the prosecutor,' he said, holding Agla's gaze, 'I have a proposal for you to reduce the debt, maybe even to become free of it.'

Agla didn't reply. Instead, she stood up, went to the kitchen and fetched two bottles of beer. She took her time opening them, then went back to the living room, handed one to Ingimar and sat back on the sofa with the other.

'Let's hear it,' she said.

9

Sonja did not say a word to Adam until they landed in Washington to catch their connecting flight. They walked through the airport in silence and boarded the Icelandic jet without saying a word to each other – not even when they went to a clothes shop at the airport to buy socks and trainers for Tómas. Adam occasionally muttered a few words to the boy. But he seemed to be gradually piecing together that the terror of that morning's road trip had been his father's doing: he stuck close to Sonja, holding her hand tightly and pulling away every time Adam tried to touch his head or speak to him. Once they were seated in the aircraft, he needed the toilet, and while he squeezed past his mother in the middle seat, he waited until his father had got up from his seat by the aisle.

'Be quick, sweetheart,' Adam said as Tómas stepped into the gangway, but as he spoke, Tómas spun around and aimed a kick at his father.

'I hate you!' he yelled. His clear voice carried through the cabin and the passengers who were busy forcing their hand baggage into the overhead lockers fell silent. Tómas rushed forwards and disappeared into the toilet, and Sonja watched Adam's face as his eyes followed his son. For a moment a look of deep hurt flashed across his features, before he leaned down, rubbed his shin and took his seat next to Sonja. She watched him fiddle with the screen in front of him as if nothing had happened, and wondered just how he had become so hard.

At one time, not all that long ago, they had been a young couple with baby Tómas, Adam was working at a brand-new job at the bank, and Sonja was looking after the home, making every effort to prepare wholesome, home-cooked meals for the family, and sophisticated dinners for when Adam invited colleagues home. They had laughed so much together – at each other and at Tómas, who had seemed sweeter by the day. And they had worked on their house in Akranes, the one they had bought just before Tómas was born, because prices there were low enough for them to be able to afford a large detached place. As she thought back, it was difficult to pinpoint exactly when things had begun to change. It had been a few years before the financial crash, just after Adam had joined the bank's management team, but Sonja was still not convinced that it was entirely due to his work.

Adam had been a jovial type, capable of bursts of laughter so infectious that everyone within earshot would also start to laugh with him; and he had had a habit of wrapping her in his arms and kissing the top of her head, which gave her a warm, secure feeling. But now he had become hard, although the anger that Sonja had always known burned inside him might well be quick to explode. It was as if his cold, hard shell had become thicker, but was simply a mantle of cooled lava over a volcanic fissure below. The gentleness and joy that he had shown before were both gone; and there was little doubt that she had played a part in that.

'How did you find us?' she asked.

Adam turned to her and grinned. 'Teddy the dog,' he said. 'Tómas sent me a Facebook message through the boy in the next trailer to you to ask how Teddy was.'

Sonja sighed. Of course, it hadn't been enough to ban Tómas from using the internet. He had been able to go online next door at Duncan's place. She should never have shown him how to use Facebook, but she had missed him so deeply, she had not been able to resist the poorly spelled, one-line messages he had sent her while he was at Adam's house.

She should have also known that Tómas would not be able to resist contacting his father. She should have paid more attention to him when he cried into the night, missing the dog so much. She simply hadn't realised how attached he had become to the animal, having only just got the dog. They should have moved on sooner, too. Staying in once place too long had been a bad idea.

'What's next?' she whispered.

'Amsterdam next week, and London the week after.'

'Two weeks in a row?' Sonja's mind whirled. There wasn't much time to prepare and previously there had been no more than two trips a month.

'No problem for you. There's always your customs guy.'

Adam ripped open the sachet containing the earphones and put them on, making it clear that this conversation was over.

Tómas returned, Adam stood up to let him past, and he climbed over Sonja to the window seat. Sonja waved down one of the stewardesses and asked for earphones for him and a blanket for her. The air-conditioning was a little too cool for someone wearing shorts.

10

Agla felt that she had only just closed her eyes when she heard the phone ringing. She cursed herself for not having switched it off and glanced at the clock; it was almost six in the morning. Ingimar had stayed until around two and afterwards she had lain awake, thinking over his proposal, but without reaching any conclusion. She reached for the phone. An unfamiliar number had appeared on the screen. It had to be some journalist – another one. For a second the thought had crossed her mind – or more accurately, her heart – that it might be Sonja, but that hope was quickly extinguished. Sonja had stopped calling a long time ago, and, quite apart from that, she would never call this early in the morning unless it was an emergency. Agla sat up in bed, her heart pounding. Perhaps it *was* Sonja, and she was in trouble.

She answered the phone. 'Hello?' she said.

'Agla...' It was Sonja's voice, but it sounded thin and tearful, as if she were wracked with sobs.

'Sonja? Is that you?'

There was no answer, but she could hear the background noise: the bustle of a crowd, and the echo of some kind of alarm bell.

'Sonja, my love, what's the matter? Is something wrong?'

Agla was on her feet and went over to the window, as if that would give her a stronger phone signal, to be sure not to lose this first contact from Sonja in such a long time.

'No, it's all right.' She heard Sonja clear her throat and sniff. 'I was wondering if you could pick me up from the airport. Something went wrong and my baggage is missing. And I don't have any money and the bus driver won't give me any credit—'

Agla interrupted. 'I'm coming, Sonja. Half an hour. Wait for me. I'm coming.'

She wasn't interested in explanations. It was enough that Sonja was waiting for her.

The shower was cold, but she stepped into it anyway. She just needed a quick wash that would wake her up. It worked, and as she towelled herself off, she felt more alert than she had been for a long time. Before the financial crash she had sometimes started her days like this – with the shock of an ice-cold shower. Back then she had needed to be up at six to keep up with her workload and to be able to weigh things up before the bank opened for business. That had been when she relished waking up in the mornings.

She snatched some underwear from a drawer; she had long given up folding it so there was the usual tangle, but she managed to find pants and a bra in almost the same colour, and socks instead of tights saved a moment or two. She opened the wardrobe where the choice was thinner than it had been. The pile of clothes waiting to go for dry cleaning was now a big one, but she hadn't had the energy to deal with it, so that left a few suits and a couple of odd jackets. Without too much time to think, she picked a Chanel trouser suit and a cream silk blouse. They were over the top for collecting someone from the airport this early in the morning, but she didn't want to look scruffy the first time Sonja saw her after such a long absence.

Precisely eighteen minutes after Sonja's call, Agla was in her car. She used the stops at red lights to apply her foundation. Her hair was almost acceptable and the perfume she sprayed over herself was Sonja's favourite. Fortunately, there was virtually no traffic, so she was quickly past the string of roundabouts around Hafnarfjörður, and at the traffic lights by the sports hall she used the waiting time to apply the finishing touches. As the urban sprawl and the aluminium factory were left behind, she put her foot down so hard that she was pressed back into the seat as if she were about to take off.

The Lexus was responsive and the road was dry, so the frost had left no ice on its surface. She'd be there in no time. Once the car was at 130kph she switched to cruise control so she could take her foot off the accelerator, holding the wheel steady with her knee so she could apply a little more mascara. That would have to do, although a touch of eyeliner would have helped. But the important thing was to be quick to get to Sonja, to show her that she was ready, that she was there for her.

Approaching the airport, she felt a knot of nerves in her belly. What should she say? How should she try to come across? They hadn't parted well last time. Sonja had said it was all over between them, but now she was calling and asking for her help in between sobs. What did that mean? Was it because she wanted to see her? Or was it because there was nobody else she could turn to?

At the airport car park gate she picked up a lipstick and as she put it to her lips, she noticed that her hands were shaking. The car had barely come to a halt when she picked Sonja out, shivering against the terminal wall; in shorts.

11

Agla's car had hardly stopped outside the terminal building before Sonja wrenched open the door and was inside.

'Thanks for coming to get me,' she said as she slammed the door shut behind her. Her words sounded dry and awkward to Agla, under such odd circumstances: the phone call punctuated by sobs earlier, and the way she was dressed in shorts and a T-shirt while the temperature outside was below zero.

'You waited outside like that?' Agla asked in astonishment. Those weren't the first words she had wanted to say, but somehow the question popped out of her mouth.

'No, I tried to figure out how long you would be, then waited in the toilets so people wouldn't stare. You said half an hour, so I reckoned it would be forty-five minutes.'

'And you didn't have a coat or anything...?' Agla asked, but Sonja stared straight ahead. There was a hard quality about her that Agla had not seen before. 'Where's Tómas?' she continued.

'With his father,' Sonja whispered, and curled into a ball in the passenger seat. Her mouth hung open and she shivered, but no sound came from her.

'Sonja, my love,' Agla said, pulling her into her arms.

Sonja offered no resistance but slipped into her embrace, putting her head on Agla's chest where she gave a weak, hoarse moan.

'What happened, my sweet?' Agla whispered into Sonja's tousled hair, an arm curled around her, feeling how cold she was. 'What happened?'

Shaken by sobs, Sonja lay in Agla's arms for a moment, before she pulled free and sat up straight. 'Let's go,' she said, wiping her face.

'What—?' Agla was about to protest.

'Drive,' Sonja interrupted.

Agla slid the car into drive and pulled away carefully, certain that Sonja was about to collapse again. She was ready to take her into her arms once more, half hoping that there would be more tears that would need soothing away. But now Sonja sat still and kept staring ahead, and the unsettling hardness had returned to her face.

They were still silent when the car turned onto Reykjanesbraut leading towards the city. Sonja had reached forwards, turned up the heater and switched on the heated seat, but her gaze was still focused on the distance ahead of her.

'I want to ask you one thing,' she said, finally breaking the silence.

'Anything you want,' Agla said, relieved that something had been said.

'Please don't ask me anything. Don't ask me what happened or why I've turned up in Iceland dressed like this, and all that. Just please don't ask me about it.'

'If that's what you want,' Agla agreed. 'I won't ask any questions.'

She sent Sonja a smile and then kept her eyes on the road ahead, her imagination taking over. The reasons for Sonja not being willing to explain what had happened to her meant that it had to be because of another woman. She must have been in a relationship with a woman who had thrown Sonja out, leaving her in shorts and a T-shirt, standing in the frost outside Keflavík airport. It had to be something along those lines. Agla felt the bile rise in her throat at the thought of Sonja with someone else and bit her tongue to keep back the avalanche of questions and accusations she wanted to unleash. Sonja had specified that she shouldn't ask, and if that was what was needed for her to be allowed out of the doghouse, then it was as well to do as she was told.

She could feel Sonja shivering next to her, so she reached for the heater control and turned it up even higher. 'You're still cold?' she said, placing a hand on Sonja's bare leg, as if she was checking to find out how cold it was.

To her surprise, Sonja placed her own hand on top of Agla's, keeping it on her leg. The palm that rested on the back of her hand was as cold as ice, but Agla could feel the heat start to rise from Sonja's leg, and the electricity, the sparks that never failed to fly when they touched, began to fizz and send little bolts of lightning into her heart.

She slowed down to eighty and the cruise control kept the speed there. She was going to drive as slowly as she could into town so this would last as long as possible.

12

'Tell me about it!' Sonja's neighbour said as she inspected her from top to toe. 'These airlines are always losing people's luggage.' She rummaged in a drawer and finally pulled out a bunch of keys. 'And did you have to travel into town dressed like that, you poor thing – in this cold snap?'

'I got a lift,' Sonja replied. 'In a warm car.'

'Thank God for that,' the neighbour said, holding out the keys almost reluctantly, as if she wanted to prolong the moment. Agla had done the same in the car outside – tried to hold onto her, hoping for explanations. Sonja reached out, plucked the keys from her neighbour's hand, smiled and turned on her heel. She could feel the woman's gaze on the back of her neck and could almost hear the questions that were already forming inside her head. Lost luggage probably wasn't quite a watertight enough explanation for her sudden and half-dressed reappearance.

Her concerns over the neighbour's opinion of her quickly evaporated as she opened the door to the apartment and the smell hit her in the face. They had left in such a hurry two months ago that she had not cleaned up first – she hadn't even taken out the garbage. She held her breath, walked straight through the apartment and opened the doors to the balcony to let fresh air into the place. She took deep breaths of the outside air, then hurried to the kitchen, took the garbage bag from the cupboard under the sink, and tied it smartly closed without wondering what was in there that had collected such a heavy layer of mould. When people went on holiday – a real holiday – they thought of things like that ... what they were going to come back to. But she hadn't really considered returning. That had been her plan C, or even plan D. In fact, plan D was never a plan, just ignominious defeat;

crash-landing into the old reality, with no cash saved up and mouldy garbage waiting for her.

She found a packet of joss sticks in the kitchen drawer, lit one and took it with her to the bathroom. She turned on the hot tap and water roared into the bathtub. The incense hid some of the sulphur smell of the hot water but couldn't quite compete. This smell, originating deep down in the island's geothermal underbelly, was something that she would get used to in a couple of days. It was strange that after only a short time away she could smell it again, and then stopped noticing it just as quickly when she got home.

Her tears began to flow freely as soon as she submerged herself in the hot water. Tómas's dismay as it dawned on him that he was expected to go with his father, the vindictive grin on Adam's face as he told her she could find her own way into town, and her own despair all now assailed her mercilessly. She was back at zero, back at square one, but even worse off than before. There was no chance now of easily negotiating access to Tómas with Adam. She would be lucky to see him at all. Life without Tómas was going to be almost unbearably empty.

What's more she was expected to travel to Amsterdam the following week and bring back a big shipment. That's the way it would be over the coming weeks and months, just as it had been during the months before she had made a run for it.

She sank deeper into the hot water, immersing herself completely. She held her breath until she felt that her lungs were about to burst, then exhaled underwater, sending a flurry of air bubbles to the surface. She waited for a moment in the complete silence, her mind on the border between consciousness and some kind of intangible reality. By the time she had hauled herself up, out of the water, and had filled her lungs again, she had a new plan; a new strategy to escape from the trap.

13

'Why's he doing that?' Tómas asked, his eyes darting in confusion from Sponge to Húni Thór and his father as they rocked with laughter. He had been playing with Teddy from the moment they arrived home from the airport that morning, and the dog had been obedient and delighted to see him, his tail wagging as he shared the breakfast his father prepared.

The doorbell rang and as soon as Rikki the Sponge and Húni Thór came in, the dog went wild. He jumped at Sponge, energetically rooting around him, not with delight as he had when Tómas had come home, but sniffing around him and pushing his nose into him. Then he froze, standing still and staring at Sponge, and occasionally barking and scratching at him. No matter how much Tómas tried to get him to come into his bedroom, the dog seemed mesmerised. It wasn't funny, Tómas thought, although his father and his two friends laughed and laughed as if this was the funniest thing in town.

'Maybe he's sick,' Tómas said, and a shadow of anxiety settled on his heart.

'He's not sick,' his father said, wiping a tear from the corner of his eye.

'Why are you laughing? It's not funny,' Tómas said, trying to pull the dog away from Sponge.

'Well, Tómas, I was wondering if we shouldn't call him Door Sniffer.'

They burst out laughing again – Sponge so hard that he had to hold on to one of the kitchen units to stop himself from collapsing onto the floor.

Tómas was furious. 'He's not called Door Sniffer! That's one of the Yule Lads!'

'Or we could call him Pointer?' Sponge suggested, still weak with laughter.

'Or Nosy?' Húni Thór added.

'Yeah, or Sherlock?'

'Stop it!' Tómas yelled. 'His name's Teddy! And I'm taking him with me to Mum when I go and live with her, because you keep laughing at him!'

His father's laughter ended abruptly. He took the ball that he had said the dog could only play with on special occasions, patted his leg and tugged at the lead, and Teddy caught the ball, magically losing interest in Sponge.

'Take him into your bedroom and let him play with the special ball,' his father said. 'The dog lives here. He's not going to your mother's place.'

'No, that's not a good idea,' Sponge added, his expression serious until he could no longer contain his laughter.

Tómas could hear them laughing in the kitchen as he shut his bedroom door behind him and threw the special ball for Teddy.

14

Agla was walking on air as she emerged from her car outside her house. The sky had shaken off the clouds and the sun shone through, and even though it was low in the sky, she felt this was a good omen. She didn't make a habit of thinking along such lines. She wasn't the superstitious type, unlike Sonja, who could see portents of all kinds of events everywhere. But Agla was happy and that chimed perfectly with the sun, which was making a valiant effort to climb into the sky. Ingimar's proposition the previous night now seemed less ridiculous than it had as she had lain awake after he'd left. It could even provide a way out of her predicament. It was as if the sunshine and Sonja had between them triggered a spark of hope inside her.

She plucked the newspapers from the post box, took them upstairs, dropped them on the table and made some coffee. While Sonja had been decidedly reserved when they parted, and in fact hadn't said much at all, at least she was back and had come to Agla for help. That had to mean something. And she hadn't pushed Agla's hand off her leg; instead she'd held it in place and absently stroked the back of it. That had to prove something. This had all been through her mind so many times over the years. From the moment they had first touched there had been a desire in her for Sonja that was more powerful than anything she had experienced before, but at the same time she had longed for some event that would bring their relationship to an end before anyone could find out about it. When it had ended – with Sonja's departure – she had experienced relief blended with pain; a greater anguish than she ever could have imagined. Now, though, she was certain what it was she wanted – even if the feeling remained that her desire was something shameful.

She took off her jacket, hung it over a chair and opened the first newspaper ... to see a picture of herself in handcuffs, being led into the special prosecutor's office. The newspapers seemed to get a perverse pleasure from using this same photo again and again, whenever there was an opportunity. It was as if this was the only picture of her they had. The pictures of Jóhann and Adam were considerably more tasteful. Jóhann looked to be striding along a street, respectable in an overcoat and with his tie knotted smartly and the bank's logo pasted in. It had to be an old photo, because in it he had a good deal more hair than he did now. Adam's picture was a passport photo. Agla avoided looking at it, determined not to let the sight of Adam and all the guilt that it summoned up spoil the joy of having seen Sonja again.

Although she knew well that Sonja and Adam's marriage had already been rocky by the time she appeared on the scene, she was still the one who was the homewrecker. And while Sonja had repeatedly told her that she was mistaken, this seemed to be Adam's take on things. The times they had met after the ruinous financial crisis, after the bank had collapsed, and after Adam had walked in on her and Sonja in bed together, she had never failed to see a look of furious accusation in his eyes.

Agla scanned the article devoted to the market manipulation case against her, Jóhann, and Davíð, one of Adam's staff, and she snorted with derision. The journalists had taken a report of one meeting at the bank, which they had found in the special prosecutor's documents, and represented it as some kind of key moment – the turning point when a conspiracy had been set in motion, sending money around the world and back again in order to buy shares in the bank itself to lift its share price. How little they knew, she thought, and how excited they got over something so trivial. It was such a small matter compared to the overall picture. It wasn't easy to imagine what the headlines would be if the media ever smelled the slightest whiff of the truth.

15

Agla remembered the meeting clearly. What the newspaper had reported was correct: Jóhann had brought out the champagne at the end of the meeting, and Adam had spent most of it laughing like a man possessed. But he had been coked up to the eyeballs and could hardly sit still. The rest of the article was complete rubbish, though. The money they were accused of handling had indeed already been on its round-the-world trip, but that wasn't what they had discussed.

'Fetch the dwarves,' Jóhann had ordered, and Davíð immediately got to his feet, went to his office and returned with the notebook. 'We'll divide it up between them,' Jóhann added, lighting a cigar and puffing out a cloud of smoke as Davíð began to read aloud which companies would have to share the burden of the majority of the bank's debts; these were the 'dwarves', their names derived from Norse mythology.

'Dvalin, Bofur, Bombur, Nóri, Onar, Mjothvithnir, Nali, Víli, Hannar, Austri, Vestri—'

'No. Not Vestri,' Jóhann broke in. 'I'll keep Vestri for myself. Because I'm from the west.'

Adam laughed loudly, and the boys dutifully laughed with him.

'Draupnir, Hor, Hlévang, Gloin,' Davíð continued. 'Yngvi, Eikin-skjaldi, Fjalar, Frosti, Finn and Lofar.'

'Excellent!' Jóhann said with deep satisfaction, dropping his cigar into his coffee cup. Agla knew he found smoking during meetings a particular pleasure, probably because smoking in the building was completely outlawed. Nobody else dared bring tobacco in, let alone light it up.

'There are two ways to straighten out the finances, my children. You either increase revenue or reduce the debt. That's basic household bookkeeping.'

With the words *household bookkeeping* he sent Agla a roguish glance and the boys laughed. No meeting was worth having without making at least one joke at her expense. She didn't care. They needed it to bolster their self-confidence, to convince themselves that they were better, cleverer and smarter than anyone else, and it didn't worry her that she was used as the butt of the occasional joke. Jóhann had a knack of keeping on top of their weak points. They were young and greedy, and used so much aftershave that it was sometimes difficult to breathe during meetings with them. Without question, every one of them would have laid down his life for Jóhann.

'You'll work with the loans department to transfer it all, and make sure it all goes smoothly, won't you?' Jóhann whispered to her as he eased the cork out of the first champagne bottle with a small pop. He poured several glasses and handed them around.

'Cheers!' he thundered, grinning broadly. 'Here's to a positive outlook for the bank in the quarterly report!'

16

Sonja was busy. Now that she had formed a plan in her mind, she could not relax until she started working on it. She had taken out all the garbage, emptied the laundry basket into the washing machine, opened all the windows and burned one joss stick after another until the smell in the apartment was bearable.

Now she searched through the wardrobe for something she could wear. Most of her everyday clothes, jeans and T-shirts, had been left behind in the trailer in Florida, but there were three sets of better clothes in the wardrobe, the clothes she wore for overseas trips. The reality was that these were a costume, an outer shell that projected the persona of a woman who could hardly have been more dissimilar to her real self – someone who had never finished college and had drifted into the security of marriage without too much thought; who was passing herself off as a corporate suit, an educated and determined woman with a business career; a woman with vision, a woman who knew what she wanted. She had even gone so far as to establish a fake company, SG Software, as her cover. It provided the reasons for her frequent trips overseas and was a way of laundering the proceeds of what she brought into the country.

She selected some black trousers, then took a jacket that was part of a grey suit and put it on over a black T-shirt. She put a touch of powder on her cheeks and a little make-up around her eyes, then wound a grey scarf round her neck and put on the silver earrings Agla had given her such a long time ago. The image looking back at her from the mirror looked convincing and smart, but discreetly so.

She stopped at a filling station on Bústaðavegur, overlooking the Fossvogur valley, which was usually thought of as one of Reykjavík's greenest spots, but was now bare, with the trees leafless, still in their deep winter sleep. Her mind went back to Florida for a moment – to the year-long greenery it had taken her only a few weeks to take for granted.

She entered the station and bought two pay-as-you-go SIM cards. One went into her old mobile phone and the other into the phone she had bought for Tómas, but which Adam had handed back, saying that the boy was too young to have it. These were the numbers she would use for anything to do with bringing in merchandise. After a while she would dispose of these and replace them with other anonymous, untraceable numbers. That was how it worked. It was laziness and inattention to this kind of detail that resulted in people being caught out. But she wasn't someone who got the details wrong.

As she approached it, Thorgeir's house looked very different from the last time she had been here. Back then there had been a Christmas party in full swing and an animated reindeer festooned with lights had stood outside. Now the grass was stiff with frost, and the whole district was quiet, the suburb's inhabitants all at work at this time of the afternoon. The house showed no signs of life. But after she had rung the bell three times with no response and was about to try the door handle, the door opened and Thorgeir peered out. He was dressed in slippers and a checked dressing gown, and his hair was scruffily awry. He had the look of an old man and Sonja had the sudden feeling that the dressing gown and slippers suited his lined face better than the tailored suits he normally wore.

'You,' he said, looking her up and down with little interest. 'What do you want?'

'A proposition for you,' Sonja replied.

Thorgeir stood aside without replying, indicating that she could come in. She followed him along the corridor, past the kitchen and into the living room. The curtains were drawn across the long picture window, so the room was dark apart from the glow of a single lamp.

'You're sitting here in the dark,' she said. It wasn't a question; it was a statement directed at the wretched figure he presented.

'Yeah. I've been out of the loop since I was arrested. They haven't spoken to me since I was released from custody,' he said. 'And they got themselves another lawyer while I spend my time here like a condemned man. And that fucking mouthy bastard Rikki the Sponge is back in with them.'

'Hmm.' Sonja raised an eyebrow as she looked around for somewhere to sit. Thorgeir swept a pile of clothes off the leather sofa and waved her towards it.

'Why's Rikki called Sponge?' she asked pleasantly, as if trying to make conversation over an awkward cup of coffee.

'You mean you don't know?'

'No. It's only recently I found out they call him Sponge.'

'Then I'm certainly not the one to explain it to you,' Thorgeir snorted as he dropped into an armchair, on top of the clothes and the pizza box that already occupied it.

'Fair enough,' Sonja said and leaned forwards to make sure she had eye contact with him. It wasn't easy, as he constantly looked aside and his gaze flitted around the room as if he was following butterflies.

Coming down off the coke, Sonja thought to herself, deciding that wouldn't do any harm. At least it was going to be better than having him pumped up with self-important arrogance.

'We could work together, the two of us,' she said, trying hard to make her voice sound friendly as she spoke to this man who she hated so deeply. He had been Adam's ally; together they'd tricked her, so she had no doubt that a large portion of the misery she had recently endured could be laid at Thorgeir's door. But now she had to replace hatred with pragmatism.

'I can't get free of Adam,' she said, tensely conscious of the risk she was taking in revealing her thoughts to Thorgeir. 'So my only option is to find some kind of hold over him. And for that to happen I need to be a more important link in the chain.'

Thorgeir's tiny, narrowed eyes stopped moving for a moment and he stared at a point above her head while he thought.

'You want to stamp out the competition,' he said, looking into her face now and smiling. Sonja nodded and he laughed. 'Fucking hell, but you're a piece of work! Adam has no idea what kind of a fucking witch he's dealing with.' He paused, calculating. 'I'm in for a quarter of your take.'

'A quarter's too much,' Sonja said. In her mind she'd already established her negotiating position. 'Let's say a tenth. And if we're smart, we might be able to take out their new lawyer so you get your old job back.'

Thorgeir jumped to his feet and started pacing back and forth in front of her. From his face Sonja could tell he was thinking over his options. If he said no, she was in trouble – having now revealed her plans to him.

To her relief he replied in an upbeat, happy tone of voice. 'Add some merchandise on top of my share and we're talking.'

Sonja didn't hesitate. 'Done,' she said. It would be no problem to let him have a small amount of cocaine. She always diluted each shipment anyway.

'This cunt pushes a hard bargain,' Thorgeir laughed, extending a hand to shake on the deal, but she stood up without paying his outstretched hand any attention.

'My name's not cunt. My name's Sonja,' she said sharply.

'Okay, okay,' he said, his hands spread wide, and he laughed as he followed her to the front door.

She turned, looked into his eyes and waited. He seemed to have forgotten what they had just agreed a moment before. A hard comedown from coke, Sonja thought and pointed towards the telephone table by the door, where a notepad lay.

'Yeah, of course.' He opened the table drawer and rooted through it for something to write with. He finally found a pen and scrawled down a name, then ripped the sheet from the pad and handed it to her. 'I'll give you the other name when you've proved you keep your word.'

'The other one?' she said in surprise. 'You mean there's only two others who are importing?'

'Yeah,' Thorgeir said and laughed. 'How much coke do you think is needed in Iceland?'

'A lot,' Sonja said, still in a state of surprised shock. 'I thought there was plenty of demand.'

'There are a few big customers who get through a kilo or more a year, but most of them are just after a few grams. So there are no big amounts needed.'

Sonja took the piece of paper from his hand and turned on her heel. After the stale mustiness inside the house, the crisp, clean air outside was like a cool, refreshing drink. She took a few deep breaths and felt her body relax a little as the oxygen flowed through her veins. It was looking like executing her plan was going to be easier than she had expected.

17

As Bragi opened his eyes he sighed with happiness. Valdís had come home and he could feel her presence, even though she wasn't in the double bed with him, but in the hospital bed that had been set up in the living room. He could smell the ointment Amy used on her all the way through the house. The radio was turned low, playing a Viennese waltz, and he could hear the indistinct sound of Amy's voice as she talked to Valdís in a mixture of English and Icelandic while she tended to her.

This was the fourth day that she had spent at home and over these four days his satisfaction had increased dramatically. He had been making plans to bring her back home for a long time; it seemed remarkable to him that it was almost as much of a challenge to take someone out of a nursing home as it was to find them a place in one to begin with. His plan had worked out, though, almost exactly as he had intended it to. Since Sonja's disappearance, however, the money side of things had become a problem, but he was confident she would show up again – the ties that bound Icelanders to their homeland were strong.

In addition to that, she was such a unique specimen, with nerves of such steel and so practical in her approach that it had taken him a long time to figure out her methods. A person like her was of too much value to whoever was pulling the strings, they would hardly allow her to stay missing for long. It was a shame, he thought, as he had a certain sympathy for her; it was clear to him that she'd been acting under duress.

Bragi put on his dressing gown over his pyjamas and went into the living room. Valdís sat on the bed and Amy knelt in front of her, painting her toenails. He smiled. This was how he wanted her final stretch on Earth to be: secure and looked after by people who showed compassion and understanding, and a little spoiling wouldn't do any harm either. Valdís had spoiled him and the children for all those years.

'Good morning,' he said, planting a kiss on the top of Valdís's head.

Not long ago she had stopped speaking altogether, but she smiled a little and pointed at Amy, crouching in front of her.

'I know,' Bragi said. 'Amy really looks after you.'

Amy looked up and Valdís's smile broadened. This was as good as it could get. It was as sweet as he had imagined it would be.

In the kitchen he put some coffee on and dropped two slices of bread in the toaster, and then went back to the bedroom to check his uniform. He was on evening shifts now, so his mornings were relaxed. Before Valdís had come home, he would have spent every free morning on his feet, washing the car or pottering with something that needed to be fixed, but now he enjoyed just being at home, relished being able to relax. That was what Valdís had always done: helped him relax.

The doorbell rang, and he walked into the hall to open the front door. It was with huge surprise – having just been thinking about her, and wondering when she might show up again – that he saw Sonja standing outside.

'Hello Bragi,' she said with a small smile.

He looked her up and down for a moment, taken by how beautifully dressed she was, then, saying hello back, he stepped aside and beckoned her in. He shut the door to the living room, where Valdís and Amy were, and gestured that Sonja should go into the kitchen.

She took a seat at the kitchen table without a word, while he – equally silent – poured coffee into a cup and put it on the table along with a carton of milk. She splashed milk into her coffee, sipped, and then coughed.

'I could do with your shift timetable for the next month,' she said, looking up at him calmly.

He nodded, understanding. He took the printout that hung on the door of the fridge and handed it to her, not hesitating for a moment, even though it meant a betrayal of the values he had held dear throughout his customs career. There was another thing he held dearer: the promises he had made to Valdís and that he had made to himself when they first got married – that he would take care of her in sickness and in health.

Sonja studied the printout, nodded to herself, folded it and put it in her bag. Her hand came out of the bag holding a phone, which she handed to him.

'I'll send a heart if everything is all right, and an exclamation mark if anything has gone wrong and I can't make it. That way you'll know whether or not to expect me.'

'I'll see that anyway from the passenger list the Analysis team sends for each shift,' he said.

But she shook her head. 'Sometimes I pull out at the last minute,' she said. 'If I get a gut feeling that something's not right.'

'Very wise,' Bragi agreed, his own calmness taking him by surprise. Even though he was about to embark on a criminal career, that wasn't how it felt. 'I'll do the same and send an exclamation mark if you need to pull out,' he said. 'That's if the sniffer dogs are brought in unexpectedly or if Analysis is up to anything suspicious.'

He suddenly remembered the bread he had put in the toaster.

'Would you like some toast?' he asked.

'Yes, please. That would be nice.'

She sat in silence as he buttered the toast and cut slices of cheese, his thoughts unexpectedly going back to when his sons had been small and he had done the same for them.

He brought the breakfast over and they sat at opposite sides of the kitchen table and munched for a while without speaking.

'There's something else,' she said, as she swallowed her last piece. 'It would help if I could get rid of the competition. It's someone else bringing in gear for the same people. And what's good for me is good for you.'

'You have a name?'

'I do.'

She took a slip of paper from her bag and handed it to him. He read it, imprinted Axel Jónsson's name on his memory, screwed up the paper and tossed it into the kitchen sink.

'I'll check him out,' he said, and got to his feet.

'The same terms as before,' she said. 'You get what you want.'

Bragi grunted his agreement. He knew he could trust her. He had known that from the moment he had come home to find the envelope she had dropped though his letterbox; an envelope stuffed with cash and a hand-written apology.

'My wife has come home,' he said. 'She has advanced Alzheimer's. I want her to be here with me for the time she has left.'

She looked into his eyes and smiled quickly.

'That's beautiful,' she said. 'It's a wonderful thing to love someone so much.'

18

'You look cheerful,' Elvar, the defence lawyer, said, smiling happily.

Agla gave him a smile back and knew perfectly well what was going through his mind. She had been far from cheerful recently. A couple of times he had tried to cheer her up in an avuncular tone that, oddly enough, suited this young man surprisingly well. But it hadn't helped. She had stuck with the bottle and the powder, letting his words wash over her without taking the slightest notice. With hindsight, it was clear that he had been getting nervous at the prospect of defending her.

'Thanks. I'm feeling a lot brighter,' she said. 'Everything you've been doing looks good and you can go ahead and take on all the assistants you need for this.'

Elvar nodded. 'I've brought in an accountant to go over things with me, and it would be good to have one more person, mainly to prepare for the bank's damages case.'

Elvar's hand dropped onto the pile of documents on his desk so Agla could see just how much paperwork needed to be examined to prepare for the damages lawsuit.

'Don't worry too much about that,' she said. 'It needs minimal attention. The case will be dismissed by the county court.'

'What?' Elvar said and stared at her doubtfully.

'That's right,' Agla assured him. 'Put all your effort into my defence; the damages claim doesn't matter.'

She had no way of explaining it in any greater detail, as she had no idea herself how exactly the bank's former chief executive, Jóhann, was going to get the case thrown out. But it was a favour he had promised her, and she presumed he'd manage it through his various contacts.

'How do you know it'll be dismissed?' Elvar said. 'How...?' He seemed for a moment to be lost for words. 'How can you be so sure?'

'Let's just say that the elves made me a New Year's promise,' Agla said, and winked.

He stared at her, his face alive with questions, slowly fading into a semblance of disappointment. That was one of the things she liked so much about him: he never showed that he was judging her, he just showed disappointment. His expression was that of a parent who has realised, through the discovery that a pack of biscuits has been stolen from the corner shop, that their offspring has failed to inherit their own moral compass.

'I guess I don't want to know any more about this,' he said.

'No,' she replied. 'You don't.' She felt a brief pang of guilt, and wanted to do something to make amends, but the moment passed.

'It'll be fine, Elvar,' she said and watched as he seemed to sag in his chair, as if all the energy had been drawn from his young body, out through his smartly pressed clothes.

She felt sorry for him. He had been keen to take on her defence. It was every young lawyer's dream to defend a 'bankster', to get to grips with a big case, to carve a career around events that would go down in history. But when it came down to it, it was as if he had somehow decided that she was innocent, that justice was on her side and he simply needed to demonstrate that. Maybe it was because she was a woman. Maybe he had come to the conclusion that she was a victim in all this, that she had inadvertently managed to get caught up in the bank management's market manipulation, and that he could somehow save her.

But over the last few months, as the reality became clearer, it seemed that little by little his aspiration to see justice done had ebbed away. Agla sighed. It was tough being young, she thought. By the time her defence was ready, there would doubtless be little left of his lofty ideals.

19

There was a queue at Múlakaffi, even though it was almost one o'clock, but Sonja decided to put up with the wait. She was longing for a proper meal, and there was fried fish on today's menu: old-fashioned, fresh-caught fish fried in breadcrumbs with onions and potatoes, just like her mother had always made. The thought of her mother gave her a moment's heartache, but it passed quickly. She was used to directing her thoughts away from all the strife between them and concentrating on something else. It was disconcerting, though, that it was often food that, in some way or another, triggered thoughts of her mother.

She took a seat by the door and wondered if she would be able to finish the portion piled high on her plate. On any normal day the toast and cheese with Bragi would have kept her going into the afternoon, but this time the jet lag was catching up with her, and as she became tired it was as if her body cried out for extra fuel and her appetite doubled. The café was full of the tradesmen who habitually came for the solid food that would keep them going through a day of hard work. There was one other woman in the place, dressed in office clothes – presumably someone working for a company in the district. She toyed with the idea of what these people might be thinking about her. She was probably too smartly dressed for Múlakaffi. Normally she made an effort not to stand out too much from the crowd, not to be too notice-able, but this time she was too tired to worry about it.

She made short work of the fish, as she did so, making a mental list of everything she would need to do before next week's trip. She would need to book somewhere to stay in Amsterdam, buy a vacuum-packing machine online and use the PayPal account to pay for it all. That was a safer option than using a credit card, as the Icelandic authorities were still enforcing currency controls – most likely as a pretext for snooping into people's affairs – and there was always the chance that the purchase of a vacuum-packing machine in Amsterdam could attract attention. She would need to book flights, and the return one would have to be on a day when Bragi would be on duty. She would also need to get her sun-bleached hair freshened up; it paid dividends to look smart, as an unkempt appearance at customs was as good as asking for trouble. And she would have to get in touch with Adam, to let him have the new mobile number and to get the contact number for the pick-up in Amsterdam. She would try to talk to him about Tómas. She couldn't bear to be without Tómas for long. That would simply hurt too much.

20

The lunchtime rush hadn't begun as Agla walked tentatively into the changing room at the Laugardalur outdoor swimming baths. Decades had passed since she had last swum. It took her a while to work out how the metal disk the woman at reception had handed her fitted the locker door, and a helpful traveller showed her how it was done. The locks on the old lockers had been easier to deal with. It was just as well that little else had changed since her last visit: so she easily found the showers; she rolled up her towel and put it on the towel rack that was where it had always been and stood under the nearest shower.

A few nervous foreigners were taking showers behind curtains, which were also something new – the last time she had been here, the showers had been open. Although a few stalls had been fitted with these curtains, the clearly Icelandic women went straight to the open shower stalls they were used to. They were mainly older women, on their way back in from the pool and their morning gossip session in one of the hot tubs. Agla noticed that they all wore Speedo or Adidas swimsuits, so her rose-patterned one was clearly far behind the times. She wondered whether to wrap herself in her towel and go to reception to rent a costume, something dark blue or black – something less noticeable – but she decided against it. Going to reception with a problem was going to turn more heads than being seen on the poolside in a brightly coloured outfit. And she was here on an errand, not to attract any kind of attention.

She emerged from the changing room at the same moment as the former bank manager, Jóhann, appeared from the men's changing room. They nodded to each other and both headed outside, towards the hot tubs, neither of them having to wait for a signal from the other, but making their way, almost step for step, to the furthest hot tub from the building – the hottest one, which was somehow fitting to start with.

Agla struggled to get into the water, her feet numb with cold from the short walk along the ice-cold poolside, and she felt herself smart in the searingly hot water. Jóhann waded in as if he were used to it, bellowing and puffing. That was the way he did everything, with fuss and noise. Agla had found a seat and was just getting comfortable when Adam came along. He was as good-looking without clothes as he was in them – his body was lean and he carried himself well, as if he completely trusted his bare feet not to take a false step or slip on the ice that formed in the steam by the side of the pool. He stepped into the tub and walked down the steps and into the water without catching his breath or his expression changing, as if the temperature change had no effect on him.

He nodded to Jóhann and focused on Agla. 'Hello,' he said, checking out her body with such a piercing gaze that Agla could almost hear what he was thinking: *What does she have that I don't?*

Even if he had asked it out loud, she could not have given him an answer. She could have compiled a long list of Sonja's delightful attributes, but she still had no idea what it was that Sonja had seen in her. That remained a mystery.

This wasn't a comfortable place to be. She would have been happier not being so scantily dressed in front of Adam, but this was the only place she could think of that she could be certain neither of them could hide a microphone. Jóhann was notorious for the recordings that he used ruthlessly, both to get the better of business rivals and to keep his own staff in line. This was exactly the kind of affair in which it would pay not to take such risks.

'Ingimar came to see me,' she said. It was as well to get straight to the point. She would be boiled alive if she had to stay for long in this heat.

'What was that all about?' Jóhann snapped, just as Adam muttered, 'Shit.'

'You're toxic, Jóhann,' she replied. 'You're being investigated for the third time so there's nothing *you* can do for him.'

Jóhann hung his head and mumbled something unintelligible.

'And Adam has been giving him chickenfeed,' she continued.

'That's because I'm dealing with creditors who are just as tough as he is,' Adam hissed. 'We agreed that it was a priority to keep them sweet.' The veins in his neck bulged in anger and beneath the water's surface he clenched his fists as if he needed to use force to keep them from punching her face.

'Ingimar has a proposition,' Agla said. 'Something that could free us of some of the big debt – maybe even all of it if we play our cards right.'

She could almost see Adam's anger subside at her words. But Jóhann got straight to the point.

'What kind of proposition?' Jóhann asked and Agla toyed for a moment with the idea of telling him about the version she had thought over in response to Ingimar's proposal – to hear his thoughts on it. That had been the way they had done things when they had worked together, running ideas past each other, each considering the other's judgement. But she decided against it. It would be safer if she was the only one to know how the game would be played out.

'Ingimar suggests that I deal with his side of things and you two keep the special prosecutor off my back. Look after your own people.'

'You're already in the shit,' Adam said, and she could make out a grin, threatening to appear on his face.

'Yes and no,' Agla said. 'The investigation as far as my affairs are concerned is over – as long as I'm not caught up in any other cases. So

I only need to deal with one prosecution and one sentence in the next few years. Apart from that, I'm free.'

Adam caught Jóhann's eye. 'Fair enough,' he said after a pause. 'I don't know how you reckon you'll be able to do anything for Ingimar – anything that'll satisfy his people. It's not as if we're talking small potatoes here.'

Agla smiled. That was quite right. The money they had borrowed was no small change. In the original scenario everything had looked watertight, but the loan had turned out to be the killer. The gamble could have given the three of them a golden future, been wonderful for the bank and have left their creditors unharmed – if only it had worked out. But it hadn't, and they had all learned from bitter experience that the only thing more important than being careful who you lent money to was being careful who you borrowed it from.

'The less we know the better, I guess,' Jóhann said and Agla nodded.

She got to her feet. Her body felt heavy and drained of energy by the heat, as if the flesh were about to drop from her bones.

'If you fuck this up, Agla...' Adam said, speaking to her back.

She turned to look into his eyes. 'I don't fuck things up, Adam. I know who Ingimar is. I know what he's capable of. So fucking this up isn't on the agenda.'

Adam had nothing more to say, so she nodded to Jóhann, who was by now lobster-red and puffed in the heat, and steadied herself on the handrail as she left the tub, feeling faint as she felt the cold again.

21

Tómas followed his father into the bathroom and watched him hang up his swimming trunks and towel.

'Did you go swimming?' he asked in astonishment, feeling the disappointment grow in his belly. Going swimming was one of his favourite things and one of the few he genuinely enjoyed doing with his father. 'Why couldn't I come as well?'

'I just had a short meeting in the hot tub with people I needed to speak to,' his father replied.

Tómas stamped off into his bedroom, slamming the door behind him. 'You're lying!' he yelled. 'You don't have meetings at the swimming pool. You just don't want me to go with you because I went to Florida with Mum!'

He heard his father walk along the corridor and stop by his door, knocking softly before he opened it.

'I'm not angry with you because you went with her,' he said as he came in. 'I'm angry with your Mum. But that's not your fault.'

He stepped on a Lego brick and winced, then swept the bricks aside with his foot before sitting on the edge of Tómas's bed. He put out a hand and stroked his back, but Tómas shook him off. 'Don't be like that, Tómas,' his father said in an almost begging tone, but Tómas's anger erupted again.

'You let that horrible man tie us up!' he shouted, curling himself up in a corner of the bed, feet towards his father.

'No, Tómas! I asked them to go and get you. I had no idea they would tie you up. That's the truth, the complete truth...' He took hold of Tómas's feet and held them tight as Tómas's fury turned to helplessness. 'Tómas, I would never, ever, want anyone to tie you up.'

'And all my stuff that was left in the trailer?' Tómas sniffed. 'When do I get it back?'

'What stuff is it that you're missing so much?' his father asked.

'All sorts. My exercise books, the cigar box with the football pictures and my basketball. The best type of basketball. Duncan said so.'

'We can buy you a new basketball here, Tommi. That's no problem. And we can get exercise books in any bookshop.'

Dad clearly didn't understand. He didn't understand that some things are important, and of course he had never seen the cigar box and all the work that had gone into decorating it with shells. Mum was the one who understood that kind of thing.

Dad pulled him close and although Tómas tried to resist to begin with, there was something comforting about giving way and lying in his father's arms, feeling his hand pat his back rhythmically as he sobbed until his heart became calmer and everything seemed a little easier than before. All the same, he would have preferred to have been with Mum, and as he thought back to how they had left her at the airport, dressed in clothes for hot weather, the anger again swelled inside him.

'I want to go to Mum,' he said, wriggling out of his father's embrace. 'I want to go to Mum now.'

His father shook his head. 'We have to wait and see, Tómas,' he said. 'You have to understand that I can't trust your mother not to disappear with you again.'

'I don't understand anything!' Tómas yelled, jumping to his feet. 'You're just bad. I want to go to Mum!'

22

It had been a strange day, and that was putting it mildly. She felt that it had been an age ago when she had stood in a pair of shorts outside the airport terminal with no idea what to do next. Now her life seemed to be back on some kind of track, and although there might not be all that strong a chance that her plan would work out, at least she had one. That was the important thing.

Since her old life – her aimless, undefined existence – had crashed down around her, she had always tried to maintain some kind of goal. Bitter experience had taught her that, if she didn't set her own path, then others would do it for her – and she had already had enough of that. Although she was still embroiled in trouble, forced to do what Adam wanted her to, deep inside herself, she had set a course with a definite outcome – one which Adam would be far from happy with. It included her and Tómas secure in a little flat somewhere. It didn't matter where, as long as it was somewhere she would look forward to waking up in the mornings and where they could play and be silly, and she would be able to go to sleep with him every night without having to worry about his safety or wellbeing.

She had been running away for so long, fighting a desperate rear-guard action, constantly afraid of being swallowed whole by a world that she feared so much, and from which she could never completely tear herself free. It was as if every time she was sure she was about to escape the trap, she was again snared in its mesh, which held her even tighter than it had before. But now she was going to mark time. She was going to stop running. It was time to turn around, look fear in the face and swim back into the net. Somewhere in that tangle had to be the way out.

She had just arrived home and closed the door to her flat behind her, when there was a soft knock, and she knew it was Agla.

Hell, she thought to herself, knowing it was inevitable that she would invite her in, and they would find their way into bed. And in the time it took her to open the door, she put aside the decision she had made before she left for Florida: the decision to keep away from Agla. It was either her exhausted mind's fault, or else some need to give in to her urges – to admit to the spark of passion she had felt ignite again in the car on the way from the airport, when Agla had put her hand on her thigh.

As soon as Agla leaned forwards and hesitatingly kissed her, Sonja threw aside all the old disappointments and the arguments that had stemmed from secrets and jealousy, and passionately returned her embrace. Right now she needed Agla so much, needed her earnest-ness, her gratitude and those hot hands that would roam across her as only she knew how.

'You don't know how much I've missed you,' Agla whispered, kneel-ing in front of her, her trembling hands rolling up her shirt. 'I almost died, I missed you so much,' she said, burying her face between her breasts, too eager, too desperate, and sucking so hard that Sonja had to shush her to dampen her ardour.

'I missed you too, my sweet,' she whispered into Agla's hair, as always stiff to the touch with too much hair spray. 'I missed you too.'

23

'Who's the guy?' Agla whispered into the ear of the sleeping Sonja. She had slept like a log through the night and once she had woken had lain still, relishing the sound of Sonja's breathing, inching closer to her, to bask in the delightful warmth of her skin. But now she was in the mood to talk. A day ago, life had done a complete about-face, and it was a long time – before the financial crash in fact – since she had had such a feeling of optimism. Her mind was clear and cool and she had a detailed plan in mind of how to put Ingimar's proposition into practice. It was complicated and would mean some work, but it could be done. She had to admit to herself that it would even be fun. This kind of work was what sparked her imagination, tested her mind and boosted her self-confidence. She had not had to do anything that challenged her since before the crash – initially because, after it, everyone at the bank mistrusted her, and subsequently, when she had become a person of interest to the investigation, she had resigned to spare the new director having to fire her. But now things were looking brighter. Now she would have work to do. While the boys had shivered with fear in the hot tub at the mention of Ingimar's name, she was not frightened. Instead, it triggered tension, and tension had always been the fuel that she ran on best.

'What are you talking about?' Sonja mumbled, her eyes still closed.

'I was asking which of us is the guy...'

Sonja sighed deeply, turned to face Agla and the familiar look in her eyes meant she had something to tease her with.

'I'm the guy,' she said. 'I wear jeans more often than you do. You're more of a lipstick lesbian.'

'A what?'

'A lipstick lesbian.'

'What's that supposed to mean?'

'Count the amount of cosmetics in our bathrooms and you'll see which of us is the guy.'

'Isn't that just because I'm older? I didn't use so much make-up when I was young.'

'No, it's because you're the woman. So I'm the guy.'

'How do you know?' Agla asked. This had somehow taken her by surprise. 'How do you know which of us is the guy?'

'You can check our wardrobes as well,' Sonja said, getting out of bed and opening her wardrobe door. 'Compare this to yours and you don't have to even ask which of us is the guy.'

She left the room and Agla sat up in bed, taking in the sparse contents of Sonja's wardrobe. It was true that Sonja didn't have many clothes, but she had always ascribed that to the fact she was badly off. Her own wardrobe was undeniably better filled, even though half of the contents were in a pile on the floor, waiting to be taken to the dry cleaner's.

'There's nothing here,' Sonja called from the kitchen. 'No bread, no coffee, nothing.'

'How do you feel about breakfast in Luxembourg?' Agla asked, standing in the doorway.

'Yes, please,' Sonja said, closing the fridge and sniggering.

'I'm not kidding,' Agla said. 'I have to go there for work and it would be fun if you could come with me.' Sonja looked at her thoughtfully for a moment. 'It would be wonderful, Sonja, I promise. I'll call now and tell Jean-Claude to clean the flat and stock up the fridge...'

'What?' Sonja interrupted. 'Who is Jean-Claude? And what flat?'

'My flat. Jean-Claude lives downstairs and he cleans for me.'

'You have a flat in Luxembourg?' Sonja stared at her in disbelief. 'And maybe millions and trillions in bank accounts around the world? Is what the papers say about you true?'

'Well, not all of it,' Agla said awkwardly, and coughed.

'Christ,' Sonja said and shook her head, while Agla wondered if it was in surprise or disgust. Surprise, she hoped.

Agla went back to the bedroom and searched around for her clothes. Two buttons were missing from her silk blouse, casualties of the previous evening's passion. She straightened her hair with her fingers and went into the bathroom, where Sonja was washing her face.

'Come on. Come with me,' she beseeched. The thought of time

abroad with Sonja was irresistible, somewhere where nobody knew them, nobody would stare at them on the street, and nobody would care what they were doing together.

'I can't,' Sonja said. 'I have to work.'

'You're going back to the computer business? Is that what you need to do?'

'Yes,' Sonja said in a low voice and a shadow of a scowl passed across her face. 'That's what I need to do.'

Agla pulled her close and kissed her.

'You know...' she began, and wondered how to put what she wanted to say into the right words; '...that, well ... I can always help financially if you get bored with this work.'

Sonja pulled away. 'I know that, Agla,' she snapped, suddenly upset, seemingly close to anger. 'I can look after myself! As I've told you many times before.'

Agla put up her hands. 'Okay, okay. No need to be angry.' She wrapped her arms around Sonja and pressed her close. 'A whole weekend in Luxembourg. Just you and me,' she whispered and felt Sonja soften in her arms. 'The two of us, together.'

'You're different,' Sonja said, pushing her away and looking at her curiously. 'You're happier.'

Agla felt a warm flush. It was incredible how Sonja could read her feelings. 'It's ... well, let's say I've been offered a business opportunity that I'm happy with,' she said, hoping that Sonja wouldn't ask for any details.

'Bank stuff?'

'Yes. Bank stuff,' Agla said and smiled.

'It's good to see you happy.' Sonja slapped a blob of face cream onto her cheek and began working it in. 'But I can't go to Luxembourg with you.'

'I hardly dare say it, but if you're short of cash for the flight...'

'Hell ... Out, Agla,' Sonja barked at her. 'I've told you once already.'

24

Bragi was waiting with impatience when at last Atli Thór, his protégé and favourite colleague, came into the surveillance room and handed him the passenger list from the Analysis team. He took the sheets of paper and, trying to hide his excitement, he scanned it for a particular name – the one that Sonja had handed him on a creased slip of paper.

'Aren't you going to read it properly?' Atli Thór asked, before his attention became focused on the coffee machine. Not only had it run out of beans, but the drawer that took the coffee grounds was full, so getting a cup of coffee was an undertaking. 'What was wrong with the old coffee machine?' he sighed. 'This lousy bean-munching apparatus that shits coffee grounds just demands constant attention. It's a job and a half to get a dribble of coffee out of it.'

Bragi grinned at his bad temper. The new coffee machine was yet another example of modern life to which he made a point of paying no notice. He had no intention of learning how to work this piece of equipment, with its menu of options and the array of warning lights that always lit up every time someone wanted a cup of coffee. Ever since the old machine had been replaced Bragi simply made his own old-fashioned coffee at home and brought it to work in a thermos. With only a few months to go before retirement, it was hardly worth taking the time to learn how to use the new one.

While Atli Thór struggled manfully with the coffee machine, Bragi went through the list, but didn't see the name, not on his shift nor the next day's. But there was no reason to despair. It was impossible to tell how often this courier travelled, and although Sonja seemed to travel twice each month, there was no certainty that this other person did the same. Bragi plucked a pen from his shirt pocket and circled a few names at random.

'Searches?' Atli Thór asked and Bragi nodded.

'Just at random,' he said. 'We could just as easily take one in every twenty.' He was about to hand the list back when he noticed that there was another sheet he had not seen behind the ones he had been through. This was the list for the Greenland flight, which the Analysis team always sent to their colleagues there, already checked and marked. For some reason this list of passengers leaving the country had found its way to Bragi with the arrivals list, probably by pure coincidence; if there was any such thing as coincidence. There on the list was the name that had been on the slip of paper Sonja had handed him and which he had committed to memory: Axel Jónsson. As usual, the Greenland flight was not due to leave from the international airport at Keflavík, departing instead from Reykjavík's domestic airport, tomorrow morning.

25

Tómas felt his stomach ache as he walked home from school. It was as if there was a huge bruise inside his belly. It was as well that it was Thursday, because tomorrow would be Friday and after that was the weekend, and by Monday he hoped the curiosity of the other kids in the class would have faded away. They asked endlessly about Florida, and why he had been away so long and why his father had come to the school looking for him and yelled at the teacher. But Tómas had no answers to give them, and just muttered something unintelligible.

When he got home, he found his father on the steps outside, with Teddy on a lead.

'Are you going for a walk?'

'No,' his father answered. 'I have an errand to run.'

'Where? And why are you taking Teddy?' Tómas stared quizzically at his father, who looked awkward.

'I ... well, I'm going to let my friend have Teddy for a little while. Because he's so good at finding things.'

'Can I come too?' Tómas asked, dropping his school bag in the hall, ready to go.

'No, that's not possible,' his father said, setting off for the car and pulling the dog along with him. 'Dísa is indoors. She'll look after you.'

Tómas stared and felt the bruise inside his belly grow. Dísa was his father's girlfriend and she was all right, but he would still prefer to go with him and the dog.

'Why can't I come?' he wailed. 'You always leave me out!'

He saw his father shake his head as he made for the car, opened a rear door and Teddy jumped inside. He thought it was stupid that first his father went swimming and left him behind, and then he wanted to go for a drive with the dog, leaving him behind again. There were few things dearer to Tómas than swimming and the dog. This was deeply unfair.

'I'm going to go and live with Mum! And I'll take Teddy with me!' he yelled with all the energy he could muster after his father, who finally turned and took a few rapid steps back towards him.

'You're not going anywhere, Tómas! You understand that?' His face was close to Tómas's, so he could smell the coffee on his breath. 'Your mother is an unfit parent, so you'd better forget these daydreams once and for all,' he hissed, spun around and slammed the car door behind him.

For a moment Tómas felt as if his heart was going to stop beating. He had never before been afraid of his father. The car's wheels screeched as it pulled away. Tómas watched the wind ruffle the surface of the puddle on the pavement in front of the house, sniffing and wiping away the tears that ran down his cheeks. The bruise in his belly contracted and tightened into a ball. He would never speak to his father again. He was going to be silent and not say a single word to him from now on.

26

Bragi fiddled with the boarding pass in his hands while he looked around the departure lounge at Reykjavík's domestic airport. The little international lounge that served flights to Greenland and the Faroe Islands was securely separated from the arrivals hall for domestic flights, but the same security procedures took place here as at Keflavík, just on a smaller scale. It was like a tiny version of an airport terminal and Bragi was enjoying taking it all in. He remembered this building being extended – it didn't feel like it had been such a long time ago; but now it seemed tatty, with the original woodwork repeatedly painted over and the linoleum flooring worn down by the footsteps of too many travellers passing through. This was one of the few places he had not worked during his long career. He had worked in the postal division, at the ferry terminal on the east coast and at the Reykjavík docks, but the longest spell had been at Keflavík.

He watched passengers enter the departure lounge and paid attention to each of the men. A Fokker 50 didn't carry that many passengers, so he should be able to use a process of elimination to narrow the candidates down to Axel Jónsson. A group of Greenlanders were already there when he had arrived, apparently on their way home from a conference or some kind of event. Then there was a family that had checked in at the same time as he had – a young couple with two sturdy children; Bragi crossed them off his mental list. After them came three middle-aged women travelling together, followed by two couples who appeared to be from central Europe. Another group of Greenlanders came in, and behind them was a man on his own who immediately attracted Bragi's attention. He looked to be around thirty years old, dark haired, with three days' worth of stubble and wearing jeans and a leather jacket. As soon as he had passed the security check, the man went to the toilet and Bragi wondered if he should follow him to see if he was doing anything suspicious. But he decided against it; it was better to stay where he was to get a full overview of the passengers getting ready to board.

While people were still arriving in the departure lounge, Bragi moved to a less conspicuous position, conscious that he should not appear to be looking out for someone. There was no one-way mirror to hide behind now. A few minutes passed before the man Bragi had been waiting for arrived. He knew immediately that this had to be Axel Jónsson. He didn't need any confirmation, as instinct told him he was right – he was like a sniffer dog following a scent. The man was around forty, slim with neatly cut dark hair and freshly shaved. He wore sporty, good-quality clothes, as if he was on his way to a game of tennis or a round of golf. There was nothing suspicious about him, and that in itself was suspicious. Bragi sat on one of the plastic chairs and felt himself relax. Now he knew who he would be tailing.

27

'Then we're almost there,' the bank manager said, shaking his computer mouse as if trying to bring it back to life. The atmosphere of strict legality had departed along with the witnesses, leaving only the issue of adding the transaction to the bank's registration system. Agla sat back in her chair and admired the view below this modern, glass-walled financial fortress, looking down at the canal that was still as a mirror as it reflected the white-and-yellow three-storey buildings that rose straight up as if they had roots in the water.

'The vendor is Nóri and Avance is the purchaser,' the bank manager mumbled to himself, tapping at his keyboard with two index fingers. Agla knew him from her banking days. She had often used his services and found him to be exceptionally flexible, plus he had a talent for handling heavyweight customers with a real, luxurious, European flair. Lunch had been served at the office: oysters, champagne, and then Stilton in delicate chocolate shells was offered with the coffee that he spiced with a dash of fine cognac from the bottle in his desk drawer.

'The debt package is based on the basic investment,' he muttered to himself, ticking boxes on the screen. Then he looked at Agla. 'I'll enter a note to state that the chairman of Avance Investment's board will arrive later today. He can simply make himself known to the desk staff downstairs and they'll know what this is about.'

'That's wonderful,' Agla replied. 'Jean-Claude sends his kindest regards, but he's terribly busy today.'

That was a half-truth. Jean-Claude was certainly busy as Friday was the day for mopping the stairs and Agla had no wish for him to meet the bank manager. She was pretty sure that Jean-Claude's style would have been to knock back far too many oysters, turn his nose up at Stilton with chocolate, hold out his glass for more cognac and crack a few coarse jokes. It was better that he could come into the bank while the taxi waited outside with its engine running, sign on the dotted line and head straight for the door. She would be there to hurry after him and discreetly point out where his signature was wanted, as any efficient secretary would.

'We do our best to make business as smooth as possible for our customers,' the bank manager said.

Agla nodded in agreement. 'You certainly do that,' she said. 'It's always a particular pleasure to do business here.'

She admired the view beyond the window and it occurred to her that she had once dreamed of an office like this; a spacious, bright room with a view – maybe out to Reykjavík's slate-blue harbour. But by the time she had got what she wanted, she had been so overwhelmed by stress that she hadn't been able to appreciate it. That had been a few months before the financial crash, when the bank's share price was in free fall, lines of credit were closing one after another and every strategy they could come up with to the fix the situation, such as transferring more debt to the dwarves, were just short-term measures.

The bank manager pushed his reading glasses a little higher up his nose and continued to tick boxes on the registration form.

'LIBOR interest rates,' he muttered. 'And the usual Deutsche Bank fee, if I remember correctly?'

'Yes,' Agla replied. 'The same terms as usual.'

'And what industry sector should I enter for this transaction? Which sector did the initial investment come from?'

'Heavy industry,' she said. 'Aluminium.'

28

The approach to Nuuk was captivatingly beautiful. Bragi gazed at the town nestling by the jagged-edged fjord with its myriad hues of blue, from the cobalt of the sea to the grey-blue steel sheets on the roofs of the houses that looked like little toys from this height, and the light, almost luminescent, blue of the snow covering the ground.

For a moment the sad thought came to him that Valdís was unable to enjoy this with him. Such thoughts came to him more rarely now that he had accepted Valdís's situation, but on the occasions that they did, he felt a pain deep inside himself, as if a heavy rock in his chest was weighing down on his internal organs. He wasn't here to admire the view, however, so he shook off such sentimental thoughts and stretched out of his seat a little to check on the man who sat on the other side of the gangway, three rows ahead of him.

Axel Jónsson sat still, apparently asleep, with his head back against the seat. He clearly had no interest in the view over Nuuk. Other passengers leaned over their neighbours to see out of the windows, but not him. Bragi thought to himself that, if the man preferred not to see out because he might be afraid of flying, then one hand would be clasped around the armrest, but that wasn't the case. His hands lay idle in his lap, and from where he sat, Bragi could see no indication that he might be stressed. Maybe he was wrong about the man. Maybe it wasn't Axel Jónsson. Maybe the man was just an innocent traveller. Or perhaps this was the right man and he'd become used to the view of Nuuk having seen it so often. According to Bragi's thinking, that was exactly the way it was.

As the aircraft's doors opened and the bitter cold swept into the cabin, Bragi silently thanked Valdís for the woollen sweater he was wearing. It was the last one that she had knitted for him; the pattern had been taken from a book, as, once she had been taken ill, she had no longer worked from her own patterns. It wasn't the finest sweater she had made, but all the same, it was tightly knitted and thick, and here in the Arctic cold it would keep him warm. In a strange way, he felt that with this sweater on, he had Valdís's arms around him and there was more than just warmth to such an embrace.

The man Bragi was sure was Axel Jónsson stood up and took his bag from the overhead locker, while Bragi did the same. He had taken hand baggage with him, with little more than a toothbrush and a change of underwear. He didn't expect to spend long in Greenland. From the log of past passenger lists he had been able to get hold of, he had seen that Axel Jónsson usually spent one or two nights here. There was every chance that he would do the same this time.

29

Agla and Jean-Claude laughed all the way up the stairs to the first floor, where he lived.

'I'm never comfortable in a suit,' he said, and Agla patted his shoulder.

'Yes, but now you're the chairman of the board of Avance Investment,' she said. 'And turning up to sign documents in janitor's overalls won't do.'

Jean-Claude extended a hand and shook hers heartily.

'Let me know if there's anything else I can do for you. Nothing's too much trouble after everything you've done for me.'

Agla nodded. 'I appreciate your help,' she said.

It was quite true. He was her representative in Avance and another company she owned, plus he had signed for three of the dwarves in which the bank had its debts. On top of that, he looked after the flat for her, forwarded her mail and in fact made it possible for her to be a legal resident of Luxembourg. For a variety of reasons, that was a real convenience. It also helped that he had no concept of numbers; he had once commented that 'there are so many zeroes'.

Jean-Claude disappeared through the door to the janitor's flat, having already taken off his tie and loosened the neck of his shirt. Agla went up the stairs to the second floor and opened the door to her flat. For a second she closed her eyes and imagined Sonja running to her. She had bought Sonja's favourite perfume at the airport and sprayed it throughout the flat, so the mirage was strong and for a moment she almost believed her own fantasy. She could see Sonja, in a dress and heels, hair piled high, throwing her arms around her in welcome. Damned stupid. Agla opened her eyes and shook off her sentimentality. She had bought this flat a couple of years ago, shortly after she had first kissed Sonja, and somehow, stupidly, she had always had an image in her mind that she would someday be here with her. Even though she had never invited her here before, the high ceilings in the living room, with rosette mouldings around the light fittings, and the dark hardwood floors had seemed to her to be something that Sonja would like. So she couldn't deny she had chosen the apartment with her in mind. Left to herself, Agla would probably have chosen a more modern-looking home.

She punched Sonja's number into her phone, and was deeply relieved that she answered. But it didn't take long for Agla to sense that Sonja was not in the best of moods, and that it wouldn't be long before she said goodbye and ended the call.

'And how's the bank stuff going?' Sonja asked.

Although Agla knew the question was being asked out of courtesy, she decided to answer in some detail, if only to keep Sonja on the line. 'It's going well, but it's quite complex. It all revolves around billing a company in Iceland to get the payments past the currency restrictions,' Agla said.

'And I guess it isn't completely legal?' Sonja suggested.

Agla laughed. 'Don't be silly!' she said.

She would have liked for Sonja to be in a better mood, for her to give some indication of whether they were to meet again, and when.

'How long is this business going to keep you over there?' Sonja asked.

That was the hint, the clue. She wanted to know when Agla would be back so they could meet.

'I'm going to Paris on Monday and finish in London at the end of the week. That should wrap things up.'

'So this is something big?' Sonja asked, again as if this were a courtesy question to keep the conversation alive and not because she was particularly interested.

'Very big,' Agla said. 'The biggest deal I've been involved in.'

'That's good for you,' Sonja said, and Agla somehow detected a note of sarcasm in her voice. And suddenly this spacious flat felt too empty and too white. She walked to the window and looked out at the canal below. Two people were paddling a double kayak, but they seemed to be struggling to keep their strokes synchronised – the boat seemed to tip and tilt on the same spot without moving forwards.

'What are you suggesting?' she asked.

'Nothing. I'm not suggesting anything.'

Agla wanted to turn the conversation around, take it in a more personal direction, ask when they would next be able to see each other, but before she could do it, Sonja had somehow quickly ended the conversation and put down the phone.

30

It was just as well the Gulf Stream was there to keep Iceland warm. Without it, the island's winters would undoubtedly be more like those in Greenland. The cold had Bragi shivering, in spite of the woollen sweater, his coat and the thick scarf he had wrapped twice around his neck. It was hard to believe that Nuuk and Reykjavík were on the same latitude. The air was fresh and still, not the damp atmosphere that he was used to at this time of year back home. And the view of Sermitsiaq – the mountain that loomed over the town – was magnificent. Reykjavík's Mount Esja was a molehill in comparison.

He had been right behind Axel Jónsson when they both checked into Hotel Hans Egede. He had even stood next to him in the lobby for a while, taking care to remain unobtrusive. Now he was hurrying after him along a street that had a long name that included at least three q's and which he had been unable to commit to memory. Axel had his bag with him, hanging from one shoulder, and it was obvious that there was some weight to it. It was made from pale-yellow canvas and looked like a school bag, of the kind that Bragi had seen more men than he could count carrying after the old-fashioned satchels had dropped out of fashion.

Axel had only just got into his stride when he took a right turn down a street with an even longer name: Samuel something-or-other. He passed a man sitting on the pavement selling fish from a little cool box. Bragi slowed down to take a look at the fish, but didn't dare stop, for fear of losing sight of Axel and perhaps missing him disappearing into one of the houses. It was as well he hadn't paused, as Axel took another right turn and Bragi had just turned the corner as he saw him go into a restaurant.

Leaving it a minute, Bragi followed him in and took a window seat, from where he could keep an eye on Axel, who had chosen a table further inside. This was a fast-food place. The menu was decorated with a Danish flag but the food looked to be American. Bragi ordered a burger and chips, rather than the pork ribs that he would have preferred, as he was concerned they would take longer to eat. He wanted to be quick so that he could follow Axel when he set off again.

Axel had to wait longer for his order, allowing Bragi to eat his burger at leisure while Axel fiddled with his phone. Bragi watched the world pass by outside and smiled to see children playing on the round, pale-grey rock across the street, which was partly covered with a layer of ice. They clambered up the slope again and again so they could slide down on their backsides. Children were the same the world over.

His interest quickened as the restaurant's door opened and a man came in. He was not an Inuit, and neither did he look to be a European; his complexion indicated that he came from somewhere a long way to the south. He went directly to the table where Axel was sitting and took a seat opposite him. Now Bragi was regretting having placed himself too far away to overhear any of the conversation between them. But he had little time for regret, because the man stood up almost immediately and made for the door. Bragi took a handful of chips to munch on the way and left a generous payment on the table. The yellow canvas bag was now slung over the departing man's shoulder.

31

Agla's hands explored the bed but she didn't have to open her eyes to know that Sonja wasn't at her side. And she could no longer detect the scent from the pillow that she had almost soaked with perfume the previous night, in order that, while her eyes were closed and before she let reality take over, she would be able imagine that Sonja had just got out of her bed.

She ran yesterday's phone conversation through her mind and swore at herself for not having said the right thing at the right moment. Somehow this was the way it so often played out between them. It was as if they could never reach a conclusion they were both satisfied with on how their relationship should be. It was always so damned miserable when things were dry and cold between them, especially now, after such a long and lonely break from each other. She stretched for her phone on the bedside table and scrolled through to Sonja's number, but the call went straight to voicemail, so her phone had to be switched off. She could try again that evening.

This was starting to feel familiar, although it was a touch too dramatic to call it a pattern. She would pursue Sonja, finally have her in her arms, and then screw things up without knowing exactly how, before starting to pursue her again. Agla could feel her cheeks flush and a familiar feeling made its appearance – guilt.

It was as if Sonja had breathed new life into the guilt that her mother had rid her of when she was just ten years old.

'Guilt is what causes women the most problems in life,' her mother had said. 'If you can lose the guilt, you'll be free.'

She'd said this after Agla had lain in bed in tears, having sneaked down to the harbour with her brother's fishing rod and lost it.

'Take a look at your brothers,' her mother had said. 'They don't have regrets. They just forget and carry on. They put it all behind them. You can't change the past anyway, so why let it worry you?'

After her mother had left the room and told the raging boy to grow up and get over it, Agla lay silently in bed and thought. She knew that her mother was right. Those nagging pangs of conscience did nothing but hold you back. That was when guilt had left her and had only made a reappearance decades later – when Adam had walked in on her in bed with Sonja, little Tómas holding his hand. The whole family's life was instantly wrecked ... by her. Ever since then it felt as if everything linked to Sonja brought back that guilt, blended with another emotion that had also started to make a habit of showing up: shame.

Agla sat on the edge of the bed, lifted her arms and stretched. A day in heels yesterday had left her with a sore back. It would be flat shoes for the rest of the week: flat shoes, trouser suits and her attention on the bank. Sonja would be occupied with her computer work, so sorting things out between them would have to wait until they were both free. However much she longed to catch the next flight home and do her best to gain Sonja's affections, that wasn't on the agenda. Now real life would have to take priority.

There was one call she had to make to ensure that everything was in order, to prevent a misunderstanding later on.

Ingimar picked up before the phone had even rung once.

'I just wanted to make you aware of something,' she said.

'Yes?' Ingimar said, and she could hear his heavy breathing.

'When the invoice reaches you, the interest is the LIBOR rate plus the usual Deutsche Bank rate.'

'Why?' Agla could hear his displeasure in the single word.

'Each payment is reduced,' she said, 'as the LIBOR interest rate is lower than you had in mind, but then there's the opportunity to offset the companies' interest payments against corporation tax, as long as the loans are on the usual terms.'

'Even though the payment ends up within the same group?'

'Yes.'

'So we get a tax break on this?' Agla could hear the laughter in his voice.

'That's right,' she said, 'as long as we use what are considered usual terms – the LIBOR rate, for example.'

Ingimar sniggered softly. 'I'm not sure if you're crazy or you're a genius,' he said and Agla smiled to herself before ending the call.

She went to the bathroom and ran the shower. Talking to Sonja would have to wait until she was back in Iceland. Now she would have to put on her hard outer shell, smother her pangs of guilt and concentrate on business. She needed to be able to think clearly. The week ahead of her was an important one.

32

Sonja reproached herself all the way to Amsterdam. The flight leaving Iceland far too early in the morning hadn't helped. It was never a pleasure to have to wake up in the middle of the night, and now she was in the airport shuttle taking her into the city. Normally she found a train ride relaxing, the rhythmic motion reminiscent of a resting heartbeat and providing a feeling of security, but this time she found the sound irritating. All she saw out the window now seemed ugly, her mind not registering the clear sky or the budding trees but only the garbage by the motorway running beside the track and graffiti tags on the walls of the cuttings the train passed through. She felt that her life had gone backwards over the last week and she hadn't been developing in the right direction. If it wasn't enough that she had let Adam trap her yet again, she hadn't withstood the temptation to sleep with Agla, which brought with it all the usual expectations and disappointments. On the phone the previous day she had gone on and on about all kinds of bank business that she knew perfectly well that Sonja had no interest in. She had heard enough of that kind of crap – about acquisitions, leveraging, mortgaging and whatever all that stuff was called. Her attention never failed to go in other directions whenever that bank stuff came up. There was probably some element of masochism in having had both a husband and a lover in the banking sector, considering how boring she found it all. But she knew that Agla had blabbered out of awkwardness, because she had no idea what else to talk about.

Sonja had so many times in the past promised herself that she would stay away from Agla, as the relationship brought her constant emotional turmoil and disappointment, but this week had left her previous promises to herself in ruins. She had once again lost control and been helplessly carried along by her passion, as if swept away by an irresistible flood.

Now there was a pick-up ahead of her and being distracted was not an option. She had to maintain her focus on the business at hand, be cautious, all her senses alert and her nerves primed. Anything that looked out of place in this business could indicate a hazard, it was vital to ensure Agla wasn't going to distract her.

Leaving Centraal railway station she walked out into damp air. It had rained recently and there was a heavy scent of approaching spring. It was clear that Iceland was only nominally a part of Europe; there was at least a month to go before any sign of spring would show near the Arctic Circle, while here there were banks of colourful tulips in flower.

She had booked a small apartment online, paying with the company's PayPal account as a way of leaving as little of a trail as possible. Now she was turning over in her mind whether or not she could trust Bragi to keep an eye on everything so that she could take a direct flight home with the shipment, or if she ought to make it a dog-leg journey. Waiting in the taxi queue, she took out Bragi's shift timetable and studied it. He would be on duty on Tuesday, Wednesday and Thursday. Tuesday would be a good day to go back with the shipment, giving her plenty of time to fetch, pack and plan.

33

Bragi sighed with relief as the aircraft's wheels touched down on Icelandic soil. He always disliked being abroad without Valdís. He had lost all interest in exploring the world when she could no longer be at his side, and although his work meant watching thousands of people as they streamed in and out of the country, he felt no envy. He was satisfied being where she was. Now she was at home, he looked forward to opening the front door to the aroma of her face cream and the sound of the radio burbling.

He had spent the whole of the previous afternoon walking around Nuuk, following the man who had taken Axel's bag. He had waited, shivering in the cold, as the man went inside a small grocery shop, appearing without the bag but with a large box in his arms. For a moment Bragi had doubted whether he should continue shadowing the man, but he was certain that the bag's contents were now in the box, which otherwise looked to be full of groceries. The man sauntered down to the dock with it and boarded a ship with a Holidays Arctic Cruise logo painted on its side. It was a substantial vessel, although nowhere near as vast as the cruise liners that called in to Iceland. In comparison, this one was a midget. A Canadian flag hung lifelessly in the still air at the ship's stern. Bragi waited a while on the dock to see if the man would reappear, but there was no sign of him. Instead, anorak-clad tourists festooned with cameras made their way up the gangway and before long the ship had left the dock and Bragi watched it steam out of Nuuk fjord.

Back at Hotel Hans Egede, as he sat in the lobby and used the hotel computer to google, as Atli Thór called it, Holidays Arctic, Bragi had formulated a theory – something that went against all of the accepted thinking that customs officers worked on. However, this time everything fell neatly into place. Holidays Arctic was one of a few shipping companies operating between Canada and Greenland. He leaned back in his chair and smiled. He felt that he had acquired an insight into a new dimension. All his years with the customs service had been about identifying patterns that everyone knew were there but which were carefully hidden. Now he could see it with his own eyes, as clearly as could be. There he sat, a time-served customs officer, not far off seventy, in a hotel in the capital of Greenland, with the biggest coup he could have imagined in his hands, and unable to tell anyone about it.

Now back on home soil, with no baggage to wait for, he left the terminal immediately. He sat in his car and headed for home. He was going to sit with Valdís after dinner, put some beautiful music on, and think. And he certainly had something to think about.

34

When Tómas came in from football practice, his father was sitting with Dísa on the sofa in the living room. Since Thursday Tómas had only seen him fleetingly, so his promise to himself not to speak to his father had hardly been tested. Tómas was soaked through. The team's coach had decided that it would be good practice to warm up with a run outside as the temperature was above zero, but it had poured with rain the whole time. It had been great to see the boys in the football team again, and, thankfully, none of them had asked where he had been. They just said 'hi' and got on with training. Duncan would have enjoyed a real football practice like this – it might even have prompted him to have a little respect for football. Instead, he was convinced that the only game worth playing was basketball, which Tómas felt was very narrow-minded of him. He liked pretty much all ball games, although football was, naturally, the best.

He pulled off his wet clothes in the bathroom and was about to turn on the shower taps when he heard his father yell from the living room.

'Take a shower, Tómas! Always take a shower after practice, remember?'

He stopped in his tracks, went to his room and put on dry clothes. He had no intention of giving his father the satisfaction of seeing him do as he was told. He would have preferred to have stayed in his room, but hunger overcame his reservations. All that running had left him ravenous.

His father got to his feet as he appeared in the kitchen. 'Shall I make you a sandwich?' he asked, but Tómas turned away and fetched the bread himself from the cupboard.

His father watched in silence as he buttered the bread and sliced some cheese, and when Tómas sat down to eat, his father sat on the next bar stool, placed a hand on his back and patted him affectionately.

'Don't sulk, Tómas,' he said, and there was something in his tone of voice that made Tómas long to punch his father in the face – hard.

He took a hefty bite of sandwich and then another, so that his mouth was full and he would not be tempted to say anything.

'Aren't you going to talk to me?' his father asked, a ghost of a smile playing across his lips, as if there was something funny about all this.

Tómas shook his head and the smile vanished.

His father coughed and he began to speak, hesitatingly. 'Uh ... I'm sorry if I was angry the other day, Tómas. It was a tough week for both of us. I hope you can forgive me one day for everything that happened in America. Yeah? I just wanted you back. Your mother had no right to take you away like that.' His father's voice gained strength now and the hesitation was gone. 'Your mother and I had an agreement, and she broke it by running away to another country like that without even telling me where you were. So of course I was angry. What was I supposed to do?'

Tómas had no answer to that. He had no solution to all this. He just wanted to be with Mum. He stood up, fetched a pad and a pen from the junk drawer and wrote on it: *I'm not speaking to you. Only to Mum and Dísa.*

His father groaned and Tómas could see the flush pass across his features.

'We'll see about that, young man,' his father hissed, left the room and slammed the door behind him.

Dísa went to the bedroom and shut the door behind her, and while Tómas finished his sandwich he could hear crashes and bangs from the garage, where his father seemed to be hurling things at the wall.

35

'Welcome to Paris!' called a cheerful William Tedd, placing the emphasis on the correct pronunciation of the city's name. He was an American who had worked for an American bank in France for almost a decade, but could still hardly speak any French, although he made an effort to put a decent French accent into his English when the occasion demanded it.

'Thank you,' Agla said, kissed him on both cheeks and took a seat at the table.

'How do you like the place I picked for our meeting?' he asked, excited, and Agla nodded her approval.

It was a homely little restaurant in Chevreuse, on the outskirts of Paris, and the smell of garlic in the air was promising. The restaurant was housed in what seemed to have once been the gatekeeper's lodge for the small chateau that stood at the top of the hill, its walls black with mould and surrounded by weeds.

Their table was in a corner of the garden, separated from the rest of the dining area by a trellis with climbing plants growing through it. If there was one thing that could be said for William, it was that, while he was in some ways a standard American banker type, he knew how to take you by surprise. He was an excitable and demanding character and it was always satisfying to do business with him. He appreciated good food and had a knack for finding places to eat, unlike the London boys, who just went for the most expensive places, expecting that quality and price would go hand in hand.

'I took the liberty of bringing a bottle with me,' he said, pouring for her.

She didn't recognise the label, but, taking a sip, she found the wine dry and light.

'Wonderful,' she said, sipping again, and seeing how William's face glowed with satisfaction.

'I always bring a bottle here,' he said. 'Because they just have house wine that's completely undrinkable. But the food – the food is a delight! Simple but wonderful.'

'Which is just what you're going to do for me,' Agla said and William laughed.

'Precisely! Simple but wonderful. Isn't that the way we've always done things, *ma chère* Agla?'

He was right. They had always done business well together. All the trouble in the wake of the financial crash hadn't been his fault. He had carefully tied up every loose end, and the proof of this was that his name had appeared nowhere in the special prosecutor's investigation into the business that he had been partly responsible for.

Agla handed him the papers that detailed the part of the plan that he needed to know about and watched his boyish face gradually suffused with wonder as he read. To begin with he raised an eyebrow, then looked at her for a moment through narrowed eyes, then carried on reading. Finally his mouth fell open. He cleared his throat, took a sip of wine and put the paperwork to one side.

'Big,' he said. 'A pretty big deal.'

'That's right,' Agla said.

'I need three days for this.'

'You have twenty-four hours,' Agla said.

He sighed. 'You Icelanders, always in a tearing hurry.'

He took out his phone, selected a number and Agla heard him ask for a broker and an assistant to be sent to them at the restaurant with the sales documents already prepared with Avance as the vendor and AGK-Cayman as the purchaser, and then he read out the loan codes from the paperwork. He spoke fast, and completely forgot to add a French accent to his closing *merci*. Then he put the papers on the table and his phone on top of them.

'This could be a fine start to a reincarnated business relationship,' he said.

Agla nodded. This would work out well for everyone who took a cut of the transfers – William, the bank in Luxembourg, the London boys, and not least, her own partners.

'To successful cooperation,' she said, lifting her glass and clinking it against his.

'I took the opportunity of ordering snails as a starter,' he said as the waiter appeared with a dish hot from the oven and placed it in the middle of the table.

'Wonderful,' Agla said, inhaling the scent of garlic and dropping the red-and-white checked serviette into her lap.

William had been the one who had taught her to appreciate a meal. Before they had met, she had always shovelled food down quickly, like a hungry dog, a legacy of having been brought up in a family of boys.

'You'll just have to do the same as they do,' her mother had said when she was eight years old and complained that she was still hungry after a meal had literally been devoured by the boys in a few moments.

'Can't you just give me a portion first?' she asked.

But her mother had shook her head. 'Is it right that someone gets a portion of their own and the others don't?' she replied. 'You'll just have to fight for what's yours. It's a hard world out there.'

Little by little, therefore, it had become speed that made all the difference if she was going to eat her fill, as the boys seemed able to eat endlessly and didn't share when it came to food. Somehow she developed the habit of leaning over her plate and shovelling it down as fast as she could. That had lasted until she met William, who had asked with a smile if she had been a hungry child.

They had spent a whole afternoon in a little place in Montparnasse, where he had ordered seven courses then urged her to chew slowly and savour every morsel of them while they spent hours planning the world tour the money would take. Over the course of that meal, she had felt something inside her relax.

Now she allowed the chocolate cake to melt in her mouth, one mouthful at a time, while William and his assistant, who had arrived and sat on a rickety chair with a laptop on his knees, put together the figures for the loan paperwork. Once this was done, she would take a look through everything herself. And then there was only London left.

36

Sonja much preferred the buzz of being active over sitting still. Being busy brought down her stress levels. It also shrank the ball of longing that always formed in her belly when she had been away from Tómas for too long.

She had been shopping and had brought all the pickled gherkins she could carry in two carrier bags back to the rental flat, and now she was busy pouring out the contents, washing the jars and drying them. She had drawn the curtains across every window, which was a shame, as outside the kitchen window was a little patch of greenery packed with tulips about to burst into red-and-yellow flower. It was a compact apartment, and it was clear that young people lived here, occasionally renting the place out to travellers to supplement their income.

The pick-up had been straightforward. A black-haired young woman had wordlessly handed her the bag as she had sat waiting on the wall under the statue of Spinoza, then turned on her heel and walked away. Sonja had quickly glanced around, making sure none of the people walking or cycling over the canal bridge had paid any attention to this encounter, but she didn't look inside the bag until she was back at the rented flat. She was amazed at how poorly the shipment had been packed. It was in powder form in two ordinary plastic bags tied with hair bobbles. The goods could hardly have come from South America like that, so it must have been a larger shipment that had been split.

She stripped off, put on a pair of latex gloves, picked up the merchandise and placed it on the kitchen table. Once the jars were lined up, she gently snipped the hair tie from the first bag and began carefully spooning the powder into the first jar. It was tempting to hurry the process along by pouring the powder, but hurrying was one of the things that would put her in danger, so Sonja continued to fill the jars, one spoonful at a time, taking care not to let even a single grain go astray. A tiny amount on the outside of a jar could cause all kinds of problems. It didn't make any difference that she had Bragi on her side, there was still no reason to take any risks and the shipment needed to be as close to dog-proof as possible.

The ninth jar was almost full when she scraped the final remnants of powder from the second plastic bag. She pulled off the gloves, washed her hands carefully at the kitchen sink and cautiously but firmly screwed tight the lids of the jars. Then she lined them up in the dishwasher, and set it to run for a quick wash.

In the bathroom she turned on the shower and saw that her phone, lying on the bathroom cabinet, was blinking. She looked at the screen and saw that it was Agla – for the third time. She turned the phone face down and in her mind went over every stage of what she had to do. Once she had showered, she would pack each of the jars in a thick plastic envelope and use the vacuum machine to seal them up. Then she would wrap each one in clothes and pack them in her suitcase so that there was no chance that any could be broken. Glass was the only material that the smell of cocaine could not permeate, making it the ideal packing material. Its fragility was the downside. It would be disastrous if one of the jars were to crack. Then there was the danger that the electronic surveillance systems customs used would identify the contents, even from a distance. And that would mean relying completely on Bragi, which was uncomfortable to contemplate. It had been a long time since she had relied on anyone at all.

37

To be on the safe side, Bragi had set the phone Sonja gave him to silent and put it in his staff locker. It had seemed a good idea to keep it there, but when he went to the staff room for the third time to check on it, his knees were starting to complain. He was getting older faster than he was prepared to admit, and any extra walking was becoming a greater effort. Now he found it most comfortable to sit.

He checked the phone and opened the messages folder to see if anything had come in. And now, the third time that he had checked, there was something: a heart. That meant Sonja would arrive on the evening flight, as he had already seen on the passenger list. He sent a heart in reply, confirming that everything was ready for her.

He had given one of the women on his shift a day off, suggesting that she ought to take an extra day, knowing that she had her son's confirmation to prepare for. The woman had been taken entirely by surprise by his suggestion and wasn't inclined to take him seriously, which was understandable, as Bragi had always been strict about attendance; but she had then thrown her arms around him and planted a kiss on his cheek. She said she could hardly tell him how much it meant to her.

He could have replied that it was very convenient for him that she was busy preparing a confirmation party. The Analysis team had also been conveniently forthcoming: they wanted customs to check on two Poles due to arrive on the same flight as Sonja, so he allocated that job to Atli Thór and a student from the customs training programme, while Bragi himself would look after the arrivals hall.

He pushed the phone to the back of the locker, locked it and left the room. His knees were very painful, but that would be all right. By now Sonja would be in the air and there would be three uneventful hours before her flight was scheduled to land. He could sit quietly and keep an eye on the windows.

He wondered if he ought to send her a message suggesting they should meet. He ought to tell her about Greenland. But straightaway he doubted himself. Maybe he was seeing a pattern in something that was a complete coincidence. Perhaps he was losing his touch, starting to imagine things. And even if his conclusion was correct, there was no certainty that the merchandise was making its way regularly through Greenland; what he'd witnessed could have been a one-off. He pulled up a chair and took a seat at the window overlooking the arrivals hall. It would be best to wait before speaking to Sonja about Greenland. He preferred to be sure of his ground first.

38

Sonja switched on her pay-as-you-go phone as the aircraft landed. It was practically an antique and took a while to connect, but as the stewardess welcomed travellers home, as was the airline's custom, the phone chirped to let her know there was a message. She sighed with relief at the sight of the heart on the screen, the heart that told her everything was ready for her. Bragi had sent it a little late and she would have preferred to have had confirmation before boarding – if there had been a warning exclamation mark, it would have been too late to do anything about it. Next time they met she would emphasise the importance of a prompt response.

As the aircraft came to a standstill and the passengers waited to be let out, Sonja went through her false persona in her mind, as she always did. This was her preparation, surrounding herself with the protective shell that she needed to help her become invisible. This would allow her to vanish into the throng of passengers without it being obvious that she was hiding. She was a businesswoman, she told herself, owner of software consultancy SG Software, and the reason for her frequent journeys was to sell and manage software installations in various countries. She repeated these statements to herself like a mantra and took care not to let her mind dwell on the reality that she was a lowly mule who knew next to nothing about computers.

The doors opened, the fresh air flooded into the aircraft cabin and people began to move. Sonja took her hand baggage from the overhead locker, slung it over her shoulder and folded her chequered woollen scarf over her arm. She was ready to face the airport jetway with all its cameras, through which the customs officers would be watching. The queue inched forwards, past the stewardesses who stood by the door to bid each passenger goodbye; Sonja smiled and said 'thanks' as she passed them. She stepped out into the jetway and after only a few steps was ready to faint. Three broad-shouldered customs officers stood there waiting.

Weak at the knees, she felt her heart melt inside her. Had Bragi betrayed her? Had his conscience become too much for him? She coughed and swallowed to try to banish the feeling that she was being suffocated, then forced herself to walk along the gangway, one foot at a time, steady, acting as if nothing was wrong and keeping her cool. She told herself to maintain the persona, the fake version of herself, play the part for as long as she could of the innocent passenger, the professional woman who travelled to sell and maintain software systems.

She kept going, heading along the jetway, acting as if she had not seen the customs officers. But as she reached them, the biggest one took a step forwards.

'Please step aside for a moment.'

In an instinctive movement, she shrank back from him, and although her mouth opened, no sound came from between her lips. She had been rendered both lame and mute, unable to speak the words of astonishment that she had so often practised in her mind for just this moment.

It took only two or three seconds to shut her mouth and continue along the jetway as she realised that the customs team were speaking not to her, but to the man who had been behind her in the queue leaving the aircraft.

She was out of the jetway, had gone along the corridor and down the escalator and was inside the terminal when she felt the endorphin rush and the infinite feeling of relief that came with it.

39

Agla put the phone down again. Sonja clearly wasn't going to pick up. Every time she called, it just rang and rang, and there were no replies to the voicemail messages she left. Her refusal to answer the phone was infuriating. But she could cope with that, as long as Sonja did not disappear again. That had been pure hell. Weeks had gone by with no sight of her; it had even been hopeless to sit in the car outside Sonja's place hoping to catch a glimpse of her.

Agla could feel the apprehension starting to grow inside her, so she quickly shifted her thoughts to money, the work she was here to do. It wasn't a good idea to be depressed when dealing with finance. It was as if optimism, and even arrogance, made the money flourish. A dose of self-confidence helped business go smoothly. It's important to believe in yourself and the business, she reminded herself. It was almost as if that was the starting point.

With hindsight, though, she saw that had been precisely what had gone wrong for them before the financial crash. Adam's nerves had been shot and stress had made Jóhann ill; he'd thrown up into a bin during every meeting.

'If we look at which of our customers will give us a loan with no questions asked, then there's one obvious candidate,' Jóhann, the bank's manager, had said when the three of them had met around two years before the crash. His complexion had been pale and there was a bead of sweat on his upper lip: his usual indicator of stress. Adam had protested, having a minor bout of hysterics at the thought of the trouble they would all be in if knowledge of what they were doing were to get out. These were his customers and he was sure he could predict how they would react if some of their cash were to disappear. Agla had sat quietly through the whole meeting, silently plotting.

'I can get William in Paris on board,' she had said as the meeting came to an end, 'but it's best if you don't know the details and I don't know where the cash comes from. That's the safest way.'

Then she had risen to her feet and walked out. Doing so had been no more than a formality, as they knew perfectly well that she was aware where the money had come from. It came from contacts of Adam's who every week paid in large volumes that Adam then laundered for them via a fake company account. She didn't know precisely what the origin of the money was, but it wasn't difficult to make a guess that it was linked to Adam's astonishingly easy access to cocaine.

That alone should have set all kinds of alarm bells ringing, but the coke in question had undoubtedly affected the judgement of all three of them present in that meeting.

After that they had been able to borrow a substantial amount every week, to send it on a journey around the world. As the money came back via some of her companies, they used it to buy shares in the bank itself. The strategy worked well to begin with, and the shares jumped in value, but as things went sour across financial markets and share prices went into free-fall these amounts were no longer enough. On top of that, the shares couldn't be sold because, by then, they were worth less than the debt, and putting them up for sale would have reduced the bank's value even further.

That was the time, when Adam was sweating out three shirts a day and Jóhann was puking into the bins, that the idea had been floated to do something radical for the bank; something much bigger; something huge.

And that was how the awkward debt had turned into the massive debt – with Ingimar's help.

40

Sonja admired Ríkharður's new scar. It was still livid, with freshly healing skin around the dark marks left by the stitches. He limped over to her, across the pier. Sonja felt as if the cries of the squabbling seagulls provided a mocking soundtrack as he made his way over to her with obvious difficulty. He silently put out his hand for the case.

'Not so full of yourself now?' she asked, as a way of saving face and not showing fear. She had been nervous about meeting Rikki to hand over the shipment, as there was no doubt he would still be furious about the last time they had met. He had to know that she was the one who had framed him – making him look like the grass who had leaked information to the police so that Adam and Thorgeir would have him beaten to a pulp. But Adam had assured her that Rikki would not be a problem.

Ríkharður said nothing in reply, but turned and marched away with the case. He obviously had no intention of talking to her. Sonja let out a long, relieved breath. Silence was just fine. Silence could be their new way of dealing with each other. It had to be better than the insults and filth to which he had previously treated her. And it was much better than having his rock-hard fingers around her throat or his fist thrust in her face. She could get used to silence.

She stood on the dock and watched him drive away. This was the first time that he had not had an Armani-clad gorilla cub at his side as a show of strength. She had the impression that she was now the one calling the shots. It was a feeling she liked.

She sat in the car and turned up the heater. She was chilled through after standing, waiting for Ríkharður in the cold drizzle. She counted to ten, took three deep breaths and punched Adam's number into her phone.

'Rikki has the gear,' she said.

'Good,' Adam said, and she could hear that he was about to hang up.

'We have to talk about Tómas,' she said quickly.

'Tómas isn't up for discussion,' he said, and ended the call.

Sonja took three more deep breaths to try and keep her emotions under control, but failed. The tears began to flow and the image of Tómas at the airport, being led away by his father, filled her mind. The helplessness in his eyes and his little body shaking as he looked over his shoulder at her broke her heart all over again. She knew perfectly well that Adam was bluffing; he was just punishing her, and sooner or later she would get to see Tómas, but waiting for that to happen was almost unbearable. There was nothing for it but to persevere. Her fate was tightly bound to Adam's; she was as guilty as he was having smuggled tens of kilos of cocaine into the country, so becoming a whistleblower was not an option. If she were to do that, there was no question that Adam would drag her down with him, and then Tómas would be left with no parents.

May 2011

41

María straightened the knot of her scarf before she left her office. She had no idea what to expect. Finnur, the prosecutor who was deputising while the special prosecutor was on leave, had just said that they needed to meet, just the two of them. She went to the larger meeting room, but found it empty, so she looked around the door of the smaller room, but there was nobody in there either. She checked the time. She was early. He had said half an hour, and now it was precisely half an hour since he had called.

'María?' a deep voice called from behind her. She turned. Finnur's dark mop of hair appeared around the door of one of the interview rooms and he beckoned to her with an index finger. She followed and he gestured towards a seat by the window, as if she were a suspect.

'What's going on?' she asked, looking him in the eye.

'Take a seat,' he said. There was something in his tone of voice that she found irritating. He talked as if the place was all his, as if somehow he was the one with the power over her. Officially, he was – being the special prosecutor, although only for a few weeks. When that was over, and the real special prosecutor returned, she and Finnur would be back on equal terms. The special prosecutor had promised that next time he was away, she would be the one to step into his shoes.

'What's going on?' she repeated, without sitting down. She had learned on an assertiveness training course to repeat questions and wishes in a relaxed and measured way, until notice was taken of them.

'I have something that you need to listen to,' he said. His voice was low, practically a whisper. He jerked his head once more towards the chair, indicating that she should sit – he had been on the same assertiveness course. She gave way and sat down, even though she felt uncomfortable. Normally, she was the one who showed suspects to a chair in this room.

'What is it?' she asked. 'A secret?'

He smiled, and lifted a finger to make her wait for a moment, then took his phone from his pocket. He fiddled with the screen and finally placed it on the table between them. First there was a hiss of interference, then the sound of a phone ringing, and finally a voice was heard from the phone; a voice she knew well.

'I just wanted to make you aware of something,' the voice said. It was Agla's voice, familiar to María from endless interviews and statements.

'Yes?' a man's voice said, and his heavy breathing could be heard.

'When the invoice reaches you, the interest is the LIBOR rate plus the usual Deutsche Bank rate,' Agla's voice said.

The man asked why.

'Each payment is reduced, as the LIBOR interest rate is lower than you had in mind, but then, there's the opportunity to offset the companies' interest payments against corporation tax, as long as the loans are on the usual terms,' Agla said, speaking firmly and fast.

'Even though the payment ends up within the same group?' the man's voice asked

'Yes.'

Finnur switched off the recording, picked up his phone and dropped it into his pocket. 'As you can hear, that was an intercepted phone call,' he said.

'Yes,' María said, holding back the flood of questions she wanted to ask.

'Interested?' he asked in a low voice, one eyebrow raised.

María was – she would have liked to have known a great deal more about this recording, but she held herself back.

'That depends on how old this recording is and it also depends on why you're letting me listen to it,' she said calmly, reluctant to reveal her enthusiasm.

He met her gaze for a moment and nodded. 'This is all confidential, obviously.'

'Naturally,' she replied. It had been a long time since she had been involved in a confidential case. 'Is this a case that's in progress?'

Finnur shook his head. 'It can't become a formal case,' he said. 'We can't justify ... what shall I say? ... according to the rules, how we obtained this recording.'

'Aha.' María smiled. It was no secret that phone-tapping warrants were sometimes used a little too freely.

'I know I can trust you one hundred per cent?' There was a question in Finnur's voice.

'You can,' María said. 'But it's uncomfortable not knowing where you want to take this.'

It was true. She intensely disliked blurred lines.

'Let's say that we need something that could provide grounds for this to become a regular investigation. And if you take this on, then you'll have to do it on the proviso that there is no formal warrant,' he said. 'On top of that, I'm the only one you discuss this with. However, I can provide assistance. Expense is no problem.'

'How old is this recording?' she asked, expecting that it was part of the chaos of the early part of 2008.

'It's ten days old,' he said, and María suddenly felt wide awake.

'I'll take a look,' she said.

42

'The overseas parent company has received the first invoice, and they'll forward it to the smelter here, so everyone's happy,' Ingimar said with a smile.

He led her into the living room, which was more old-fashioned than she had expected, with an antique sofa and chairs, cups and plates decorated with seabirds in a glass cabinet and liberation hero Jón Sig-urðsson's likeness on the wall. His room gave the impression of having been set up in the Árbær Museum as an example of the home of a well-to-do, turn-of-the-century burgher.

'Can I offer you a drink?' he asked, going to an old-fashioned bar on wheels.

'Yes. Thanks,' Agla said, taking a seat in the armchair that faced the window. There was a magnificent view over the lake in the centre of Reykjavík. The street lights were gradually turning themselves off and the daylight seemed to emanate from the lake's mirror-smooth surface. 'Beautiful view,' she commented, taking a sip from the glass Ingimar handed her.

'It's complete bullshit that money isn't important,' he said, taking a seat in the chair next to hers and waving a hand at the window. 'This is what money can bring you.'

'True,' Agla agreed, taking another sip.

Ingimar swirled the drink in his glass so that the ice cubes rattled. 'You've never made much use of your money,' he said.

Agla shook her head. 'Only investments,' she said apologetically.

Ingimar smiled, wagging an amused finger at her. 'I know your type,' he said. 'For you this is a game. Everything's a competition for you.'

'Almost everything,' she said, thinking of Sonja. For Sonja she would buy a house like this one, complete with all the trinkets, including a dinner service painted with seagulls in a glass cabinet, so she could pretend to have come from a better family than she did. For Sonja she would do that. The idea made her feel more emotional that she was prepared for, and it wasn't as if Sonja was likely to accept a house from her anyway. She never wanted anything from her, and now she wasn't even answering her phone.

'Accounts here are delighted with the tax they can offset. We're talking a few hundred million krónur every year, so it could hardly have worked out better,' Ingimar said, lifting his glass, and Agla did the same. 'Cheers,' he said. 'To us.'

'Cheers,' Agla echoed, and they touched glasses.

'Another drink?' he suggested.

Agla shook her head. 'No. That's not a great idea before lunch.'

'Coffee, then?' he said and stood up. 'I'll get our morning cup?'

'Yes, please,' Agla said and followed him to the kitchen. It was a strange, dreamlike feeling to be having a friendly chat with Ingimar, in his house. Jóhann and Adam would quail with a mixture of fear and reverence if they knew. But her dread of Ingimar had seemed largely to evaporate as she had got to know him better, being on his side. It was undeniably better to be with him than against him. She knew plenty of people who had set themselves against this man and come off worse. He was like a spider, with a web that stretched into the most unlikely places.

She sat at the kitchen table and watched as Ingimar counted the spoonfuls of coffee into the percolator.

'So, now that all your dreams have come true,' she said, 'we'll have to discuss what you can do for us.'

43

Bragi took a seat in the inspection room and leaned on the steel table with a deep sigh. His legs were killing him and he was too old to pretend to be more cheerful than he actually was. Atli Thór glanced at him, but Bragi wasn't worried that he would think less of him for having tired legs. As far as Atli Thór was concerned, Bragi was the hero of the moment.

They had been standing by the observation window when Bragi pointed at Axel Jónsson coming down the stairs.

'Let's take a look at this one. He gives me the creeps every time I see him.'

Atli Thór had grinned slightly, but his expression had become one of astonishment when seven large packages of cocaine were taken from the base of Axel Jónsson's case.

'It looks like almost four kilos!' Atli Thór whispered as if he was in church and the contents of the case in front of him were holy relics. 'I'll get the police in here.'

He left the room and Bragi was alone with Axel Jónsson.

'So, now you're sat here and you're trying to comprehend that the moment you've always feared has arrived,' Bragi said, watching Axel sit completely still and expressionless against the wall on the other side of the room, staring at the floor.

He had stopped talking as the suitcase was opened. Until that moment he had chatted happily – about travel, about this and that. His words were cheerful and rapid, convincing Bragi that he had a large shipment with him. Innocent people don't talk so much. They seemed to be more frightened when taken aside by customs, waiting silently as their luggage was X-rayed, asking in surprise why they had been picked. Smugglers were the ones who acted as if nothing was wrong.

'A shame about the next trip to Greenland,' Bragi said now.

Axel flinched. He looked up, met Bragi's eyes and immediately looked away, staring at the floor again as he rocked impatiently in his seat. Bragi smiled to himself. That was the confirmation he had needed. He said nothing more, but waited, massaging his right knee with his knuckles. It had to be some kind of arthritis.

Atli Thór returned with two police officers, and once the paperwork was completed and Axel and the goods had been handed over to the police they went to the coffee room where the team were waiting in excitement. Someone had gone to fetch a large cream cake that stood on the table.

'The man has a sixth sense!' Atli Thór called out and slapped Bragi on the back in delight to celebrate their achievement. 'A sixth sense!'

44

Thorgeir was in much the same state as when Sonja had seen him last. He was still wearing the same dressing gown. She wondered if it had been washed in the meantime – it didn't look like it had. She stepped into the hall but declined his invitation to sit in the living room. She took an envelope of cash from her pocket and handed it to him.

'And ... y'know?' Thorgeir asked, clearly agitated.

Sonja smiled and put a hand into her other pocket to take out a small bag of cocaine. There was no mistaking Thorgeir's obvious relief.

'Good,' he said, dropping the bag into the pocket of his dressing gown. 'It's a royal pain having to buy this stuff on the open market. You know how much this stuff costs? It's insane what they charge for it now. Insane.'

Serves you right, Sonja thought, delighted that he had been given a taste of his own medicine, even if it was in just a small way.

'And you have something for me?' she asked.

Twenty minutes later she was standing outside Bragi's place. It was a terraced house with a drive and flowerbed at the front – a sensible home; exactly the kind of house she would have expected him to live in. She waited, holding the slip of paper with the two names on it, as he pulled up in a car that seemed to be two sizes too small for him.

As he approached her, he seemed to sense what she was thinking. 'Economy. I no longer spend anything on things that don't matter,' he said as he walked towards the door.

She followed him inside and this time he beckoned her to follow him into the living room. The sofa and coffee table were in a corner of the room while the centre was occupied by a hospital bed. A small old lady sat in a wheelchair next to it and looked at them with empty eyes as they entered the room. In the glass-fronted display cabinets, in between the porcelain figurines, Sonja could see plastic medicine bottles. Bragi stooped to kiss the top of the woman's head and her expression brightened for a moment.

'This is my wife, Valdís,' Bragi said. 'Valdís, this is Sonja, who is working with me now.'

Valdís's eyes focused on the visitor, but Sonja could not be sure if the introduction had been understood. It was obvious that this broken person had once been beautiful, with high cheekbones and thick waves of silver hair that lay over slim shoulders.

'Hello,' a young woman with Asian features said as she came into the living room with a fashion magazine in her hands.

'Good afternoon, Stephanie,' Bragi said. 'This is my colleague, Sonja, who has dropped by for a cup of coffee. Did everything go well today?'

'Fine,' Stephanie said and took a seat next to Valdís, opened the magazine and began pointing to the pictures.

The old lady seemed to be immediately engrossed in a dream world of beautiful dresses and parties, as if Sonja and Bragi were no longer standing there at her side.

They left the room and Sonja had just sat at the kitchen table when her pay-as-you-go phone rang. She saw Adam's number and excused herself, going out into the hall to take the call.

'You have to go to London right away,' Adam told her, his voice agitated. 'Everything's gone to fuck!'

'Oh, dear,' Sonja said with poorly feigned sympathy, and with a fixed grin on her face, unable not to gloat. 'I'm supposed to go next week, aren't I?'

'You have to go this week,' Adam hissed.

'I can't. I had planned to go next week,' she said hearing him gasp for air as he made an effort to keep control of himself. She could imagine him standing with his fists clenched and the veins in his neck pulsing.

'Now, if I were to get to see Tómas...' she began, and to her amazement Adam immediately responded positively.

'One evening, Sonja. He'll come to see you this evening and you go to London tomorrow.'

'Okay,' she said quickly. 'Okay.'

Her heart swelled with delight. She would see Tómas today.

Bragi handed her a cup of steaming coffee as she came back into the kitchen.

'I'm going to London tomorrow,' she said. 'And I'll be back during your Sunday evening shift.'

Bragi nodded.

'You can expect to have to travel straight to Greenland with the goods,' he said, and groaned as he lowered himself into a kitchen chair. He was clearly having trouble with his back or his legs.

'Greenland?'

'Yes, and it's a fantastically smart idea,' he said. 'All the effort that goes into tracking drugs is south to north. If you travel from north to south, then customs are pretty much just for show. This stuff goes from Greenland over to Canada by sea and who knows where it ends up? Probably in some big city over there.'

'The stuff I'm bringing in to Iceland ends up in Canada?'

'That's right,' Bragi said. 'At least, a large proportion of it. And that's logical, considering the volumes you're carrying. I'm relieved that Iceland is just a jumping-off point for material that's on its way to America. This stuff isn't all going up Icelanders' noses.'

He sipped his coffee and looked thoughtfully down at the floor. Sonja wordlessly handed him the slip of paper that Thorgeir had given her.

'The mule is Illugi Ævarsson. The other name, Thorsteinn Thorsteinsson, is the lawyer who makes the payments and hides the cash,' Sonja explained. 'I don't know if you can do anything towards putting him out of action.'

Bragi nodded and folded the slip of paper into his uniform shirt. 'Let's see,' he said.

Sonja finished her coffee and stood up. She was already mentally planning a trip to Greenland.

45

María went through the collection of sound files Finnur had sent her. She had been surprised that he had sent them, not from his office email address, but instead via a personal Gmail account. She realised that he wanted to be cautious, as these recordings had been carefully excluded from any official records. There were fifteen files, all phone calls, and most of them lasting less than two minutes.

She had already requested a listing of Agla's phone calls over the last month; doing this was by now practically a formality and the phone companies routinely handed over phone data and no longer argued about it. She had placed the request for Agla's calls among a pile of others that were being sent, so nobody noticed that an extra one had been sneaked in.

She disliked this kind of working practice – and that was putting it mildly. It would have been closer to the mark to say that it upset her to step outside the rules, although she had been aware from the outset, from when she started investigating cases related to the financial crash, that sooner or later she would have to get her hands dirty. This, strangely, was the first time that she had needed to bend the rules in person, though. She could find solace in the request having come from higher up. This was Finnur's responsibility.

It was almost dinner time, so she packed everything up and decided to listen to the recordings at home. They always had dinner at seven, even when Maggi cooked – her preference for regularity had infected him over the ten years they had been together. She appreciated the routines they had built up and which were her lifeline, part of the persona she had, with great difficulty, forged for herself, and that made her wild younger years increasingly distant – a painful memory that became fainter as time passed. She had been a crazy teenager, completely at the mercy of her own whims. It was not until she was into her twenties and woke up one morning after a party with a raging hangover in a heap of naked strangers that she decided it was time to change.

She held her jacket closed around her on the way out to her car. It was blowing hard down by the sea. She had parked some way from the office in order to secure a space where the doors of the cars parked alongside would not damage the paintwork on hers. It wasn't as if this was some classy car – it was just an economy model that she had selected after carefully comparing figures on fuel consumption and breakdown frequency, but any tiny dents in the paint infuriated her. She could simply not understand why people didn't take more care when they opened their car doors in public car parks.

When she arrived home, Maggi was about to put food on the table. It was five minutes to seven; she smiled with satisfaction.

'Hi, darling,' she said, planting a kiss on his cheek. 'What's for dinner?'

'Tuna and pasta,' he replied, and there was no need to say more. There was always a healthy salad with dinner.

This lack of friction in their relationship was something she always treasured. She sat at the table and he spooned food onto the plates. She had established a rule that the portion on the plate was dinner. Seconds were only at Christmas. This was how they both stayed slim.

'I need to work after dinner,' she said. There was an agreement about that as well. Weekday evenings were available for work, if required, except for Friday, which was movie night.

'Okey dokey,' Maggi said. 'I'll go for a swim.'

She cleared up after dinner. This was another household rule: the cook didn't have to wash up. She filled the kettle to make some tea. She was tired and needed a dose of caffeine before listening to all fifteen phone conversations.

46

Tómas shivered with impatience while his father searched his pockets, patted his stomach and ran his fingers inside the waistband of his trousers.

'You know if you have your passport with you, or there's any trouble, then you'll never see your mother again,' he said.

It was like the dream he had so often. He would be walking up the stairs in his Mum's block and the smell of the place would set his heart racing as it brought with it the promise that soon ... soon he would be able to throw himself into his mother's arms, she would kiss the top of his head, crush him to her and whirl him around. But the staircase was long in his dream, stretching away above him, so he had to climb and climb without getting any closer to his mother.

Now the same thing was happening. They were at the bottom of the stairs, inside the outer door, so close to Mum, but his father was reluctant to let him set off up the steps.

Tómas wondered if he should break his oath of silence and tell his father that it would be fine, but he decided against it. He understood that his father was frightened because he and Mum had run away to Florida, but all the same, it was lousy of him to threaten that he might never get to see her again. Tómas's stomach tensed into a tight ball at the thought that his mother could be lost to him forever. He was determined not to speak to his father again until this was behind them and he got to see Mum more often – much more often.

By the time his father finally did let him go, Tómas was starting to grind his teeth in irritation. Dad waited down below and watched as he ran upstairs, making sure that he went to his mother's flat. As if he was going to go anywhere else! All he wanted was his mother, who already had her arms wrapped around him, whispering 'my darling' into his hair. The second the door closed behind them and they were alone, the floodgates inside him opened and he sobbed.

Mum held him in her arms for a long time, rocking him back and forth like a baby, and after a while the sobs subsided.

'Don't bottle up the anger,' she whispered. 'It's not good for you.'

He nodded and sniffed, but inside he knew better. Anger was good. If he was angry and unpleasant enough with his father, he wouldn't want to keep him for much longer and would let him go to Mum. And once he was with Mum, then he could stop being angry.

47

Agla's jaw dropped as she opened the door. Adam immediately walked in, without waiting to be invited.

'I'd like some news,' he said and marched into the living room without taking his shoes off, taking a look in the bedroom on the way, and growling like a dog making up its mind whether or not to bark.

'It's all over between me and Sonja, Adam. The whole thing was crazy. I still don't know what came over me.'

Her denial bubbled over, even though she had only just put the phone down after begging Sonja to call her back. Adam's presence had that effect: the shame drenched her like filth from a sewer.

'I meant news of Ingimar,' he said shortly and turned around. Agla could not make out if there was more contempt or hatred in his expression.

'Ingimar, yes. Of course.' She could have bitten off her own tongue. It was stupid to start blathering about Sonja. Of course he wasn't here to talk about her. 'We can expect to have halved the debt by the end of the year and be debt-free next year,' she said. 'That's to say, they'll write off the debt, if everything goes to plan. If everything works out as Ingimar and I expect.'

Adam stared at her in disbelief. 'How the fuck did you do this?' he demanded.

Agla shrugged. There was nothing she could say. There was no telling if he was carrying a microphone and, anyway, it was none of his concern. This was her business, which she had taken on. She had struck the deal with Ingimar and she would complete it.

Adam snorted again and went back to the front door. Agla followed him and the instinctive thought popped up that maybe she should offer him a beer or coffee, but she swiftly banished the notion. This was no courtesy visit.

'We all come out of this well,' she said. 'And the other debt – the one that's in your name – that'll be small change if everything works out with Ingimar.'

Adam twisted round in the doorway and sent her a poisonous look. There was no trace of gratitude or relief on his face, even though she had lifted the noose from around his neck. All that could be seen in his expression were bitterness and maybe a little envy. This was all very familiar. They had all been like this, the boys at the bank, whenever she had been successful at something. They showed their annoyance and envy, as if she had taken something that was rightfully theirs. And she had always had the feeling she had grown up with in the little room that Dad had built for her at the end of the corridor at home.

'You can shut up, you spoiled brat, with your own room and everything!' was the endless refrain from her brothers whenever she protested about anything. But when she lay there alone in her tiny room and listened to the whispers and the giggling from the boys in their bunk beds in the room across the hall, she could not understand why they envied her solitude.

48

Sonja had to summon up every ounce of persuasion she could find to get Tómas to go back down the stairs to where his father was waiting for him. It had been a wonderful evening. They had played and read comic books and talked. But there had been no dancing. Somehow it was too short a visit for them to be able to lose themselves in something so frivolous. They would dance when he came for a weekend, Tómas said, certain that this curtailment of their time together was a temporary arrangement. And she agreed. She was in no mood for dancing. That was their way of being joyful together, with a pounding salsa beat in their ears, bouncing and laughing on the sofa.

'London, tomorrow,' Adam hissed to her as he took Tómas's hand and led him away to the car.

'See you soon, Tommi,' she called after him as Adam pushed him into the back seat, his face wet with tears. That would hopefully stop shortly. She had told him he didn't need to be too brave– didn't need to hold his tears in. The truth was, she wanted him to demonstrate to his father that it was good for him to spend time with her.

He seemed to have understood it at the time, but that had undoubtedly been forgotten by now.

She held back until the car was out of sight then sat on the steps outside the block of flats and wept. Parting was normally hard, but this time it had been especially tough. They had just begun to reconnect when it was time for him to go, and she desperately needed this con-nection with him. It felt as if there was an invisible umbilical cord that kept them linked to each other, transporting vital sustenance – not just from her to him but the other way as well. If that flow was interrupted for too long, they both began to shrivel up.

She wiped away the tears with the back of her hand and took deep lungfuls of cold air. There was a taste of iron to it. The temperature was well below zero, and even though it was getting towards spring, the pale-green northern lights swayed in the night sky as if they were trying to cheer her up, even though they knew it was a hopeless effort. Without Tómas she could never be happy for long. Her dreams of how their life ought to be were not so grand that it was unfair to expect that they could become a reality, though. She simply longed for a safe place for the two of them, somewhere they could be unafraid and beholden to no-one, and the height of excitement would be deciding what to have for dinner at the weekend. She had experienced enough tension in the last few months to last her a whole lifetime. Plus, she had had enough of being without Tómas. She would have to put her plan into action as fast as possible. This couldn't continue for much longer. She couldn't stand it.

49

Amy was late that morning, which gave Bragi more time that usual with Valdís. He didn't mind. His shift wasn't until four that after-noon, so he was in no hurry to leave the house. He stirred the porridge, took a little on the tip of the spoon and fed it to Valdís. These days she ate such tiny amounts. She took cod liver oil and vitamins, and the girls did well persuading her to eat, but little by little she was fading away. She seemed to be declining, not just in spirit, but physically too; her body was wasting away, as if collapsing in on itself, and she had become as light as a feather. He had no illusions about his ability to prolong her life. She would leave when her time was over, but until that moment arrived, he would ensure she was comfortable. He owed her that.

'Hello!' Amy called from the hall, and appeared with a smile on her face. She kissed Valdís's cheek, as if she were her grandmother or an elderly aunt, and Bragi went to the kitchen to make coffee. On the way he picked up the Fréttablaðið freesheet from the hallway and saw that there was little by way of news in it, just the same rumblings of discontent as the last few months: fuel prices were rising, struggling companies were laying off staff in droves, and elderly and disabled people collected empty cans around the town to earn a few pennies for food. He leafed through the paper while the coffee brewed, marked the good news items with a cross, filled three cups and took them into the living room. He settled in his chair while Amy brought Valdís back from the bathroom and helped her into her rising chair. Her joints had become so stiff and she struggled so much to stand up that Bragi had bought the chair to make life easier for her. Amy blew on her own coffee and sipped at it between lifting a cup to Valdís's lips so she could drink.

Bragi began by reading out a news story about Bobby Fischer's widow and how she stood to inherit from him, according to a regional court. Fischer's name seemed to ring no bells with Valdís, but Amy nodded in satisfaction. He left out the story about the aftershocks that had followed the earthquake and tsunami in Japan, as he knew that it would leave Valdís sad and even frightened. Natural disasters had always been upsetting for her. Instead he read out the obituary for Elizabeth Taylor, and held up the page so they could see the picture of her, resplendent in a white dress with diamonds at her throat and a glass in her hand.

Finally he read a news item that he liked, describing how a young MP, Húni Thór Gunnarsson, had been cautioned by police for interfering when staff from the financial crimes unit fetched some bankers out of a party where he had also been a guest. Bragi wasn't a malicious type, but there was something about that stuck-up mummy's boy that made his skin crawl.

'Today's reading is over,' he said, and handed the paper to Amy, open at the society pages that Valdís had always read.

He went to the bedroom and laid out his uniform on the bed. The shirt he had worn on his last shift was still clean and neat, so that could be worn again. He took the slip of paper Sonja had given him with the two names on it and put it in the pocket of his uniform trousers.

50

Walking through the doors into the special prosecutor's offices, María had the feeling that everyone was watching her. As usual, she went straight to the coffee machine, and while the dark-brown liquid dribbled into a cup, she discreetly looked around. She must have been imagining things; her senses going haywire. Nobody was paying her any attention. The staff were all absorbed in their own work, every one of them with a workload that precluded any kicking back in office hours. On top of that, none of them had any idea about the side project that Finnur had handed her – based on the recordings of fifteen intercepted phone calls that did not officially exist.

There were two meetings ahead of her before lunch; the first was in an hour, so she went to her office and shut the door behind her. Her emails could wait while she listened to Agla's phone calls again; this time just the ones that might have a bearing on financial misconduct.

The call that Finnur had played to her had certainly been the most interesting one. The sound file had been date-stamped, but it was difficult to tell if that was the date of the recording or the date the file had been copied from one computer to another. It was 16th April. María scrolled past two recordings that she now knew almost by heart having listened to them last night, and concentrated on the next most interesting one, in which she recognised the voice on the other end of the conversation; the voice that belonged to former bank manager Jóhann, a key figure in the special prosecutor's investigation. There was no doubt that when the recording had been made, Jóhann had been drunk.

'*You've done a fantastic job,*' he said and she could hear him gulp down another slug. '*But Adam and I are naturally concerned that things could turn out badly.*'

'*You boys don't need to worry about that,*' Agla replied shortly. It was clear that she was irritated. María was familiar with that dry, vexed tone with a note of sarcasm behind it. It was precisely the tone that Agla had used throughout all the interviews María had conducted with her concerning market manipulation.

'*You'll have to watch yourself with Ingimar,*' Jóhann said with a groan. '*You'll really have to.*'

'*I know all about that,*' Agla said, still dryly, but with impatience in her voice.

'*He's far more dangerous than you imagine—*' Jóhann droned on, and it was obvious that he had a story to tell.

But Agla cut him short. '*You don't need to tell me,*' she said firmly. '*We can talk about that later.*'

Then there was a click as the recording came to an end. María wished Agla had let him carry on ranting so that she could find out more about this Ingimar. Maybe that would have given her a clue as to who the man Agla and Jóhann regarded as so dangerous might be.

The answer came sooner than she could have hoped. There was a soft knock on her door and a messenger handed her a brown envelope clearly marked *Confidential*. She signed for it, and quickly tore the envelope open.

Inside were Agla's phone records. But for the past month they were strangely sparse. Could she have another phone? Or was she simply not in frequent contact with many people? María highlighted in yellow the number Agla called most frequently. This was an unregistered number, and by comparing the dates with the recordings, she could see that this number belonged to her lover, Sonja, whom Agla seemed to call most frequently when she was drunk, judging by the recordings she heard the previous night. There was one overseas number on the list that she appeared to have called repeatedly. María consulted an online phone directory and saw that it was a Luxembourg number. According to the Luxembourg phone book, it belonged to someone called Jean-Claude Berger. She recognised the address; it was the same block as Agla's registered domicile. That was something that had irritated her many times; an overseas residence complicated all kinds of formalities in the market manipulation case. Another quick search revealed that Jean-Claude was listed as the building's concierge. She highlighted all the calls between them.

Next María went to an Icelandic directory and tried some of the Icelandic numbers on the list, and found that these were all food outlets that offered home delivery, apart from the last one. That had been the conversation on 10th April, the same day that the call Finnur had played for her had taken place, according to the date stamp. The name next to the number in the directory was a familiar one: Ingimar. Ingimar Magnússon.

María was startled by a colleague putting his head around the door. 'Aren't you coming to the meeting?' he asked.

She jumped to her feet. She was notorious for her fanatical punctuality, and now she was already ten minutes late.

51

The same gloomy atmosphere seemed to exude from the house, despite its immaculate exterior. The steps were swept and the front door had recently been treated with oil so that the hardwood fragrance carried down to the street in the quiet, elegant London district, where all the houses were inhabited by the wealthy and the privileged.

Sonja stood for a few moments below the steps before she managed to muster the courage to knock. She had dreadful memories of this house. She felt that the place was so steeped in terror and pain that she could practically hear the echoing screams of the victims of the person who lived here, Mr José ... and of the terrible pet he kept.

There was no person Sonja feared more, and although she tried to contain her emotions, her experience of him was such that the only option she had was to be terrified of him. She felt the goose pimples break out on her legs as the heavy door creaked open. Allowing the door to creak like that had to be deliberate – an extra measure to instil fear in visitors. Everything else about the house was well looked-after and a few drops of oil to do away with that sound would have been no problem for the occupants.

'You must be Sonja,' said a warm female voice with a Mexican accent. 'Welcome.'

Sonja followed the woman and without meaning to be was mesmerised by her rear. She wore a skin-tight dress and her hips swung seductively as she walked. Her shiny black hair hung almost to the middle of her back, and a cloud of perfume surrounded her.

'You have met my husband, Mr José,' the woman said, turning and gesturing towards the stocky Indian who was dressed as he had been the last time Sonja was here – in a singlet and shorts – and who glistened with sweat even though the temperature was more bearable than it had been during Sonja's previous visit.

He made straight for Sonja and planted energetic kisses on both cheeks, pulling her so tightly into his arms that she was sure her clothes would be soaked with his sweat.

'He's very affectionate,' the woman said with a smile, extending a hand. 'I'm Nati. *Mucho gusto.*'

'*Mucho gusto,*' Sonja mumbled in reply, conscious that her voice was half an octave higher than usual. Fright seemed to have tightened her vocal chords. But she was relieved that there was a woman here. Her thinking may not have been entirely logical, but she felt a female presence would reduce the odds of this coming to a bad end.

'Dinner is ready,' Mr José said, to Sonja's complete surprise. The last meal she had eaten here had ended in bloodshed, so she had hoped that this time she would be able to pick up the goods and make a rapid exit.

The couple stood either side of her, and between them led her to the dining room, which was more tastefully decorated than it had been last time she saw it. A finely woven Spanish-style rug occupied the centre of the floor, there were comfortable sofas in the corners and the dining table was laid with silver and porcelain. Mr José took a seat at the end of the table, while Nati pulled back a chair for Sonja and slid it under her as she sat down. Then she took her place at the end opposite her husband and rang a tiny silver bell. The tinkle of it was still echoing when the pale servant Sonja had seen the last time appeared, bearing a tray with three bowls of soup.

As he placed the bowls on the table, Sonja heard a dark, menacing growl coming from somewhere in the house. Sonja felt her belly tighten into a frightened knot. The sound was like nothing else – neither a hiss nor a bark, but instead the cruel pain from the mouth of a hungry, caged animal.

The tiger was still here.

'Things have not gone well in Iceland,' Mr José said, noisily spooning up his soup, but still not loudly enough to drown out another growl from the tiger. 'First you disappeared, and then customs caught someone. That's apart from all the trouble with the lawyer, Thorgeir.'

Sonja could feel the sweat break out down her back. Now she was sure to be punished for running away. Unbidden, a thought came to her – would she prefer to lose a hand or a foot to the tiger; the choice that had been put before a disobedient fool called Amadou during the last time she had sat over dinner here? She wondered whether she should apologise, or try to explain, to find an excuse in words that would somehow reach this man's heart.

'I ran away to escape from Adam,' she said. That she had gone straight for the truth took her by surprise. 'He's treated me very badly. We have a little boy, as you know, and he refuses to let me see him. So I took the boy and ran. The same as any mother would do.'

'As any mother would do,' Nati repeated, nodding emphatically and glancing at her husband with a serious look in her eyes.

'Hmm.' Mr José lifted his soup bowl and drank what was left in it. Then he took a pack of cigarettes from his pocket, took out a cigarette and rolled it between his fingers to loosen the tobacco. He fished a little packet from his shirt pocket, and poured carefully from it into the paper tube of the cigarette, stuffed some of the tobacco back in the end and lit up. The cigarette burned away in a few puffs, and once he had regained his breath, he seemed much better disposed.

'I'll talk to Adam,' he said. 'It's not right when a man refuses to let a mother see her child.'

'Not right for a man,' Nati agreed.

'I would be very grateful,' Sonja said.

'You want to have your boy a lot of the time?' Mr José asked.

'Absolutely,' Sonja said without hesitation. 'I would like to have him with me *all* the time. He could go to his father when I am travelling.'

'Not a problem,' Mr José said, stretching a hand out to one side, at a right angle to his body.

Sonja looked at him without understanding, until Nati coughed, and motioned with her head, puckering her lips, so that Sonja understood that she was expected to kiss his hand in gratitude.

She stood up quickly, knelt before Mr José and kissed his outstretched hand. She was genuinely grateful. If this was all she needed to do to get her son back, then she would be happy to spend all day on her knees in front of him, covering his sweaty hand with a thousand kisses.

'In return you have to do something for me,' he said as he withdrew his hand. That practically went without saying. Kissing someone's hand was likely to be too small a payment in this business for the return of one's child; and probably not enough to escape the tiger's jaws.

'Anything,' Sonja said. 'Anything at all.'

52

When Agla arrived at the Grill Bar, Ingimar had already ordered the eight-course menu for all of them, and was at the bar with another man, both of them with drinks in their hands.

'Agla, I'd like to introduce Jón. Jón, this is Agla.'

They shook hands and Agla was surprised at how small a grown man's hands could be. He was delicately built, although he looked to be Ingimar's height. He put her in mind of a bird.

'Jón is the chief financial officer of the aluminium company, as I told you before,' Ingimar continued. 'And I thought it important that you two meet. It's vital to build up personal connections, to establish trust.'

Jón nodded, and Agla smiled politely. Then she caught the waiter's eye and ordered a glass of white wine. It would be as well to keep to the grape this evening, and steer clear of beer and the hard stuff so she wouldn't get drunk.

'Agla is absolutely in a class of her own,' Ingimar said, nudging Jón with an elbow and giving her a roguish wink. 'There are money men I've worked with who are constantly bolstering their own egos, who can't withstand the temptation to live it large. But after the financial crash, pampering yourself like that just leads to trouble. And Agla is the competitive type. Competitive people don't need to feed their own egos. They just need to win.'

'That's the kind of people you can trust,' Jón said, raising his glass in his delicate hand.

Agla raised her own glass and sipped her wine. They lapsed into silence as the waiter fetched something from the corner bar behind them.

'When Ingimar suggested this strategy, I have to admit that I was doubtful,' Jón continued when there was no longer any risk of them being overheard. 'But when the paperwork arrived I could see that it had been done so skilfully that it's watertight. It's pure genius to run this through an international hedge fund. How on earth did you persuade a big fund like Creek to handle this?' he asked with delight in his eyes.

'It wasn't cheap,' Agla said. 'Far from it.'

'I can well believe it,' Ingimar said, and Jón nodded understandingly.

'That's why substantial costs are built into it. Every fund that handles this kind of debt takes a fee.'

She decided not to enlighten him with the fact that most of the companies and funds that the debt was filtered through were hers.

'Of course, of course,' Ingimar muttered in a low voice.

Then he cleared his throat and Agla understood that now he was going to move the conversation on to important matters. That was what this meeting was all about: the big debt.

53

'You don't have any idea what these people are like,' Adam had snapped, his voice almost a falsetto with agitation, restlessly pacing the meeting room. A dark-blue patch of sweat had spread across the back of his light-blue shirt like a waxing moon. This was six months before the financial crash and worry had deprived every one of them of a full night's sleep for weeks on end, so the atmosphere in the bank's top-floor meeting room was becoming increasingly tense.

'It would have been worth knowing right at the beginning what you were getting us caught up in,' Jóhann hissed, dropping a stomach tablet into a glass of water, where it fizzed into a little storm of bubbles.

'You two were keen enough to take their money,' Adam said, and both Agla and Jóhann knew he was right. They had welcomed the new customers to whom Adam had introduced them. Even though they didn't know who the customers were, they could have worked out for themselves that the flow of cash hadn't come from any legal source.

'That's right,' Agla said. 'We were all happy enough to get the money that we could use as we saw fit, and it's nobody's fault but ours if it's a mess.'

'An international recession isn't exactly our fault,' Jóhann mumbled, sipping the white liquid in his glass. 'It's tough dealing with lines of credit that close down.'

'We all overestimated how much this cash could influence the bank's share price. If our predictions had worked out, then it would have been a perfect solution for all concerned,' Agla said. Sometimes she liked to think out loud, and when it was just the three of them together, they listened to her. 'There were just too many factors working against it going up,' she added. 'On the other hand, if the strategy as a whole had been bigger then it would have worked out as it should have done, with us selling at a top rate, paying off the loan and taking a healthy slice ourselves.'

Jóhann put his glass aside and stared into the distance in front of him. 'So you say,' he said. 'So you say.'

Adam continued to pace back and forth from one end of the meeting room to the other, while Agla's attention was on Jóhann's face. She could see from his expression that he had something in mind.

'If we run the same strategy again, but ten times bigger, then we're safe,' he said and Agla's heart skipped a beat in anticipation.

'Yes,' she said, suddenly understanding.

'What?' Adam asked, and without waiting for an answer continued with the same speech that he had kicked the meeting off with.

'If you reckon you have a way out, then it had better be quick, because I don't feel like being beaten to a pulp. You two don't know who these guys are that we owe money to. But I do!'

'If we fix a loan and send the money the same route – via Tortola, the Cayman Islands and Switzerland,' Agla said, putting Jóhann's thoughts into words so that Adam could take it all in, despite his agitation, 'then it'll work out. On the condition that the amount is that much larger that it'll be enough to lift the bank's share price when it comes back.'

'I know someone with ten times the muscle who might be persuaded to do it,' Jóhann said.

And with that Adam finally sat down, and there was a moment of silence in the room as they gradually realised the sheer scope of what they were about to do.

That was how Agla met Ingimar, and the big debt came into being.

54

Sonja waited in silence as Mr José prepared another cocaine cigarette. Nati was clearly used to dealing with his behaviour, so it was best to follow her example and wait patiently.

'It's not good when routes close,' Mr José said after he'd puffed on his cigarette and recovered from the violent bout of coughing that followed. 'It upsets the balance of everything and I don't like that.'

'You mean Greenland,' she blurted out, realising immediately that fear had taken hold of her. She normally kept her cool under stress, but somehow, sitting at Mr José's table had robbed her of her usual caution.

Sonja wanted to bite her tongue, but it was too late. Mr José's eyes narrowed and he stared at her with an enigmatic look that was impossible to interpret.

'*Muy bien*,' Nati said. 'You're smart. She's smart, *mi amor*.'

'Maybe too smart,' Mr José said, getting to his feet. 'Maybe much, much too smart. How do you know about Greenland?'

'I can go to Greenland,' Sonja said quickly, making up for her mistake, and to give the impression that she was ready to work, hoping that they would not see her as any kind of threat.

Mr José took leisurely steps towards Sonja until he stood directly behind her. She sat as if unable to move, her heart pounding in her chest. She was about to explain her knowledge of Greenland when she suddenly felt Mr José's hands around her throat, squeezing.

Darkness began to appear before her eyes and she felt a wave of nausea ripple through her body. She heard Nati muttering something and the tiger growling in the distance, and then nothing, just the silence that endured until he relaxed his grip and she could hear again.

'You understand that Greenland is our goldmine,' he said slowly, still standing behind her.

She was unable to say a word, as if her voice had entirely deserted her, so she simply nodded her head vigorously.

'The problems getting stuff to America are just crazy, and the costs are astronomical. There are guys building submarines to move coke, for fuck's sake! And even that isn't enough, as every second boat gets caught.' By now he was angry and paced the floor as he spoke. 'So, Nati, God bless her, my beloved, mother of my children, had the idea of trying small regular shipments – via the usual Europe route, and then from north to south through Greenland.' He stopped at Nati's side and kissed the top of her head.

'It's a dog-leg halfway around the world,' Nati laughed. 'But it's worth it – it really is.'

'And the bonus is that, if someone's caught, it's just a small amount that's lost, not the five hundred kilos a submarine can carry – which is what's happening to some of them.'

Mr José laughed out loud and Nati smiled alongside him.

Sonja nodded repeatedly, although she didn't feel that the amounts she had been carrying were exactly small. But she wanted to make it plain that she understood and agreed with everything they said. Her mind was still clouded and for some reason an image had appeared before her eyes of a new-born Tómas, lying in his cot in the maternity unit.

Mr José patted her on the back so that she jumped and the tears started to flow. He appeared not to notice and left the room.

'Ay, linda, que te pasa?' Nati said gently and laid a hand on her shoulder. 'We need to let you take a shower, my darling. Come with me.' She pulled Sonja's hand. She tried to stand, but her legs refused to obey, and she was still weak with terror, so weak, in fact, that her mind hadn't even got as far as comprehending the humiliation of having wet herself.

55

The point had arrived, during the eight-course meal at the Grill Bar, when, with help from Ingimar, they had to come to an agreement about how to write off at least a large portion of the big debt.

Jón pecked like a bird at his food, an indication of why his physique was not more robust. He took each course as it was placed before him, started by dividing it in two, and then ate just one half. The young trainee waiter who cleared the plates looked so worried that Agla felt compelled to compliment him on the food.

'In the light of this substantial project that Agla is working on for us, it seems reasonable to ask what the outcome will be for her and her colleagues,' Ingimar said, dabbing at his mouth with a napkin and letting it fall back into his lap.

He had finished his steak and wiped up the remaining sauce with what had been left of the bread, so his plate was practically clean. His eyes flickered towards Jón's plate, where half a steak was untouched.

'We'll see in the next quarter what the overall effect is,' Jón said. 'There has been only one invoice so far and the next invoice on the loan will arrive in September...'

'August,' Agla corrected. 'And it shouldn't be a problem to work out an accurate forecast – what this arrangement should return. The amount of the loan payment is pure profit that can leave the country and go straight to the parent company, without having to worry about currency controls.'

'And on top of that it's such a substantial figure that it's enough to give us a healthy tax break, so the benefit is significantly more than we could have predicted,' Ingimar added.

'So the smelter shouldn't have to pay any tax for at least the next three years,' Agla said. She had taken a look at the smelter's quarterly figures and worked out an estimate in her head. Anyone could do that. Jón's hesitation wasn't because of any uncertainty. There was something else that was holding him back.

'I imagine you and your people will be looking for a write-off,' Jón said. He didn't meet her eye, but instead looked down at the table, at his half-eaten meal.

Agla didn't reply, as in her eyes this didn't merit a response. Of course they were looking for a write-off. It wasn't as if she had done all this work for nothing.

'A loan can disappear just as easily as it can appear,' Ingimar said. 'There's nothing complicated about it.'

'Well, we are talking about tens of billions,' Jón said, with the emphasis on *billions*, as if this word, symbolising all of those zeroes, needed to be treated with some kind of respect.

Agla sighed silently. She knew all about men like this, men who used money as a tool to wield power, the little middlemen who held on tight to every bit of power they could. But she wasn't frightened of zeroes. As far as she was concerned, there could be three of them, or six, or six hundred. Neither was she frightened of men like this.

'We all know that this cash never appeared in the company's public figures, which is why we were able to borrow it,' she said, catching Jón's eye and smiling. It was as well to try pushing first. 'So it should be no problem to write it off.'

'Well, maybe over a few years—' Jón began, before Agla cut him off.

'No,' she said firmly. 'It needs to be written off in one go. Now.' It was time for a threat. 'Otherwise I don't see the point in making it possible for you to move tens of billions out of the country every year if I am still personally in debt.'

She placed the same emphasis on *billions* as he had, more for her own amusement than to snipe at him, and he looked awkward. Ingimar sat in silence, riding the tension, and his eyes flickered from him to her and back again, as if he were watching a tennis match.

'Hmm,' Jón picked up his fork, pushed his half-eaten steak around his plate, hummed again, put down the fork and waved for the waiter. 'We would like a dessert.'

The waiter nodded, cleared their plates and disappeared.

'It would be convenient,' Jón said, leaning back in his chair, 'if a little company I have in Switzerland could handle the write-off. For a fee, naturally.'

'Naturally,' Ingimar said, a satisfied smile on his face.

'Of course,' Agla said. She had won. She felt the rush that came with victory. Ingimar had been right when he had said that she was someone who needed to compete. This birdman, Jón, on the other hand, was simply greedy.

56

When Sonja came to, she found that Nati had put her under a shower and was now crouched at her side, washing her lower half in warm water.

'Thank you, I'll do it myself,' she said, taking the shower head from her hand. There was no shower curtain for her to hide her nakedness behind, but there was a towel on a hook by the shower that she took and wrapped around herself with one hand as she turned off the water with the other. 'I'm terribly sorry,' she said, and Nati waved a careless hand as if there was nothing unusual about guests wetting themselves in her dining room.

'He can be dreadfully heavy-handed,' she said. 'He's a monster.'

Unsure how to react to this, Sonja did not dare agree, although she was convinced that Mr José was certainly a monster. She stood awkwardly, wrapped in the towel in front of this strange woman who had shepherded her, helpless and almost unconcious, into the shower, undressed her and washed her as she would a small child.

'I thought he was going to kill me,' she whispered.

Nati looked up and their eyes met in what Sonja interpreted as mutual understanding.

'I'll lend you some clothes,' Nati said quickly, and was gone. Sonja wrapped the towel more tightly around herself and followed her out of the bathroom into what appeared to be a guest bedroom. Her legs still felt shaky and she steadied herself with a hand against the wall so as not to lose her balance. She had never been so terrified before. She had genuinely believed that he was about to kill her.

As she sat in the taxi on the way back to the hotel, everything about this trip seemed to have taken on a shade of unreality. It was like a long nightmare, her mind playing tricks on her, stress and fear stacked up into an absurd hallucination. But the sparkly blue leggings that Nati had lent her and the soreness in her throat when she swallowed convinced her it had been real.

She tried to concentrate her thoughts elsewhere, to look to the future and focus on the job in hand. She sat with a bag in her arms, five kilos that she now needed to pack and take to Iceland, and from there to Greenland, if everything was as she thought it would be.

She was still unsteady on her feet as she walked into the hotel, and her mouth was full of saliva because it hurt too much to swallow. The lobby was quiet; there were only a group of women sat in armchairs with desserts and three men in suits stood with beer glasses in their hands as they watched the TV news. It took Sonja a while to realise that the familiar footage was from home. For a moment it occurred to her that this was old news, until it dawned on her that this was something that was going to wreck her plans. The running text under the footage of a thick pall of smoke rising to the heavens like a gigantic mushroom read: *Icelandic Volcano Erupts*.

57

'What's special about that guy?' Atli Thór asked for the second time. Bragi's eyes were fixed on the screen where he was sure he had found the right person, the man whose name had been on Sonja's slip of paper: Illugi Ævarsson. He had googled the name, found him on Facebook and painstakingly looked through the pictures. According to the passenger list, he was arriving from Glasgow and was one of the few men travelling alone on the flight. Normally this man would not have attracted Bragi's attention. He was dressed in a light-grey suit, with an open-necked shirt, and he pulled a large computer case on wheels behind him along the terminal walkway.

'Shouldn't we just call it a day and go home?' Atli Thór patted Bragi on the back. He was in a fine mood, as the eruption had resulted in the airport being closed down and this was the last of the afternoon's flights. The evening flights had been turned back, so the only thing for it was to send the staff home. Nobody was going to be unhappy at the prospect of an unexpected weekend off.

'Wait a moment,' Bragi said and peered at the man's face on the screen. He wasn't the best at recognising faces, but this certainly seemed to be him.

'What is it?' Atli Thór asked quietly, his voice now filled with tension. 'Goose bumps? The sixth sense?'

'There's something about him,' Bragi said. He was certain this was the man.

'We'll check him out,' Atli Thór said and was gone, heading for the arrivals hall.

Bragi strolled after him; the pain in his knee was getting worse.

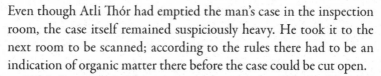

Even though Atli Thór had emptied the man's case in the inspection room, the case itself remained suspiciously heavy. He took it to the next room to be scanned; according to the rules there had to be an indication of organic matter there before the case could be cut open.

While he was out of the room, Bragi sat quietly and looked the man up and down. His dark hair was cut short and greying slightly at the sides. He was clean-shaven, his clothes were of good quality and even his shoes were polished. This was a good-looking man and somehow there was nothing remarkable about him. He didn't appear to be nervous, nor was he impatient. He just sat, watched Bragi and waited.

Bragi felt in his pocket and took out Sonja's slip of paper. He read the second name: Thorsteinn Thorsteinsson. He folded the slip of paper and put it back in his pocket.

'Thorsteinn Thorsteinsson,' he said, staring at the man. 'Is that the lawyer you'll be wanting to call?'

The man snorted in surprise. 'No. Who told you that?'

'Isn't that what you said?'

'What? I didn't say anything. You're the one who mentioned this Thorsteinn.'

'...Thorsteinsson.'

'I didn't say anything about a lawyer,' the man growled. There was an angry look on his face. He stood up and took off his jacket, and Bragi decided that he must be starting to sweat.

'So you've decided not to ask for a lawyer?' Bragi sat still and tried to maintain a neutral expression as he watched the man.

'I didn't ask for any fucking lawyer,' the man said, folded his arms over his chest and looked away, focusing on the wall next to Bragi.

Atli Thór returned with the case and there was an amusing look of wonder on his face.

'There appears to be a considerable volume of organic material in the case,' he said, placing it on the table. 'I'm afraid we're going to have to cut it open.'

Bragi stood up and took a pocket knife from his tool belt.

'He just said he didn't want a lawyer,' Bragi told Atli Thór, and that was enough.

'I didn't say I didn't want a lawyer,' the man snapped. 'I just said I didn't want that Thorsteinn.'

'Thorsteinsson?' Bragi said. 'The Thorsteinn Thorsteinsson you mentioned just now?'

Atli Thór listened to the exchange carefully. That was perfect, as it would find its way into the police case file. The report would state, in both his statement and Atli Thór's, that the man had asked for this Thorsteinn Thorsteinsson, and then changed his mind. As Bragi's knife punched through the lining of the case, there was no doubt that there would be a report: a river of white powder flowed out through the hole.

'You're amazing,' Atli Thór whispered to him as he took out his own knife ready to cut the side out of the case. 'Totally amazing.'

58

The most reliable information about the eruption seemed to come from the Icelandic news media, so Sonja went through their websites anxiously, hoping to find anything that would tell her that the vol-canic activity would not last long, and that she would be able to get home soon to deliver the goods. Sipping her morning coffee in the hotel restaurant, she looked through the images of south-coast farmers battling to save their livestock – to get them under shelter, away from the ash, and she knew she was being selfish. While her compatriots back home struggled to tape over every tiny gap in their houses so they could sit it out, and new-born lambs suffocated in the deluge of ash, her only worry was to be able to get home with five kilos of cocaine. But that's simply the way things had to be. Cocaine provided her living, just as the lambs did the farmers – and now her livelihood was threatened.

Staying in the same place in London with the goods was always hazardous and a hotel room was far from ideal. Chambermaids would come in to clean the room and other staff would be there to replenish the minibar. Each visit brought with it the risk of someone sensing something suspicious in the room – or simply deciding to do some snooping. But it was also dangerous to move around with it. She had hardly begun to think through her options when her phone rang.

'*Buenos dias*, Sonja,' Nati said.

Of course, they must have seen the news and were aware she wouldn't be travelling to Iceland with the shipment today.

'Good morning,' Sonja said, unsure of what she could say that would put their minds at ease.

'I'm sorry to see what has happened in Iceland,' Nati said. 'You must be worried for your son.' The concern in her voice seemed to be genuine.

'No,' Sonja replied. 'The volcanic ash cloud is over the south of Iceland and my son lives in the west. So he shouldn't be in any danger.' She could hear the artificial levity in her own voice as she discounted any mention of concern.

Of course she was worried about her son, although not because of the volcano. That could upset things, but it still wasn't what threatened her relationship with Tómas. What was constantly in her thoughts, reminding her that her son was not safe, was the situation she was in, and Nati had a part to play in that.

'Good, good,' Nati said. 'It's comforting to know he is not in danger. But you are not going to be travelling for the moment, so it's best that you bring the merchandise back here and we will keep it until the eruption is over and the flights are back to normal.'

This wasn't a suggestion. It was an instruction.

'Sure,' Sonja said. 'I'll bring it right away.'

Although she had no desire whatsoever to set foot again inside this couple's house, this was unquestionably the most sensible thing to do. The goods would be safe, and she could wait without having to worry. Now she just had to hope that the eruption was going to last only for a matter of days, rather than weeks or months.

59

There was a buzz in the air, as there always was when something big happened. Most of the staff were in the concourse area, where the television was, talking excitedly among themselves about the eruption, but not loudly enough to drown out the newsreader describing the terrible effects it was having on the south of the country. María had seen enough clips of drifts of ash and gloomy farmers, and there seemed to be no respite from the volcano. Predicting the behaviour of these things was hopeless, although Iceland's leading volcanologists gave it their best effort. When a volcanic eruption began it was impossible to tell how long it might continue to spew out ash and lava. That made standing in there with a mug of coffee, listening to colleagues guessing how long it might last, a pointless exercise.

Her phone rang.

It was Finnur. He offered no polite greetings and got straight to the point. 'Have you figured out who Ingimar is yet?'

María wanted to bite her tongue to stop herself snapping at him in irritation. 'I've got as far as working out that there's someone called

Ingimar who Agla was talking to on some of the recordings,' she said. 'And if you knew that already, why didn't you say so?'

'So you haven't?'

'Ingimar Magnússon; lives on Tjarnargata, and I have his identity number, but apart from that I haven't had time to chase up this sideline. As you're aware, I'm up to my neck in a big tax-evasion case.'

'Hmm.' Finnur's voice echoed oddly over the phone. 'I can promise you that you'll find Ingimar a lot more interesting once you've taken a closer look.'

He put the phone down and María shook her head. She had a pile of tax-avoidance documentation to go through before she could allow herself time to dig into Ingimar's background. She stood up, shut the door and sat down in front of the spreadsheet she had been examining. Her eyes flickered over the figures on the screen for a while before she realised that her mind was not on her work.

'Hell...' she growled to herself, and closed the spreadsheet. Finnur had destroyed her concentration.

She opened Google and punched in Ingimar's name.

To her surprise there were only a few entries. The most recent was a link to a newspaper interview that was all about the house on Tjarnargata. He had bought the badly neglected building and restored it to its original condition. The picture was of him standing with his stick-thin wife in front of one of the handsome wooden houses that stood on the street. He was a burly man in middle-age, dark-haired and wearing a suit but with an open-necked shirt. María zoomed in on the man's face as far as the browser would let her, checking to see if she had seen him anywhere before; but she didn't have much success, as the further she zoomed in, the coarser the image became. There was little to the next entry, where his name appeared in a document detailing the shareholders in a shipping company. He seemed to be one of the smaller shareholders, and that was of little interest. In the third link she didn't find his name anywhere, in spite of reading it all the way through, and was about to close the page when she noticed the name in a picture caption. The photo showed the minister of health shaking hands with the managing director of an aluminium smelter that had donated a new X-ray machine to the National Hospital. Behind them stood the people whose names were listed in the caption: Húni Thór Gunnarsson, chairman of the parliamentary health committee; the smelter company's CFO, Jón Jónsson; two doctors; a radiographer; and at the far right stood Ingimar Magnússon. He had been given no job title or description, and had no obvious reason to be there, other than that he seemed to be happy to congratulate the hospital on its acquisition of new equipment, and had a grin that stretched across his face.

María tried other search terms with the name, but with no results. Words such as *hospital*, *health* and *X-ray* all took her back to the same article, so there was apparently no other connection to be made. Next she tried *smelter* as a search term, alongside Ingimar's name and had two hits. One was an account of the AGM of the smelter's operating company, in which Ingimar was mentioned as a consultant. The second was a blog by some weirdo who called himself The Voice of Truth, and who seemed convinced that the Moon landings were one big hoax and that the CIA had bombed the Twin Towers. The blog post about Ingimar was written as if in a fever, going from one thing to another, and the sentences seemed to go on forever, with only a few breaks. The Voice of Truth appeared to be someone with a lot on his mind. The title was no more sane than the rest of it: 'The Smelter's Spin Doctor – the Man who Milks Iceland'.

60

As Sonja approached the house, she found the door already half open. She tiptoed up the steps and knocked softly on the heavy hardwood. She had taken a cab to the gardens outside Burton Court and walked from there, and although she was puffing and hot, for some reason she held her breath. There was something strange about the place. She wondered whether to venture inside, or if she should simply turn back and call Nati to ask if she could come right away. But before she could come to a decision, Nati appeared in the doorway and Sonja could tell immediately that something was very wrong. Her mascara had run down her cheeks, her hair was askew and her dark eyes were full of fear.

'Come inside,' she whispered. There was consternation in her voice and she grasped Sonja's wrist to pull her inside. Then she carefully shut the door. 'I opened the door so you would not have to ring the bell,' she said. 'I'm not sure if any of the servants are in the house.'

She led Sonja into the hall and then into the living room, where she quietly shut the door behind them. Like the rest of the house, the room was overheated. It was sparsely furnished, with two big leather chairs and an overstuffed sofa, that looked like it would be uncomfortable to sit in, but where you could easily fall asleep in front of late-night TV.

'What am I going to do?' Nati whispered, walking on tiptoe across the floor and pointing to something behind the sofa.

Sonja's instinct was to turn and run as far as she could from this unlucky house. Whatever was waiting for her behind the sofa had to be something bad. But the fear in Nati's eyes was such that she could not abandon her, even though she had the feeling as she stepped forwards towards the sofa that she would forever regret not having taken to her heels right away.

She edged closer, leaned forwards and looked over the end of the sofa. Then jumped back quickly at the sight that greeted her.

Mr José lay there in a pool of blood.

Sonja pulled herself together, looked again, and when she saw that he lay motionless, she moved closer and scanned the scene before her. There was no need to feel for a pulse or to check if he was breathing to see that the body was lifeless. His eyes stared blankly upwards and the blood pooled around him was already congealing at the edges. A kitchen knife had been sunk up to the handle in his chest.

'I found him like this,' Nati said. 'And I can't call the cops. I can't have the police snooping around the place. What am I going to do?' She shuffled awkwardly from one foot to the other, her eyes flashing from Sonja to the bloody corpse on the floor.

'Who stabbed him?' Sonja asked, her mind in a daze.

'I don't know!' Nati whined, the terror in her eyes growing. 'I went to take a bath and when I came back, I found him like this. You know what he was like – he was a complete monster. There are plenty of people who wanted to kill him.'

Sonja had no doubt there was a long list of people who would have wanted to see Mr José dead. If there had been a kitchen knife on the table the previous day when his hands had been choking her, she would undoubtedly have stabbed him herself. And for some reason, she had the feeling that Nati would have helped her.

'Do you know anyone who can help you?' she asked, certain that Nati had no shortage of dubious acquaintances who would have a better idea than she did of how to dispose of a bloody corpse.

'I can't trust anyone,' Nati whispered. 'I don't know who did this, so I can't go to any of José's people. You'll have to help me. I know I can trust you.'

'I don't know what you think I can do,' Sonja said, inching backwards towards the door. She longed to run. Every fibre in her demanded that she flee, as fast as she could, far, far away from this house and its endless horrors.

'I'll help you with your boy,' Nati said. 'I can see to it that Mr José's promise to make sure Adam lets you have your son stands.'

As she spoke the words, Sonja realised what she had lost with Mr José's death. He had been going to speak to Adam. He had been going to make sure she got Tómas back. But now it was down to Nati.

'Get some towels,' she said, suddenly in action mode. 'A whole lot of towels, and black rubbish bags.'

Nati disappeared while Sonja was left alone with the man who had made her suffer. It had never occurred to her that one day she would be standing and looking down at a dead man under such circumstances, but as it had to happen, it was just as well that it was Mr José. Without him, her world had become slightly less dangerous. He wouldn't frighten her or torment her ever again.

She sat down on the arm of the sofa and let out a deep sigh. She felt dizzy and the sensation came over her that she was being carried away on a violent stream, was floating down a rushing river, unable to resist. Mr José was trouble. Alive or dead, he was always trouble.

61

It turned out that the Voice of Truth's name was Marteinn and he lived in a basement flat on Grettisgata, one of the residential streets in the downtown district close to Laugavegur, mostly lined with small, traditional-style timber houses clad with corrugated iron in various colours, so the street would have looked like a rainbow if it were not for some planners in the 1970s allowing hulking concrete blocks to be built between the wooden buildings.

The smell that hit María as the door opened was so sharp that she almost pulled her scarf up to cover her nose.

'I don't normally invite anyone in,' he said, pushing his smudged glasses further up his nose. His shoulders were dusted with dandruff, which had snowed from hair that had probably not seen a pair of scissors in at least a couple of years.

'That's all right,' María said with relief, as she had no desire to brave the stench in the apartment. 'I just wanted to ask you a few questions.'

'Who did you say you work for?' Behind the grimy spectacles María could make out the suspicion in his eyes.

'The special prosecutor's office,' she said. 'We investigate financial crimes connected to the banking crash.'

'I know what you do,' he said. 'But I can't tell if you're corrupt or honest. Are you honest?'

His eyes narrowed and María smiled.

'I think I'm honest,' she told him. 'At least, I've made every effort to work according to the rules, and I don't take any money other than my salary. On the other hand, the nature of corruption is such that it's not easy to tell if you're working for someone's individual interests or in the interests of society as a whole.'

It was an entirely honest answer. She knew too little about Finnur, where he stood in politics, who his family were and exactly how he had obtained the recordings of the calls between Agla and this Ingimar. It could well be that there were shady motives behind his determination to investigate the matter.

'Hmm.' Marteinn looked her up and down once more, as if he thought he might notice something he hadn't seen before. 'So why are you interested in what I know about Ingimar?'

'I'm investigating his links to Agla Margeirsdóttir, who I imagine you're aware is waiting to appear in court on charges of market manipulation. I'm managing that investigation.'

'Agla laundered money for Ingimar,' Marteinn said.

'O-kaaay,' María said, drawling out the second syllable in the hope that he would continue unprompted. She didn't much enjoy talking to strange people like this.

He remained silent as a woman holding a young child by the hand walked slowly past on the street. As the entrance to his apartment was on the side of the building, there was little danger that the woman would hear their conversation, but Marteinn´s silence bore witness to his paranoia.

'What money?' María asked, when the woman was out of sight.

'Ingimar is Iceland's aluminium kingpin,' he added and stared at her as if waiting for a reaction.

'The aluminium kingpin?'

She stared at him questioningly, and this seemed to be the moment he had been waiting for. He suddenly opened up and the words gushed out of him.

'Yeah, didn't you know? Everyone knows that. He's the one who has managed the aluminium producers' contracts with the government and brokered deals for them that are so favourable that nobody is allowed to know just how favourable they are. So why are these contracts so secret, eh? Because they're so favourable – to the aluminium producers. Do you know how they treat their workers in China? Before the crash the smelters paid for energy, but the agreement with the state, which Ingimar brokered, dictated that the state reimbursed the energy costs while the aluminium companies were finishing their "establishment investments". But companies like this never finish paying for their establishment costs. They keep on sending invoices. It wouldn't surprise me if they were still invoicing the government. Iceland's politicians are idiots. Thank God for the currency controls that keep it in check, for the moment at least. Not that I have any belief in God. Religion is a drug for halfwits. But before the financial crash, Agla and Jóhann Jóhannsson made sure that the bank hid the trail of money that streamed out of the country. Isn't that money laundering? The currency controls ought to stop it, shouldn't they?'

María shrugged. She felt as if an avalanche had rolled over her.

'Do you have any evidence to back this up?' she asked. 'Or is this just a theory?'

'That's the thing with these people. You can never prove anything.'

'Misconduct can often be proved,' María protested. 'But that needs documents. It's not enough to come up with wild theories.'

'Wild theories?' Marteinn retorted, suddenly agitated. 'I'll give you all the proof you need.' He spun on his heel, back into the apartment, then turned and pointed a finger at her. 'Wait here,' he said and María nodded humbly.

There was no chance that she would sneak in behind him. She would die before she would step inside this rat hole that Marteinn inhabited. The smell told her that he wasn't in a hurry to empty the rubbish bin, and there was no certainty that there was room for another person in there. The hall on both sides was lined with tall stacks of newspapers, leaving only a narrow passage between them.

'There you are,' he said, returning with a thick folder that he held out to her. 'Here's all the proof you're going to need.'

María took the folder. 'What am I looking for?' she asked.

He sighed as if she were a dim student and he were her patient teacher. 'Look through the annual reports,' he said. 'You'll see what I mean.'

María thanked him, said her goodbyes, and had hardly set foot on the steps outside when he called to her.

'Remember, you didn't get this from me,' he said. 'If they know that, then you're putting me in danger.'

'What kind of danger?' she asked.

'If I wake up in a psychiatric ward, doped to the eyeballs, then I'll know you were the one who grassed.'

María stopped herself from sniggering until she was in the car. This visit hadn't yielded all that much, but it would be as well to take a look through the folder. Any information about the mysterious Ingimar Magnússon would be welcome.

62

Sonja used one towel after another, watching them soak up the viscous, dark-red fluid.

'More,' she told Nati. 'Get more towels.'

Nati hurried away and returned with another stack of towels. Sonja took them from her and told her in a determined voice to go and make sure there was nobody in the building, and if any of the servants were in the house, to send them away. She balled the blood-soaked towels and stuffed them into a black rubbish bag, relieved to see that the flow of blood from the corpse seemed to have stopped. Maybe the body had lost all its blood. She debated whether or not to pull out the knife that was still sticking out of Mr José's chest, but decided against it. It was as well not to touch the knife at all. She could feel her heart pounding so hard that she was sure that she was about to faint. She dared not touch the corpse, half-convinced that if she did so, Mr José would jump to his feet and lock his hands around her neck again.

A strange blend of disgust and sympathy filled her thoughts. The iron-tinged smell of blood left her feeling nauseous, and at the same time she couldn't help but feel a touch of sympathy for the person lying dead in front of her. At one time Mr José had been a little boy, and it was as if the innocence of a child had once again taken up residence in his body. There was a vulnerability in his face that she had not seen in him when he was alive.

Sonja shook her head as if to remind herself to shake off this sentimentality. She could not afford to be thinking of vulnerable little boys now, because that would lead her mind to Tómas, and she was certain that if she started to think about her son, she would not be able to finish this task.

She groaned quietly, and clenched her teeth together, then continued to press the towels down on the blood, to soak it up more quickly.

'What do we do now?' Nati whispered behind her, and Sonja surprised herself by having an answer at her fingertips. It jumped into her mind, as if it had been waiting for just this occasion. Maybe that was exactly what had happened, and for an Icelander, the cold option was always one that was closest to home.

'You're going to go online, order the biggest deep freezer you can find and have it delivered.'

'And then what?' Nati wailed. 'I can't keep him in a freezer for ever.'

'Not for ever,' Sonja said. 'Just a few weeks.'

Unsure of herself, Nati hesitated, and Sonja could see that she was close to breaking down.

'Go on. Do as I told you,' she said sharply, trying to inject authority into her voice. It was enough having to deal with a corpse in a pool of blood without needing to cope with the hysterical wife as well.

Nati left the room and Sonja sat on the sofa, pinching her arm. Wasn't that what people did when they wanted to be sure that they were awake and not in a dream? The pain in her arm was clear, so there was no doubt that there would be no easy escape. This was no nightmare, but cold, hard reality; *her* reality. She'd done everything she could to flee, to keep herself and Tómas out of the reach of the man in this house, but it seemed his arms stretched everywhere. She'd been grabbed and pulled back in, right to the centre of the web. But what she found here was not what she could ever have expected.

The vast pool of blood had become another vast problem to be solved. She would approach this in the same way she did everything else that life had thrown at her up to now. With practicality. With pragmatism. It wasn't as if she had been the one who had murdered him. There was no need for her to feel the slightest guilt over this man's death. She drew a deep breath and then sighed.

She would do what must be done.

'The freezer will be here after two o'clock,' Nati said as she tiptoed back into the room. 'What do we do now? What can we do?' she moaned, the horror close to taking complete control of her body.

It was then that the animal that had been present in Sonja's mind since the first time she'd seen it all those months ago seemed to open its jaws. She could almost hear its hungry growls coming from somewhere in the house, telling her the solution to the most bloody of problems she'd had to face.

'When he's completely frozen it'll be easier to saw him into pieces,' Sonja said. 'Then the tiger can have him, a piece at a time. That way he'll disappear completely.'

'I can't cut him up!' Nati yelped, her hands over her face. 'I can't do it!'

Sonja groaned. It wasn't a job she would trust herself to do either. But there was someone who would chop up Mr José into tiger food; someone who would even relish the task.

'The Nigerian man who worked for you – Amadou? Is he still in London?'

June 2011

63

All the anger appeared to have been sucked out of Adam. He leaned against the frame of Sonja's front door, seeming more relaxed and speaking unusually slowly, as if he wanted to be certain that she understood him.

'These trips to Greenland are no problem, Sonja. Just dress like a tourist, hang a big camera round your neck and you'll be let straight through. The only thing they're looking out for is Danes smuggling hash. So that's all their dogs are trained to sniff out.'

Sonja nodded, taking care to maintain the look of doubt on her face. She had already been prepared for a trip to Greenland, but had dragged her heels over agreeing to go, so as to give herself some leverage over time with Tómas. The week she'd spent in London, waiting for the eruption to subside enough to allow air traffic to Iceland again, had sapped her strength, and the energy had leaked out of her like the charge from a cheap battery. She would have liked a few quiet days to rest, but the hope of some time with Tómas outweighed her fatigue. If there was a chance that she could see him, wrap her arms around him and breathe in the smell of his hair, then she would gladly have left that minute. For him she would have set off for anywhere on Earth.

'And what do I get out of it?' she asked, and saw a momentary crack appear in Adam's composure as he gritted his teeth and clenched his fists. During their marriage, that had always been the signal that his temper was about to snap, and Sonja had always given way. She had always dropped her demands or hidden her opinions to keep him quiet and to ward off the bubbling anger that threatened to boil over when he was challenged.

But now she waited. She no longer cared what the consequences might be. She wouldn't even have cared were he to punch her in the face. Having pushed herself beyond her own stress thresholds with the smuggling trips and everything that went with them – and most recently clearing up after a murder, and having the body fed to a tiger – there no longer seemed to be much that frightened her. She reflected that there had to be something in the saying that what doesn't kill you only makes you stronger.

'You get paid, as usual,' Adam said, his equilibrium regained. 'You get paid,' he repeated. 'That's what you get out of it.'

'Of course,' Sonja said. 'But you know what I'm driving at.'

Adam smiled thinly and Sonja wanted to clench her own fists. Only a few years ago, when they had been curled up together on the sofa, laughing with Tómas as he did his best to crawl across the floor in front of them, it would never have occurred to her that he would become the bone of contention between them. He had become more than that, turning into a bargaining point in his parents' jockeying for position.

'How can I trust you not to skip the country with him again?'

'You can hold onto my passport while he's with me. I won't be able to go far without it.'

'You're so sly that you might have a spare passport hidden away,' Adam said, stubbornness written across his face; he was never easy to deal with at his most stubborn.

'Adam, before I figured out that you were the one pulling all the strings, I did everything I was told to do out of fear for Tómas. I was terrified that he would be harmed. But now that I know you're the kingpin, I don't need to be frightened for him any longer because I know you would never hurt him. That means you no longer have the same hold over me. Give me what I want and I'll be on my way to Greenland.'

Sonja took a step back and grabbed the door with one hand, wanting to suggest that she was about to close it. She wasn't in the mood to use the wheedling tone that had always worked on Adam when they had lived together, the pleading tone. She was not begging anymore. She started to close the door, and this seemed to work as his expression softened.

'You can have him one weekend a month and I keep your passport while he's with you.'

'Every second weekend, at least,' Sonja countered.

Adam thought for a moment. 'Okay,' he said. 'Every other weekend.'

64

'Let's say there's been ... er ... a certain amount of pressure applied ... to encourage you to retire.'

Senior Customs Officer Hrafn had an embarrassed look on his face, and rubbed his palms together continuously, as if he were applying hand cream. His office desk was huge and Bragi felt that Hrafn seemed a bit small, sitting on the other side of it. He had come by the customs office in downtown Reykjavík to pick up a new tool-belt and somehow Hrafn had heard he was in the building and called him in.

'Yes,' Bragi said. 'I've been aware of that.'

If he had given way to the pressure from above, he would have left long ago. It had been four years since the first hints had been dropped, but he had stood his ground. He had every right to work up to the age of seventy, and that was exactly what he was going to do. He had needed these last few years to put everything straight, to ensure that Valdís's own last few years would be free of worry – at home with him.

'I needed the cash,' he continued, although he kept to himself that it wasn't his customs officer's salary he meant, but the extra he had been able to earn on top of that.

'I understand, of course,' Hrafn mumbled, still energetically rubbing his hands together. 'Your leaving date is set for August,' he added.

'That's right,' Bragi said. 'I'll turn seventy on the second of August, which is when I'll be on my way for good and I'll be out of your hair.'

Hrafn shifted uncomfortably in his chair and let out a dry laugh. 'Well, getting rid of you isn't exactly a priority, Bragi.'

'How so?' Bragi's raised a questioning eyebrow.

Hrafn squeezed out another awkward laugh. 'Well, you see ... How shall I put it? ... The Analysis team is pretty pleased with what you've managed in the last couple of weeks, so they are naturally wondering if there's anything that others can learn from you, whether or not you have any more information that could turn out to be useful.'

This was what Bragi had been expecting. Those two big busts had not gone unnoticed.

'No, I'm not keeping anything back,' he said with an apologetic smile. 'I suppose I've been going more on gut feeling these last few weeks, considering I'm on the way out anyway.'

'Gut feeling?'

'That's it. I haven't been sticking too closely to the Analysis team's instructions, and I haven't been scheduling searches as much in advance. I've not been overthinking, but simply watching people and letting instinct take over.'

'Hmm.' Hrafn was clearly unsure how to respond. His eyebrows danced up and down on his forehead and he nodded eagerly as if wanting to somehow agree with Bragi but not understanding what it exactly was he wanted to agree with.

'I reckoned that, as I was leaving anyway, it wouldn't do any harm if I make a few stupid mistakes. But you can see what the results have been.'

'I see,' Hrafn said, laughing again. 'Could we ask for a few more stupid mistakes?'

'I'll do my best while I'm still here.'

'Ah. About that...' Hrafn resumed rubbing his hands together. 'There are people wondering if you could be persuaded to stay on, in some way or other. Maybe in some kind of advisory role?'

By now, Bragi was genuinely astonished. This was not what he had expected. 'People?' he said. 'What people?'

'Well ... the Analysis team. And me.'

Bragi prevented himself from letting a grin spread across his face, even though he longed to. Up to now, Hrafn had done everything in his power to ease him out, apparently determined to recruit some keen young thing for the chief inspector's position, and he had done nothing to hide his opinion that Bragi was out of touch and too old for the job.

But by staying on until August he would have enough time to build up a fund from his earnings from Sonja, enough for him to keep Valdís safely at home for the time she had left to live. There was no more that he needed.

'No, thanks,' he said, rising to his feet. 'That'll do me. Thirty years is quite enough.'

65

'What's that smell?' Maggi asked, wrinkling his nose.

'Oh, sorry.' María sat up in bed then got to her feet. 'It's an old file that's been in a damp store room for a long time. I'll put it in the other room.'

She had no intention whatsoever of mentioning this murky additional assignment to Maggi, and she certainly wasn't going to explain the Voice of Truth to him or where the folder had come from. Dubious that there would be much to learn from the folder, she had left it in the boot of the car for a few days, hoping that the smell would fade and that reading through it would become less onerous. The smell seemed to have been less pungent when she took it indoors with her, but its foul odour again flooded out the moment she opened it.

She took the folder to the other room and laid it on the dining-room table. She had already taken a quick look through it, checking the annual reports of the overseas parent company as well as those of the Icelandic aluminium company itself, but as far as she could see, everything looked fine. The invoices had been prepared along the usual lines and the key figures all appeared to be perfectly normal. She sighed. She should have known that there wasn't much behind the Voice of Truth's claims. He probably just had an overactive imagination.

She went to the bathroom, washed her hands and lifted them to her face. There was still a faint musty smell to her palms, an aroma of mould with the same sour undertone that came from a rubbish bin on a hot day, so she scrubbed her hands a second time and rubbed hand cream into them.

Back in bed beside Maggi, she looked over at him, lying on his back with his reading glasses halfway down his nose and a book on his belly. She was unsure if he were reading or asleep, but couldn't be bothered to disturb him by switching off the reading light. She wondered as she began to doze herself whether she should be taking on this extra assignment that Finnur had handed her. She hadn't been able to dig up anything significant linked to this Ingimar or his phone calls to Agla, and had to admit to herself that if Agla hadn't been involved and if it had been about someone else, then she wouldn't have had any interest in the case. It was probably best to return the folder tomorrow to its malodorous owner, and then let Finnur know that he could deal with bugged phone calls himself.

It was clearly far into the night – the room was now dark and Maggi was fast asleep at her side – when she woke suddenly, as if a vision or a message had come to her in a dream. There was nothing wrong with the annual reports. Each was perfectly normal. What was wrong was that the two failed to tie up. The parent company's figures showed staggering profits from the smelter in Iceland, while the Icelandic company's figures showed a loss.

66

Sonja sat at the computer, scanning one web page about Greenland after another, but found herself unable to concentrate; her mind was on Tómas. The anticipation at being able to see him again left her practically unable to sit still. She would let him choose what to have for dinner, and then they'd go swimming, play silly games, dance around the living room and then she would read to him until he fell asleep.

There was nothing more wonderful than reading to him until he dropped off, his head resting on her arm, and she would lie there and breathe in the smell of him. The aroma there at the top of his head was always as fresh as a spring day and it never failed to send her on an emotional journey back to the first weeks of his life, when she had hardly dared put this new-born miracle down, for fear that he could vanish from her sight. The days up to the weekend weren't going to be easy ones. But until then she would use the time to organise the trip to Greenland.

She had just managed to fix her attention on a street map of Nuuk when the phone rang. Sonja regretted answering it as soon as she heard the low voice on the other end of the line. There was only one person who began a conversation by saying, 'Yeah, hi,' on the in-breath, and that was her mother.

'Hi,' Sonja replied quickly, and realised straightaway that was too informal, as her mother came back with a stiffer greeting.

'Hello,' she said. 'I was hoping to speak to Tómas.'

So that was it. Her mother thought that Tómas was with her. She wouldn't call Sonja for a casual chat. It had been made plain when she and Adam had gone their separate ways that her mother had nothing more to say to her.

'Tómas isn't with me at the moment,' Sonja said.

'Well, there was no reply at their place, and since Adam told me that you had access again, I thought—'

'He'll be with me next weekend,' Sonja said. 'Then every other weekend after that.'

'That's good of Adam, considering you ran away with the boy.'

'That's something of an exaggeration,' Sonja said, making her words sound normal despite the anger she felt welling up inside at the thought of Adam and her mother sharing confidences. He mother seemed to be able to chatter endlessly to her beloved son-in-law about Sonja, without feeling a need to talk to Sonja – her own daughter. 'I took Tómas for a break in Florida, and Adam wasn't happy about it so he threw his toys out of the pram.'

'Really? Is that the way it was?' There was a disparaging tone to her mother's voice.

'Yes,' Sonja said. 'That's the way it was. You're welcome to call back at the weekend if you want to talk to Tómas.'

'I expect I'll have caught up with him by then.' Her mother sniffed. 'We stay in pretty close touch, me and Adam.'

'So I see,' Sonja said drily, and put the phone down. She could feel a burning sensation behind her eyes and sniffed hard to keep the tears at bay. It was a long time since she had promised herself never again to let her mother reduce her to tears.

She had only just put the phone down when the doorbell rang. She had got into the habit of checking the spyhole first before opening the door, and this time she could not believe her eyes. She instinctively stepped back and gasped before leaning forwards and taking a second look to be sure that she wasn't mistaken. After the call from her mother, Sonja could hardly have expected the day to get any worse – but it certainly had. She flinched as there was a knock on the door.

'Sonja! Open up! I know you're there!'

There was no way out. She would have to open the door.

When she did, Nati waltzed in as if it were the most normal thing in the world, dropping a huge suitcase and a clutch of smaller bags. She was dressed from top to toe in figure-hugging leather and Sonja could not prevent her eyes from resting for a moment on her magnificent cleavage.

'I'm on a stopover!' Nati declared cheerfully. 'And now you can show me your country!'

67

'Yes?'

There was expectation in Finnur's voice and María almost regretted that she had no news to give him. She closed the office door behind her and sat down on the chair in front of his desk.

'You told me I could get some help,' she said. 'Anything I needed.'

'Right,' he said. 'But maybe not something that would stand up in court. You can have assistance for a preliminary investigation with the aim of finding something that could then stand up, in a formal sense.' He opened his desk drawer and took out a bar of chocolate. It was one of those new tweaks on traditional Icelandic milk chocolate, and seemed to be addictive, because suddenly everybody seemed to be wolfing down huge amounts of this confectionary, which only a few months back had seemed uninteresting. Finnur tore open the wrapping, broke a couple of pieces from the bar, put them in his mouth and handed it to María.

'Sea salt and caramel,' he said.

She shook her head. She ate at set times, not just anytime she felt like it.

'So I gather there are no active investigations in place,' she said, suddenly doubtful and becoming aware once more of the discomfort she had felt before.

'You know how it goes,' Finnur said, chewing on the chocolate. 'There are no active investigations in progress. But if you find something, then we can account for the costs incurred afterwards.'

'And they'll be registered to you?'

'Yes,' Finnur said. 'What do you need?' Finnur broke another two squares off the chocolate bar.

'I think it would be worth following Agla to see what she's up to; where she goes, who she meets, and see what comes out of it. And if it can be done, it would be worth keeping her phone tapped.'

'Surveillance is no problem,' Finnur said, his mouth full and shrugging his shoulders as if this were some trivial matter. 'I'll put Steini on to her and he'll give you regular updates. The phone is more of a headache.'

'How so?'

'The one we know about is her Icelandic phone that she doesn't use a lot. She has another number that we can't get into as it's registered abroad.'

'I see.'

That explained why her phone was so little used. It was one of two. María would have to find out about the other number if there were to be anything useful from this investigation; if it could be called an investigation.

68

Agla sat still, trying to keep her attention on what Elvar the lawyer was saying to her, but her eyes flashed back again and again to the table where Sonja sat with a stranger. The woman looked to be a foreigner, with glistening black hair, golden skin and Latin American features. Sonja's back was to her, but Agla could see the other woman's face as she talked and talked, without a word being discernible. Sonja seemed to be transfixed, judging by the position of her head, and the way she was nodding.

'Are you listening?' Elvar asked, and Agla nodded, sipped her wine and redoubled her efforts to cut her steak into pieces manageable enough for her to swallow, but it wasn't working as her throat was getting tighter and her appetite had disappeared.

This woman had to be the reason why Sonja wasn't answering her phone. Maybe she was also the reason for Sonja's disappearance and her mysterious arrival in Iceland clad only in shorts. And now she was here, sitting by the fire with this tart in Agla's favourite restaurant, ruining the steak she would have otherwise been enjoying. She had brought Sonja here a couple of times, so it felt even more like a betrayal that she had chosen this place in which to entertain another woman. In fact, it was the only place in Reykjavík that offered a decent steak. Icelandic beef would never be listed among the world's tastiest, but the Argentinians at the grill seemed to have a way of bringing the best out of the meat they had. The open fire cast a warm glow on the diners, providing an ideal atmosphere for trading confidences and flirting, just as Sonja and the woman seemed to be doing.

Agla glanced repeatedly in their direction and saw that the woman was tapping her foot under the table, no doubt waiting for an opportunity to touch Sonja's leg. Agla felt her stress levels going off the scale. She sipped her wine again and nodded in agreement with whatever Elvar had been saying, just as if she had been paying attention. She wondered whether she should go over and say hello, simply to intrude on their moment, but she didn't dare. She wasn't sure that she would be able to keep herself together.

Elvar burbled on about the hearing ahead of them, while Agla emptied her glass and hoped that Sonja would make for the toilet. She didn't have to wait long.

'Excuse me,' she said to Elvar as she stood up and followed Sonja.

Inside, there were two cubicles, both of them unoccupied, and there was no one at the sinks. Sonja was alone, standing in front of the mirror, her black dress hugging her body tightly, her hair loosely wound into a bun at the back of her head, and around her neck hung the necklace Agla had given her for Christmas.

Agla wrapped her arms around her from behind, her lips seeking out the soft skin at the back of her neck. The tension that built up in her belly as she touched her was almost painful.

But Sonja twisted out of her embrace with a jerk, and knocked away the hand that was instinctively stretching for the neckline of her dress.

'I'm here with a friend, Agla!' she hissed angrily.

'Friend?' Agla snorted. 'Is that what she is?'

She tried to pull Sonja back into her arms, but she pushed her away. Her lips quivered and her eyes looked as if they might emit furious sparks.

'Leave me alone, Agla,' she said. 'You're drunk and being horrible.'

Agla steadied herself against the wash basin, suddenly feeling drunk and wobbly on her feet. She couldn't understand it. Sonja attracted her with some kind of force that could not be resisted, while Sonja herself seemed to be able to set her own terms for how things should be, and could walk away so easily when they didn't suit her.

But she had another woman to go home with, and Agla had nobody.

Maybe that was the problem. Maybe, if she was to shake off the spell of this endless longing, she needed to do the same as Sonja.

A half-formed, mad idea appeared from the back of her mind as she recalled seeing a news report about a place in Kópavogur where women showed off their bodies.

A few minutes later she had – rather abruptly, it was true – dismissed Elvar then stormed out of the restaurant, making sure to pass the table where Sonja sat with the other woman and to knock over a glass with her handbag, as if by accident.

Heading to Kópavogur in a taxi, the desire for the feelings that swirled inside her at Sonja's touch were so powerful that she felt her heart was going to burst, and at the same time she was so furious with her that she was hell-bent on finding the same emotion with some other woman. If Sonja could do without her, then she could do without Sonja.

69

It only took a moment for Agla to choose a girl. There was only one dark one, with black hair, in the place. She was determined to find out what it was that Sonja was looking for with her raven-haired tart. Some of the guys she used to work with at the bank had said that there was a special smell to dark women.

The girl took her to a cubicle, where Agla sat back in an armchair, taking gulps of poor-quality champagne that she hadn't ordered. The girl got into position, but over the smell of cigar smoke, the stink of spilt beer and a sour undertone that Agla tried not to contemplate might be ancient semen, she couldn't detect any special scent about the young woman. She had booked a ten-minute lap dance and the girl was already peeling off her clothes, her hips jiggling rhythmically and one foot on the arm of the chair.

'Are you okay with dancing for a woman?' Agla asked.

For the first time the girl looked into her eyes and smiled. 'Sure,' she drawled, turned away, squatted down and deftly unhooked her bra. Life would be so much easier if all women could do that, thought Agla. Then the girl turned around, breasts on display. She had a fantastic figure, with a narrow waist and a large, full chest. Her skin darkened around her nipples, which looked almost black in the dim light, and Agla felt a lump develop in her throat. The girl danced for her, twisting and shaking in a way that would have looked good on a stage but which seemed absurd in this cramped space. She stepped out of her thong, but Agla's eyes remained fixed on her breasts.

A moment later her time was up. Agla was so certain something important was welling up inside her, she booked another hour.

The girl continued where she had left off. The music merged with Agla's pulse, which now followed the beat of the dance, quicker and quicker, faster and faster. It became a wild jungle whirl, with drums beating in the distance – a humid rain forest, dark skin that shone in the gloom, salty sweat and a pounding heart; South America right here in Kópavogur.

Then the girl's hand stroked her hair and the spell was broken. This woman didn't have the touch. It was uncomfortable to be touched by her. Agla was suddenly consumed by her desire for Sonja – so over-whelmingly that she felt she couldn't breathe. And on top of that was the thought that Sonja was now at home with the woman from the restaurant. The thought hurt her like a stab to the heart and it was too painful to bear silently, so she leaned into the stripper's breasts and let the tears flow.

Agla came to as the girl handed her a tissue and told her that she still had twenty minutes left.

'Let me make you happy?' the girl suggested.

But Agla shook her head. All she wanted to do was to cry and tell her about Sonja – the whole story. So she told her how they had made love every day, sometimes twice, and could hardly keep their hands off each other. She told her how happiness flowed through her veins like blood rich with oxygen every time Sonja smiled; how she sometimes lay and watched her sleep, her heart glowing with thankfulness.

'You love her very much,' her stripper said.

'Yes. I do.'

She loved Sonja. This was so much more than a moment's infatuation or madness. She simply loved Sonja.

The stripper and one of the bouncers took her to the taxi. She had cried herself into a heap and was now unsteady on her feet. However, she demanded that the taxi take her to Sonja's place. She had to tell her she loved her. She needed to tell her she loved her.

Outside Sonja's block, she let the taxi go, certain that Sonja would let her in once she had announced her love. She would throw the foreign tart out and wrap Agla in her arms, while Agla would tell her again and again how much she loved her. She would tell her a thousand times, one for each time that Sonja had longed to hear her say those words, each time that she had been unable to say it.

Agla staggered up the steps and rang the bell for the top apartment, as she knew the old guy there would sound the buzzer without any fuss. Inside she lumbered up the stairs and hammered on Sonja's door with both fists until she could see the light come on through the tinted glass above the door.

'I have something important to tell you,' Alga said breathlessly, when Sonja finally opened the door, dressed only in her burgundy dressing gown, her hair loose around her shoulders.

'You're drunk,' she said, shutting the door in her face and switching off the light inside.

70

The jet gathered speed on the runway and then soared into the air. Its movements were gentle but quick, and Sonja felt as if she were sitting on a flying sofa. The leather seat was heavily upholstered and the table that separated her from Nati seemed to be polished wood inlaid with glittering, many-coloured tiles.

'What do you think of the décor?' Nati asked with pride.

'It's ... very beautiful,' Sonja replied. With her limited experience of private jets, she had nothing to compare it to. This was her first time in such an aircraft. Adam had flown occasionally in private jets to meetings in London for the bank, but she had never gone with him as she hadn't wanted to be away from Tómas when he was a baby.

'I designed it myself,' Nati said, waving a hand at the designs on the walls – cacti, and birds and snakes surrounded by heavy green vegetation. Sonja wasn't sure whether some sort of a plastic film had been glued up or if the insides of the plane had actually been hand-painted.

Nati snapped her fingers to summon the stewardess, who got to her feet and came over, even though the seat belt light was still glowing.

'Champagne,' Nati said. 'And some snacks.'

'I don't know why I'm going to Mexico with you,' Sonja said as the stewardess appeared and poured champagne into glasses for them.

She was exhausted after twenty-four hours in Nati's company. The helicopter flight over Thingvellir and the waterfall at Gullfoss, the visit to the Blue Lagoon and the snowmobile trip had all made her feel as if she were a tourist herself. It was as if Nati was showing her a side of Iceland that she had forgotten existed. This was something she hadn't experienced since before the financial crash. The previous evening Nati had told her to choose a restaurant and she had been through all the smartest places in town in her mind, and finally decided on one with a South American feel to it; one that she had felt would come up to Nati's standards. And then Agla had to be there, drunk and jealous.

'I need a friend,' Nati said, raising her champagne flute. 'A really good friend who can always be on my side, whatever happens. It's a man's world and we girls need to stick together.'

Sonja lifted her glass in agreement but barely tasted its contents. Over the last twenty-four hours there had been more than enough champagne for her. But not for Nati. She soaked it up as if it were her only sustenance, but it seemed to have no effect on her.

'Do you want to be that friend?' Nati reached out, laid a hand on Sonja's and stroked it tenderly.

Sonja gently pulled her hand away and smiled awkwardly. Within just a day, it had become a practically automatic reaction to turn away from Nati's touches and caresses without appearing to be rude.

'To tell the truth, I dream of a simple life with my son, just doing an ordinary job,' Sonja said quietly. 'If I'm completely straight with you, I'm not sure that I'm the right person to be your friend.'

She immediately regretted being so honest: Nati's face clouded over, and her dark eyes, which continued to stare at her, turned cold.

71

'No, she wasn't just in there drinking. I followed her in and saw her going into a lap-dance booth with one of the girls. And she was in there a long time.'

This was news almost too good to be true. This could be the opportunity María had been waiting for. She had sat in her office, with her back to the window, and listened with growing disappointment as Steini gave his report, reading out from a little notebook the times and places of Agla's movements the day before. But then he'd mentioned the visit to the strip club. This could give María an opening, a chance to get closer to Agla, without her suspecting that she was being investigated again.

'And she went home alone?'

'Yeah. She was completely arseholed, could hardly stand on her own two feet. She was helped out into a taxi at ... eleven forty-three, and it took her to...' Steini flipped through his notebook '...Eskihlíð sixteen. She went inside but came out shortly afterwards and went home on foot, pretty slowly – she was all over the place. She reached her home, on the west side of town, at twelve thirty-seven.'

'Thanks, Steini. That's all I need for the moment. I'll be in touch if there's anything else.'

Steini got to his feet without a word and silently left her office. His brawny figure moved with a quiet grace – it was as if he floated a couple of centimetres above the linoleum floor. She had always found him to be an odd type. He was one of the special prosecutor's staff, and, like the rest of them, held temporary police powers, but he never mixed with the others and never stayed long in the office; he simply gave his reports and was gone.

This was the first time that María had used him for an assignment. Up to now, she had always been turned down if she had requested surveillance of a suspect, on the grounds that it was either too expensive or there was no basis for it. She wondered why Finnur had decided that it was worthwhile having a tail put on Agla this time, when all they had was the hope that it might turn up something useful. The special prosecutor would be quick to ask questions when he came back from leave.

It went without saying, of course, that Finnur was hoping for something that could be grounds for a formal investigation. She was hoping for the same thing. She had dreamed of nailing Agla – or, rather, nailing her harder than she already had. The market-manipulation case would put her away for only a few months, at best, but everyone knew that she was one of the big fish in the whole financial crash. She was one of those white-collar criminals who got away with off-the-scale villainy and then sat there grinning as they were questioned, only a fraction of their crimes coming to light.

María swivelled around in her chair so she could see out the window. The wind hit the glass, peppering it with the little clicking sounds that came from the dirt that always seemed to fill the air these days – fine-grained volcanic ash and the salt-and-sand mix the road authorities seemed to spend the entire winter spreading on the streets of Reykjavík and the entire summer sweeping up. She tapped her fingers in time with the hammering on the glass while her mind worked in overdrive.

She was not certain that she would find anything that could be pinned on Agla. In order to follow the money – the trail that led to the whole truth, she needed names. She needed the names of the people Agla was in contact with about whatever she was plotting with Ingimar Magnússon; and it wasn't certain she would get them.

But she had found a way that would take her into Agla's home – and hopefully to her phone.

72

The video gave a startlingly inaccurate account of what had really happened, even though it was put together from genuine events. Sonja realised that a completely false narrative could easily be formed from the elements that were left unsaid. Her padded plane seat was suddenly feeling very uncomfortable.

'It doesn't look good for me,' she said and handed Nati's phone back to her. She had no need to watch it a second time to understand what Nati wanted to make clear by showing it to her. The first images showed Mr José standing up from the table at the house in London and locking his hands around Sonja's throat. From the chokehold, the sequence jumped to Sonja stumbling across Mr José's body and mopping up his blood with towels. Finally it showed her and the one-handed Amadou wrapping the corpse in builder's plastic sheeting and dragging it towards the steps leading to the cellar. The video had no sound so the events it depicted seemed very different from what Sonja remembered. She and Amadou manoeuvring the body out of the living room now looked easy, as none of the cursing, or sighing they had let out while struggling to manhandle the heavy-set dead man could be heard.

'Amadou will testify that you were the one who asked him to chop the body up and feed it to the tiger.'

Nati smiled sweetly and Sonja ground her teeth, annoyed with her own stupidity. It was quite right that she had asked Amadou to help dispose of the body, although she had stressed that she hadn't stabbed him, not that it mattered now.

'Just in case, we kept a small piece,' Nati continued. 'What could be called a sirloin steak if darling José had been a bull.' Nati made the sign of the cross over her face and muttered something that Sonja failed to make out over the whine of the jet. 'And I know that Amadou keeps the head in the freezer at his place so he can take it out and spit on it when he's in a bad mood. He was terribly upset with José after that business with his hand.'

Sonja lay back in the leather seat and closed her eyes. She felt strangely numb inside. It felt as if it was no longer enough to be angry, to be devastated that her hopes of being free with Tomas were smashed to pieces. Instead her mind searched coolly for some loophole, some tiny gap in the tightly woven netting that she felt was wrapping itself around her. But there was no loophole to be found, so up here, thirty thousand feet above the Atlantic, she finally gave up; gave up the hope that the nightmare she had stumbled into a year and a half ago would one day be over. It was never going to end. There was no way out and she would have to accept that. It made no difference how hard she fought, she would never be free. Even if she were to break away from Adam, then she would be bound to Nati instead. Every path that might have taken her back to some kind of normal life seemed to have finally been closed to her.

Sonja took a deep breath, sat up in her seat and looked deep into Nati's brown eyes.

'Now that I've thought things over,' she said. 'I'd really like to be your friend.'

73

Agla couldn't remember having met María or her husband. As deep as she dug into her memory, the evening remained shrouded in a fog, and the things that weren't foggy were the ones she would have preferred to have forgotten. María said that they had run into each other as she and her husband had been going into the club and Agla was leaving, but Agla has absolutely no recollection of it. Her mind seemed to go into a strange version of panic mode and she kept thinking that she was relieved that the cleaner had come in yesterday so the apartment looked pristine. Not that María was here to inspect Agla's housekeeping skills. She sat on her sofa, hunched into a ball, with all her trademark determination swept away. She was slumped like a sack of misery and regret.

'You mean I've humiliated myself by coming here to ask you for discretion for no reason? I was sure you had seen me. We made eye contact.'

'There's nothing humiliating about it,' Agla mumbled. She was completely confused. It was obvious that the woman was deeply distressed, and in some strange fashion that helped overcome her own disgrace at having encountered someone she knew at a strip club in Kópavogur. She knew precisely how María must be feeling. She just needed to find some way to comfort her, to cheer her up.

'Would you like a line?'

'What?' María looked up, then shook her head when she realised what Agla was offering her. 'I work for the special prosecutor, remember?'

'Or a beer?' Agla asked.

'Yes, that would be better,' she replied with a wan smile.

Agla's mind was in overdrive as she went to the kitchen to fetch two beers; she decided she needed a snort herself, even if María didn't want one. She took a jar from the kitchen cupboard, screwed off the lid and shovelled a little coke into her nose, using the end of a teaspoon. A little injection of self-confidence was what she needed right now.

Back on the sofa she sat next to María and, after a few sips of beer, she cleared her throat and tried to think of something to say that would calm this unexpected guest's fears.

'You don't need to be concerned about me,' she said. 'There's plenty you can say about me, but I'd never use this against you in any way. Whatever happens in the investigation into me and my affairs, you can rest assured that this isn't anything that I would ever use to your disadvantage. I wouldn't mention this to any of your colleagues at the prosecutor's office, or to anyone else. In fact, I have no recollection of having met the pair of you at that club.'

'Thank you,' María whispered, and Agla saw that the hand that held her beer trembled. 'Oh, I really don't know what we were thinking.'

She blinked rapidly as if she were holding back tears and Agla felt the sympathy well up in her heart.

She had said she had been there with her husband, that it had been his idea, but Agla wasn't going to believe that María had agreed just like that to go down to Kópavogur to watch women peeling off their clothes – unless her own interests lay in that direction.

Maybe it was the ridiculousness of the situation, or maybe it was the buzz the coke had given her, but without thinking, Agla leaned over and kissed María on the lips.

74

María knew she had taken things too far. She had taken herself by surprise, and now that she was back in her car, the everyday items that symbolised normal life and that now surrounded her – Maggi's best jacket still neatly packed in the cellophane in which it had come back from the dry cleaner; the tatty old gloves she only wore to scrape snow off the car; the Elvis CD in the player – all somehow seemed to accuse her of deceit. Of course, it had been just that: pure deceit; a betrayal of Maggi and their whole life together. There could hardly be anything further removed from them and their lifestyle than a drunken visit to a strip club. Maggi would never be seen dead in a place like that. She had played out the lie simply to try to win Agla's trust by pretending to be in a similar situation, and somehow the strip-club scenario had been a perfect way to build a bridge.

It was when Agla kissed her that she realised she had gone too far – further than she trusted herself to go – and that she was about to lose control of the situation she had created. Bewilderment had taken control of her, and the anger and revulsion she had often felt for Agla as they had sat opposite each other in the interview room during the market-manipulation case had found its release in the ringing slap she delivered to Agla's face.

But she had achieved what she had set out to do. Agla's secret phone was now in her pocket; she had snatched it from the table as she swept out with her nose in the air. This was the phone registered in Luxembourg, and there would be a lot more interesting activity on this one than on the Icelandic number. Now she would have to work fast, before Agla could discover that the phone was missing and that this bizarre visit had not been personal after all, but linked to a live investigation on which María was working.

This kind of approach was completely at odds with María's character – the personality she had built up, shaped and polished over the years. Maybe she would have done thoughtless things like this when she was younger. But now it felt as if Finnur's discreet request that she step outside the usual framework of rules had set her off down a slope where the ground was loose under her feet and there was no safety rope to hold. She didn't like it. This was too close to her old self.

She sent Maggi a text message to say that she would be working late that evening and wouldn't be home for dinner. Now she would need to be quick to clone the data from Agla's phone before she could notice its disappearance and put two and two together. It would be as well to do it while the office was almost deserted.

75

Giving up was truly a remarkable experience. Sonja was unable to remember when she had last been so relaxed. She had fallen asleep during the flight and hadn't woken up until the jet was on the ground, after which she had humbly walked over to the car that was there to meet them and watched sleepily out of the window on the way through the city. She had stopped caring what was going to happen to her. Nati was in control, and she was just following. Her life was no longer in her own hands; it was pointless trying to fight, like an animal caught in a trap.

Next to her, Nati spoke to the driver in rapid Spanish, while the front seat was occupied by a man wearing sunglasses who said not a single word, but who had escorted them from the aircraft to the car, opening doors for them. There didn't seem to be a great deal of attention from customs when arriving in this country. She reflected that her life would have been so much easier if Iceland had such a free-and-easy attitude.

The car sped through what appeared to be a virtually deserted neighbourhood. Only the odd figure could be seen outdoors, and a solitary yellow dog ran down the street, past the long line of single-storey storefronts painted pink, blue or soft yellow, and street-food restaurants, all of which looked to be closed.

'Where are all the people?' she asked Nati, who glanced at her in surprise.

'So, you're alive?' she said. 'Siesta, *mi amor*. Siesta. Everyone hides away during the hottest time of the day.'

Sonja understood. The car's air-conditioning was running at full blast, but she was still running with sweat. The burning sun was directly above them, in the centre of the sky, so no shadows fell and the road ahead of them undulated in the heat haze. The black surface sweated tar, which glittered like metal in the sunshine.

The car turned into a neighbourhood that looked densely packed. The imposing houses stood shoulder to shoulder. They were painted pastel colours, with gilded decoration, and each house had a cross on its roof so that the district looked like a collection of little churches. The car came to a halt outside a yellow house, larger than those around it, with stained glass in the windows and a half-moon of steps leading up to a pair of carved hardwood doors.

The silent man got out of the car and opened the door for Nati while the driver simultaneously did the same for Sonja.

'We're staying here?' Sonja asked, admiring the massive carved angel on the roof that had been placed to look as if it was about to take to the air.

'No, silly!' Nati laughed quietly. 'This is a mausoleum.'

'A mausoleum?'

'That's right. My husband's mausoleum. May God bless his wicked soul.' Nati crossed herself.

'Mr José's mausoleum?'

'Yes. The memorial service begins at four, so we have to be quick.'

Sonja was too surprised to ask any more questions and followed Nati into the building, relieved to be back with air-conditioning after the crushing heat outside.

From the main door they went into a large chamber that was empty apart from a few chairs along the walls and a vast altar at the far end where countless candles burned before a giant photograph of Mr José. The picture showed him with a gentle expression on his face, wearing a suit and with his hair combed smooth. Sonja stared at the picture, and although it showed a very different side to him than she had known, just looking at him gave her a chill that merged with the drops of sweat down her back. Blended with the fear the photograph triggered, Sonja suddenly felt nauseous as an iron-tinged smell of blood filled her nose and everything before her eyes became tinted red, like the pool of blood she had found Mr José lying in.

'The candles have been burning here since he died,' Nati said and it was obvious that she was touched. 'The people here loved him, monster that he was. They absolutely loved him.'

76

Agla had showered, dried her hair and applied a thick layer of foundation in the hope that she could hide the soreness across her cheek. María had lashed out pretty hard when she had kissed her. The redness had disappeared, and although she could still feel it smarting, that had to be just her imagination at work. It was actually shame that was making her skin glow. She felt herself tremble slightly as she dressed and once again ran through the confusion that had enveloped them both after that slap had been delivered.

Agla had apologised half a dozen times while María gathered her bag and then yanked her coat from the hook by the door so hard that it came off the wall, and all of the coats landed in a pile on the floor. María had marched out without glancing at them.

Showered and fresh, Agla screwed the coat hanger back onto the wall and hung all the coats up again, and then realised that her phone was nowhere to be found. Her Icelandic phone was there, but the other one was gone – her main phone. She was certain that it hadn't been far away. She recalled using it to search for something on the internet earlier in the day, before María's visit. She looked around in the bedroom and then back in the living room, lifting all the cushions, but without any luck. Maybe it was in the car? She decided to take a look once she had got over the slap and no longer had the feeling that one cheek was glowing bright red.

Despite her discomfort, Agla felt that this unfortunate event had been a victory of a kind. It had been strange and awkward, but a joyful triumph all the same. She felt that she had conquered a barrier by getting closer to María. Even though her head had been full of coke, she had managed to misread the situation completely and she didn't know herself where she had found the courage to kiss her, she still had. And that was where the triumph lay.

She had always been much more curious about girls than boys. Boys were just boys; she saw enough of them at home. But girls were something of a mystery and she had always been half afraid of them. She had always found it hard to read their thoughts and never understood why they preferred to be shut away chattering in a bedroom when they could be outdoors playing football. It wasn't as if she didn't have female friends; she found plenty of them. But they never lasted long. All the friends she made had no interest in sport, had no ambition to get good grades and were more likely than not offended when Agla preferred to go home to finish her homework rather than going with them to the pictures. On top of that, she was bored by their endless talk about boys. It was astonishing how much they could talk about them. She was crowded out by boys at home, so they were the last thing she wanted to think or talk about when she finally met some girls.

Agla finished replacing the cushions on the sofa and was startled by a knock at the door. She tiptoed out into the hall, peered through the spyhole and was surprised to see Ingimar there. Previously, a visit from him had set her nerves jangling. But now she found she enjoyed

Ingimar's company. It helped that he had taken up knocking on the door instead of letting himself in uninvited.

She welcomed him in, then went to the kitchen and opened two bottles of beer and handed him one without asking if he wanted it. Ingimar took the bottle and sat down in the living room, this time taking the sofa and leaving Agla the armchair. These were the kind of interactions she could understand. Boys and men were so easy to deal with, so straightforward. The world of men was a structured hierarchy that they constantly rearranged, and a single chair that faced the entrance demonstrated a position of power. A sofa with its back turned to the door signified subservience. Agla had become fluent in reading the symbols of the male environment among the horde of brothers she had grown up with. She settled in the armchair and smiled at Ingimar as he stretched out on the sofa and swigged his beer.

'I heard from Jón,' Ingimar said. 'The big debt write-off should go through during the week.'

Agla raised her beer, leaned forwards and they clinked bottles.

'It wouldn't do any harm to keep this to ourselves, just for now,' she said, and Ingimar raised an eyebrow. 'I'd be happy to be able to keep the thumbscrews on the boys for a while,' she explained.

Ingimar grinned. 'You're a competitor,' he said. 'You think several moves ahead, don't you?'

'Yep,' Agla agreed. 'Most of the time I manage to do that.'

She could keep the screws on the boys' thumbs for as long as she needed to. She would tell them that half the debt had been written off and they would be delighted with that. Then she could tell them that she was working on the remainder, and that would buy her peace and quiet. That way they would make sure that none of their former bank colleagues would mix Agla up in any of the special prosecutor's investigations.

77

María withstood the temptation to pour herself a coffee. It was too late in the evening, and in any case, her conscience would cause her enough problems, preventing her from sleeping. She had also made up her mind to stay at the office until she could be sure that Maggi was asleep so she wouldn't have to speak to anyone at all tonight. She was sure that he could tell instinctively when she had behaved badly. And she knew she had. In fact, as the time passed since she had stormed out of Agla's apartment, she increasingly wondered what she had been playing at. What the hell had she been thinking?

She had prepared a spreadsheet detailing all of Agla's calls – both to and from the few numbers on the Icelandic phone, which the phone's provider had supplied, and those numbers she had extracted from the phone she had stolen from Agla. There were two numbers that were in both: an unregistered number that María knew belonged to Sonja Gunnarsdóttir, who Agla seemed to call at any time of the day or night; and the number of Jean-Claude Berger, the concierge of the building that was Agla's legal residence in Luxembourg. María clicked on the rows of calls to Sonja and Jean-Claude and tagged them in yellow. These were the personal calls, the ones that were of no importance.

Then she set to work to mark the numbers according to nationality. Most began with 352, which was Luxembourg, and then there had been a cluster of calls over a week to 33 numbers, meaning France, every one of them beginning with a 1, which indicated Paris. On two occasions Agla had called numbers starting with 32 and María had to look that up to find that it denoted Belgium. After that were a few calls to numbers with a 44 prefix, meaning Britain, and of these most began with 20, which meant London.

Arranging the calls by date showed her a pattern that began in Luxembourg with a call to Belgium, went from there to France and ended in London. María used the Luxembourg Yellow Pages and began typing in numbers. Two were restaurants and she quickly gave these yellow tags. The others belonged to banks and one to an investment fund. María was already sure that, once she had been through all the numbers, she would be able to see a trip calling at financial institutions across Europe.

Scattered across the spreadsheet were dozens of calls to numbers she had seen many times in the call registers of suspects during the financial crash investigations: they were 1-345 and 1-284 numbers; the Cayman Islands and Tortola. There was no doubt that Agla was up to something.

78

A crowd had gathered around the mausoleum and most of the guests were anxious to pay their respects to Nati. She stood by the photograph of Mr José at the far end of the building, accepting embraces, kisses and garlands of flowers from the people, some of whom dropped to their knees to kiss her hands. Sonja watched in growing astonishment as figures in rags, most of them indigenous people, pressed bank notes into Nati's hands as they muttered their condolences, while she laid a hand on their heads as if she were a priest blessing children at their confirmation.

Nati had carried an imposing earthenware urn in for the ceremony, placed it on the altar in front of the photograph and knelt down in prayer for a moment, crossing herself repeatedly. She was dressed from head to foot in black, and the tailored dress two seamstresses had brought to her before the ceremony showed off her figure perfectly, while her face was half hidden behind gauze that fell from her hat. Sonja stood and tried to adjust the synthetic material of the dress the seamstresses had brought for her, and which clung to her like plastic, as she wondered what was in the earthenware urn. The only sure thing was that it didn't contain Mr José's ashes.

From a short conversation with their driver she had learned that Mr José had had the mausoleum built long ago, and up to know it had been used for banquets. The driver had told her with pride that it had long been the finest mausoleum in the cemetery; his face then darkened as he whispered that it was as well that Mr José hadn't lived to see the mausoleum that another narco was building not far away. That one had three storeys.

As the driver turned away, another man appeared at Sonja's side. She was about to greet him politely when the smile froze on her face. The broad cheekbones and the buzzcut hair were instantly familiar. This was one of the two men who had kidnapped her and Tómas in Florida. She felt her body react instinctively, a wave of nausea passing through her; she could almost feel the tape wrapped too tightly around her wrists.

'My name is Sebastian,' the man said in English, extending a hand while Sonja automatically took a step back. 'I know you must be mad at me, but we need to talk,' he said, taking her arm and steering her into a little side room.

'Don't shut it!' Sonja said, flustered as he was about to close the door, stiff with fear even though common sense was telling her that the man was hardly going to kidnap her a second time, whisking her away with the memorial service in progress.

'This is a life-and-death matter. You must listen to me,' Sebastian said. 'There is more at stake than you can imagine. I implore you to listen!'

He dropped to take a seat on a bench by the wall and clasped his hands together as if in prayer. Sonja felt the tension disappear from her body now that the man was no longer looming over her. Of course she could listen to what he had to say.

As Sonja came back into the hall, a small woman in a colourful poncho approached her, handing her a dish covered with silver foil and muttering something in Spanish that Sonja could not understand. She tried to apologise and push the dish back into the woman's hands, but she shook her head, crossed herself and turned on her heel. This left her standing dressed in a sticky synthetic dress with a dish of food in her hands, watching the people flow out of the mausoleum. A kaleido-scope of thoughts spun through her mind, triggered by the conversation with Sebastian and the proposal he had made. This could be the solution to all her problems. Or it could cost her life.

It had all become a bizarre dream, the kind of nonsense that someone on the verge of heatstroke would imagine. Thinking it through, she could see a clear line, a string of events. It was a road – admittedly one with plenty of twists and turns – leading from her initial decision to earn some extra cash by running that mysterious errand for Thorgeir the lawyer a year and a half ago, and taking her to this moment; standing awkwardly in a Mexican mausoleum in Culiacán and staring at a decision that she was ill-prepared to take. The problem with seeing the sequence of events like this was that, with hindsight, it was all pretty obvious, but there was no possible way to have anticipated any of it.

79

Sonja's ears were still ringing after the endless string of songs played by the mariachi band. The only thing she could make out of from the lyrics, though, was Mr José's name – *Meester Hozee* – as it sounded on the lips of the gaily dressed singers. The music had clearly been appre-ciated by the guests, who repeatedly raised their glasses to the band.

Nati had said that the music was called *narcocorridos*. 'The songs are about what a gangster José was. It's pretty popular music.'

They had departed from the mausoleum as the party was at its height, escorted by the men who had fetched them from the airport – the driver and the silent man who still sported sunglasses even though it was now fully dark. Sebastian had joined them, crammed into the back seat between her and Nati.

The car came to a halt outside a low building and they got out, fol-lowing the driver. A smell of gas and charcoal floated on the warm air as most of the city's population prepared an evening meal. The driver walked to one of the steel doors and hammered on it. A skinny wraith of a man in filthy clothes immediately opened the door. They went inside and stopped in front of something that stood on the bare concrete floor – it resembled a giant metal salad bowl.

'What's that?' Sonja asked.

'It's a limpet,' Nati said. '*Parasito*.'

Sonja waited for a better explanation, but for some reason the group stared at her as if they were waiting for her reaction to the metal thing on the floor.

'And?'

'You fix the limpet to a ship that's going from Europe to Iceland, and then move it to a ship that's going from Iceland to the US. It's a wide-open route! And then we don't need to worry about Greenland anymore. In the US they check ships that come from the south, but not the ones that come from the north. We can carry forty kilos in each limpet.' Nati smiled with satisfaction.

'What do you mean, that I'm supposed to put this on a ship?'

'You dive,' Nati said. 'And fix it under the ship.'

If Sonja hadn't been so frightened, she would have laughed. 'I don't know how to dive.' This was ridiculous.

'You can take a course. I'll pay for it. Anyone can learn to dive.'

Sonja sniggered helplessly. 'I really think you're crazy,' she said. 'I can't fix this to a ship. I don't reckon I could even lift it.' She bent down and tested the weight of the metal dish. It was as heavy as it looked. 'I'd just sink to the bottom with this,' she said.

The skinny man in the filthy clothes waved his hands. 'No, no! There will be floats on it,' he said in stiff English. 'No problem to swim with it when the floats are there.'

'No problem,' Nati echoed. 'No problem for you. There's a rubber sleeve inside that the goods go in. This is a system that has been used many times. Sebastian will show you exactly how it works.'

She turned and headed for the door, but stopped and asked the skinny man when the limpet would be ready.

'In two weeks,' the man said and bowed. 'Sebastian can collect it in two weeks.'

Nati turned around slowly, eyes flashing at the man, and switched to Spanish, and while Sonja could not understand the words, her tone left no doubt that she was heaping abuse on him. The man muttered something that appeared to be an apology and began to tremble so violently that his teeth chattered.

Nati snapped out something that seemed to be her final word, spat on the floor at the man's feet and nodded to the driver, who reacted fast, picked up a length of pipe from the bench and swung it hard against the man's leg. He sank to the floor, whining in pain.

Sonja would have instinctively gone to his aid if Sebastian had not held her back, steering her towards the door.

'Pretend you've seen nothing,' he whispered in her ear as Sonja swallowed the terror that had mushroomed in her belly at the man's pitiful cries. 'A blow like that for every week's delay, Nati says.'

Sonja wished that he had not bothered to translate Nati's threat, as, no matter how hard she swallowed, again and again, forcing herself to take deep breaths, she could not overcome her fear. Her legs refused to obey her and she felt faint. As they left the building, Sonja could see the man curled into a ball on the floor, his arms around his damaged leg.

'As you see,' Nati hissed, turning to Sonja. 'It's best that my people keep their word.'

Sonja got into the car and as Sebastian shut the door, she saw the knowing look on his face. All of a sudden the suggestion he had made in the mausoleum no longer seemed so far-fetched.

80

'Where are we going now?' Sonja asked, pretending to be curious. Her head was still numb, and she felt as if she were on the point of passing out. Sebastian had left them outside a nightclub, whispering 'We talk later' to her as he'd got out of the car. Sonja had nodded almost imperceptibly.

She would have to think over their conversation carefully. She needed to consider it at home and in her own space, with the usual reality in front of her, the overheated madness of Mexico far behind her.

'Now we'll take you home,' Nati said.

'We're going to the airport now?'

'That's right, *mi amor*. I don't sleep well in Mexico. You never know when a grenade is going to come flying through the window. Poor José might have been popular with the people around here, but he also had plenty of enemies. Now I've inherited them all, and probably a few new ones as well.'

Passing the same street they had driven down on the way from the airport earlier – the one that had seemed abandoned – Sonja saw it was now very much alive. Not only were the storefronts open, the street was filled with people with shopping bags and the food stalls had multiplied, and she asked herself how big the market in this area could be for tacos and *sopes*, which, judging by the signs, was what they mostly sold.

Even the darkness seemed swelteringly hot as they walked out to the aircraft, which was lit up on the runway. Sonja still had in her hands the dish of food the old native woman had handed her, and it seemed important to Nati that it came with them. On board the jet, she took the dish from Sonja and passed it to the stewardess.

'Heat this up,' she said. 'We're hungry.'

As the words left Nati's lips, Sonja could feel how desperately hungry she was. She felt completely empty and the sinews in her belly began to cramp at the thought of food. She had hardly eaten a thing since the steak at the restaurant in Reykjavík, but could not for the life of her recall how long ago that evening had been. Time and space had stretched and twisted since Nati had knocked on her door.

The stewardess appeared with the dish soon after take-off and Nati clapped her hands in delight.

'Mama's *molé*!'

'Mama's?' Sonja asked. 'Your mother's?'

'Yes!' Nati said. 'Chocolate and chilli sauce with chicken. Just taste it; it's wonderful.'

'Was that your mother who brought the food?' Sonja asked, thinking of the tiny native woman who had handed her the dish instead of standing in line to wait for a chance to speak to Nati. There had been no indication that she recognised her daughter, or had any desire to speak to her.

'That's her. We don't talk. She's ... what shall I say? ... She doesn't approve of my lifestyle. But she still wants me to eat properly and thinks I'm too thin,' Nati laughed.

'But she came to the memorial service,' Sonja said, with a sudden need to defend the little woman, even though she would have hardly taken it well if someone had sought to defend her own mother's shortcomings.

'She's no doubt delighted that José is dead. She never approved of him. And he tried his best to be good to her – even bought her a house that she refused to move in to. But if she wants to live in a mud hut and cook over an open fire, that's her business.' Nati fell silent for a moment and gazed out of the window. 'Taste it,' she said. 'There's nothing that tastes as good as your mother's food.'

The food was indeed excellent and Sonja felt herself becoming calmer as she ate, taking a second helping of the thick, dark sauce. Nati watched in satisfaction.

'It's fantastic,' Sonja said, and Nati beamed with delight. It was as if Sonja had heaped praise on her own cooking and not her mother's.

They ate in silence for a while and the stewardess filled their champagne flutes. Sonja gulped it down, as, despite being sweet, there was a heat to the sauce that burned her throat.

'I was wondering,' she said at last, putting her plate aside, 'when you were going to help me get my son back – when you were going to make Adam agree on custody.'

Nati swallowed the final morsel and wiped her lips. 'I don't work like José,' she began. 'Now that I'm taking over, there will be changes to the way things are done. And I want to see how you manage with the limpet.'

'But you promised me when I helped you with the body, remember?'

'Helped me?' Nati said and there was a look of astonishment on her face that would have convinced Sonja if she hadn't known better. 'You were the one who killed him! I have it on tape.'

Sonja leaned back and sighed. This conversation had gone in completely the wrong direction. The friend card that Nati had played on their journey south and the female solidarity idea had evaporated.

'You said you needed a friend, and friends help each other,' Sonja said, aware of the hurt tone in her own voice. 'Why did you want me to travel with you to Mexico if I'm not your friend?'

Nati bit a toothpick, sucked it for a second and spat it out onto the carpet. Her eyes narrowed as she glared at Sonja. 'I wanted to let you see who you're working for. You work for me, and I'm not José. I don't need to buy love by doing favours. I don't need any *narcocorridos* or a magnificent mausoleum. I don't give a fuck if people love me or not. I'm a thousand times happier if they're afraid of me.'

Sonja closed her eyes, unable to look at Nati any longer. The conversation with Sebastian returned to her, and now she fully understood what he had meant when he had told her that nobody could ever trust Nati.

81

María had highlighted in red every one of Agla's calls to financial institutions. She'd put the spreadsheet together to track the pattern of her calls and now it was almost complete. There were still two numbers to be accounted for: one in Luxembourg and one in Paris. These had to be mobiles registered to individuals. She started with the number with the Luxembourg code, but, regardless of where she searched, nothing came up. She toyed seriously with the idea of calling the number, but that could be dangerous. She had no desire to let Agla and her friends know too early that they were being watched. The tracks could disappear quickly, as she knew from her own bitter experience of working for the special prosecutor's office.

She decided to concentrate on the other number, the French one. María typed the number into a Paris directory and the owner's name appeared instantly: William Tedd. Presented with a name that seemed to be English rather than French, María put it through Google to see where it might take her. There were a great many links, so she added *Paris* to the search terms and immediately saw from the first entry that she had found what she was looking for. This William Tedd worked for an American bank and was based in Paris. She sighed. She had found from Agla's phone records exactly what she had expected to – confirmation that Agla was involved in some kind of financial activity. But this still did nothing to assuage her pangs of conscience over how she had come by this information.

She looked at the clock and saw that it was close to midnight. She picked up her phone and car keys, and was about to activate the alarm system when she hesitated. That name, William Tedd, was one that rang a bell somewhere. This wasn't a name that they had checked out as being linked to Agla, but she was certain that she had seen it somewhere in connection with some of her overseas funds. She turned round in the dark office and went to the archive room. She tapped in a code that opened the doors with a hiss. It didn't take long to find the folders she wanted. She took them to the canteen, where she switched on the coffee machine, which flashed a red light to confirm that it was heating up. Now she definitely would need a dose of caffeine if she was going to get through all these documents.

The coffee machine hadn't even got as far as buzzing to announce that it was ready when María found William Tedd's name in the case files. He had witnessed a financial transaction they had given up trying to trace, so that didn't mean much. But in the same file she came across another interesting name. In hindsight, there was nothing about the name that she would have remembered if she hadn't stumbled across it again recently: Jean-Claude Berger. But he wasn't a concierge this time; rather, he was the chairman of the board of Avance Investment, the largest investment fund that Agla used and which the prosecutor's office was keenly aware was hers, even though it wasn't in her name. María leaned back in her chair and laughed out loud. Concierge and chairman of the board. Could Agla really have been so carelessly overconfident?

82

Tómas could see that his mother was glowing with joy at the sight of him. He could barely contain himself – and he had been revelling in playing the fool since his mother arrived. He had hardly been able to believe his ears when his father had told him that Mum was coming for a visit. A visit! She had not been inside the house since she had left, and his father had always made him run out to the car when she came to collect him, and never once invited her in. And now she was sitting on his bedroom floor, laughing as he did a handstand on his bed while Dad made coffee in the other room.

'Because I have to go abroad for work, you won't be coming to me until Sunday,' Mum said. 'But we have the whole of the next weekend together.'

Tómas did a back flip onto his bed. He didn't care that his weekend with her had been delayed, now that she had come to see him. There was so much that he needed to show her, and she had never played with Teddy, who seemed to like her, trying again and again to lick her face as she sat on the floor.

Dad called from the kitchen that the coffee was ready. When they went to the kitchen, they found that he had made hot chocolate for Tómas so that he could sit at the breakfast bar next to Mum and slurp from his mug like a grown-up.

'Everything all right in London?' his father asked.

'I think so,' Mum replied.

'Be careful,' Dad said.

'I always am,' Mum told him.

'We'll talk when you're back,' Dad said.

'I'll let you know,' Mum said.

It was like a normal conversation between normal people, and Mum seemed so happy, tugging at his earlobes and ruffling his hair, and Dad didn't seem to be angry at all. There was just a normal expression on his face, as if he was quite happy to have Mum coming round for a visit. Maybe things were better between them? The teacher at school had told him that it was always difficult after a divorce, and people would argue a lot, but that would get better with time. Maybe now that time had come?

83

Sonja went straight from the airport to Nati's house in Chelsea. At the front door she took a single long breath and knocked immediately, so as not to let the fear inside her turn into hesitation. Best to get it over with. Amadou opened the door and Sonja walked straight past him and into the hall.

'Sonja!' Nati called in delight, coming out into the hall. 'Come in!'

Sonja greeted her with no great warmth. There was no reason to pretend that years had passed since they had last met, considering it was only two days ago that they had parted at Reykjavík airport.

Nati showed her into the living room and Sonja felt the goose pimples rising along her legs. But now the room looked completely different, so much so that it hardly seemed to be the same place. It had been filled with plants and lamps, colourful paintings had been hung on the walls and the furniture was pale bamboo. They sat in armchairs either side of a small table and Amadou appeared with a tray of coffee. Sonja was about to stand up and take the tray from him, but a shake of Nati's head told her to sit still. Amadou supported the tray with the stump of his hand, placing it with a clatter on a side table so that coffee spilled from the pot. He placed cups, a sugar bowl and a jug of milk on the table between them and poured the coffee into the cups. One-handed, it took him a long time while they sat watching in silence. Then he leaned down, used the stump to take hold of the tray and left the room.

'It's a little painful,' Nati said and Sonja was sure that she could see something mischievous in her expression, as if she enjoyed watching the one-handed man's tribulations.

'How much am I carrying now?' Sonja asked.

'Four,' Nati said. 'And it goes straight to Greenland, where my guy will take delivery. Well, he lets his partner in Nuuk have a small amount that he uses to mix cheap crack for the locals. They seem to be obsessed with getting out of it any way they can. I'm telling you this so you know I'm aware of what goes on. It's best if my people realise that I know everything. None of them should imagine that they can go behind my back.'

'Understood,' Sonja said and sighed. The feeling of resignation that had enveloped her like a blanket on the flight to Mexico wrapped itself again around her. She would just do as she was told. It was pointless trying to change her circumstances – for the moment. But Sebastian's proposal was still on her mind.

'If I turn a blind eye to that kind of thing,' Nati said, 'it's because it's to my advantage. But if someone's cutting and stealing, and I reckon that it's bad for me, then neither God nor a thousand angels will be able to save that person. You understand me?'

'Completely,' Sonja said, taking a mouthful of the coffee that Amadou seemed to have added sugar to without her noticing.

'This is your last flight. You can find someone else to carry small shipments by air, and you can take over the big shipments with the limpet.'

'I don't have any people in Iceland,' Sonja said. 'I've always worked by myself and have no idea how to find someone for the flights. Isn't it best if Adam continues to look after this?'

'No,' Nati said in a flat tone.

Sonja waited for her to say more, but she sat with a smile on her face while Sonja wriggled like a fish caught on a line, as she tried to think of a way to escape.

'How about Adam looks after the limpet? He has plenty of men around him who can learn to dive and who are strong enough to carry something that heavy. That way I could carry on with the flights and the Greenland route—'

'Adam has done nothing but fuck up these last few months,' Nati interrupted. 'His people keep getting caught by customs so I don't trust him any longer. But I trust you. You're someone who has talents. You take over the limpet next week and find someone to look after the flights from here to Iceland. And you can let Adam have the little bit he needs for distribution in Iceland.'

'Adam won't be happy with that,' Sonja said.

'I've told him how things are going to be. He has no choice but to do as he's told.'

Sonja was taken by surprise. 'When did you tell him this?' she asked. 'When did you tell him that I'm supposed to take over?'

'The day before yesterday,' Nati said, pouring more coffee into her cup.

This was astonishing. Could Adam be happy to have been taken out of the game? He had been more friendly towards her yesterday than he had been at anytime since they had parted. He had been courteous, invited her in and his welcome had almost been warm. Could Nati have said something to him that put her in a stronger position when it came to him? Was being Nati's friend such an influential thing? Sonja decided to tempt fate by reminding her of the favour she had asked, and which Nati had promised.

'When will you tell Adam that I need to get custody of our son?'

Nati put a finger to her lips. 'Shh,' she said loudly. 'Don't push, Sonja. We'll see how things go over the next few weeks, and if you work hard, then we'll see what can be done.'

It was the reply Sonja had expected. She got to her feet, ready to say goodbye.

'I had better take the gear up to the hotel and get it packed,' she said.

But Nati shook her head. 'You're not going to any hotel,' she said. 'You're staying here. And I expect a better welcome than last time I knocked on your door. Understood?'

Sonja nodded and sat down again. She took a gulp of the over-sweet coffee and it seemed to stick in her throat so that she was unable to swallow. It made no difference how much she wriggled like a fish on a hook. She should just as well forget all her own plans, give up and go with the flow. It made no difference what she did, the trap continued to close around her.

84

'Do you have to bring this stuff to bed?' Maggi asked as she dropped the stack of papers on the bedside table and got in beside him.

'I was just going to go through a few of the annual reports,' María said. 'Is that any different to reading Yrsa?' She pointed a finger at the book in Maggi's hand. 'I read this kind of stuff because I enjoy it, just the same as you and your crime books.'

'I know,' he said and rolled onto his side.

That wasn't a positive sign. Turning his back was a signal there was something he wasn't happy with. It was as if he had sensed something. Maybe she should tell him the truth about what had happened with Agla. Maybe it would clear the air if, as she feared, he had sniffed out that she had been up to something underhand. Perhaps he'd be amused if he told him she had lied her way into a 'bankster's' house with a story about the pair of them going to a strip club.

'Is everything all right?' she asked.

Maggi rolled onto his back again. 'Of course, everything's fine,' he said, and smiled.

She smiled back at him, pleased that he had looked over at her, relieved that he had laughed.

'I'm just concerned that work is eating up every minute of your time. Last night you came home in the middle of the night and now you're crawling into bed at nine o'clock, bringing paperwork from the office with you.'

María breathed a sigh of relief. If that was all that was bothering him, then it would be best to let sleeping dogs lie. Best to keep quiet about that ridiculous incident with Agla.

'You're right,' she said, put the annual report she had opened to one side and wriggled closer to him. 'Is Yrsa's book any good?'

'Bloody good,' Maggi said, putting it down and switching off the light. He turned to her, wrapped his arms around her and pulled her tight. María lay still, enjoying the closeness while she waited for him to fall asleep so she could sneak into the other room with the stack of paperwork from the bedside table and make another effort to figure out the contents.

These were the certified annual reports for the last ten years, including one that hadn't been in the Voice of Truth's folder. It was the latest one. She had briefly scanned the financial outcome and seen that for the first time in a decade, the smelter had turned a profit. That in itself was odd, in the first year following the financial crash. The exchange rate had certainly changed, but she had a suspicion – a strong one – that the currency restrictions imposed during the crisis had played a larger part. It had become more difficult for the smelter to pay its parent company's invoices overseas since the central bank had decided that it needed to approve all major payments leaving the country.

85

There was one message on Bragi's phone; he grunted his satisfaction when he saw the little heart. Everything was going according to plan. Sonja would arrive on the afternoon flight from London and he would ensure that there would be no trouble – no random checks around this flight. And tomorrow there would be an envelope on the floor by the door containing enough to keep Valdís for four months. He had already saved enough to pay Stephanie and Amy for several months, but sooner or later Valdís would need overnight care as well, and that would be even more expensive. So it would be worth putting as much by as he could. Her pension and his salary were enough to keep them going, so far, but from August he would retire and then he would need their savings. But Sonja had assured him that there would be more trips now, so that would be more cash for him.

He pushed the phone to the back of his locker and locked it. The aircraft would be in the air by now and it would be on the runway in two and a half hours. He could keep the staff busy until then, and there was nothing unusual about slowing things down – having them clear up and getting paperwork done, while he looked after the arrivals hall himself. He strolled out of the locker room and wrote the day's tasks on the whiteboard. He went through the passenger list, checked on Sonja and then wrote on the board that he wanted one passenger in twenty checked from the Copenhagen flight that was landing before hers. That way the boys would be happy to take a break by the time the London flight landed and would jump at the chance of a breather when he came to relieve them. Maybe he could even splash out on Danish pastries for the coffee break to encourage them to not return to their posts too quickly. But that might be a little too obvious. It didn't pay to depart too often from routine behaviour. It would arouse suspicion.

He was still pondering the pastry idea when the office door opened and two of the customs officers he recognised from Reykjavík came in, followed by a drug-squad officer with a sniffer dog.

'Well, good morning,' he said, trying to appear cheerful, as his mind started to go into overdrive.

'G'day, g'day,' one of the customs officers said and the other echoed him. 'G'day.' The three of them crowded around the coffee machine, which immediately and loudly began to grind beans to order.

'To what do we owe this honour?' Bragi asked and felt pressure mounting in his head.

'Just the usual,' the drug-squad officer said. He dropped heavily into a chair, picked a biscuit from the packet on the table, snapped it in two and gave half to the dog, which chewed it into the carpet.

'Increased security status, or what?'

'Nope. Just a tip-off on the drugs hotline just now. A big shipment coming through.'

'So,' Bragi said. 'Copenhagen?'

'Nope,' the drug-squad officer said and dipped the remaining half of the biscuit into his coffee. 'London.'

86

Bragi's hands shook so hard that he dropped the phone as he picked it up, so it clattered to the floor and came apart. It would be just his luck if this wretched phone were to break just as he needed to rely on it. On his knees on the floor, he picked up the parts of the phone and tried to figure out how they fitted together. The phone didn't appear to be broken, but the back had fallen off and there was a loose square piece that had to be the battery. He made a couple of attempts to slot it all together, and realised there was no point in hurrying. His hands were shaking so much that he could hardly control them, and his head felt as if it was going to burst. He could hardly think.

He realised eventually that inside the phone were three little square electrical contacts that had to match those on the battery, so everything at last fitted together and it easily snapped into place. He pressed the ON button three times before the phone responded. Then it took a while to start up and connect to the mobile network.

Now he was facing the possibility that Sonja could be caught, and the thought hit him that he could also be in danger. They had never discussed whether or not she would keep quiet about how he had helped her. He had assumed that she was the type who could be expected to do that. She had been to his home and had seen Valdís. She knew why he needed the money. It had never occurred to him that she would implicate him. But now, it felt as if all of the things he had previously taken for granted had been swept away. His dissatisfaction with the nursing home where Valdís had been looked after, the fact that he had missed her terribly, and his concerns over the bruises that had appeared on her body were suddenly all minor considerations in comparison to what could be awaiting them. All of a sudden, he was facing the prospect that Valdís could die alone and abandoned while he was in prison. That would be his gratitude to her for a whole lifetime of care – a whole lifetime of love.

When the little icon had finally appeared in the corner of the screen, Bragi opened the messages and sent an exclamation mark to Sonja's phone. But that single exclamation mark seemed too little, considering how serious the situation was, so he sent a second message with a row of three exclamation marks. She could hardly misunderstand that.

He sighed. The aircraft would be landing before long, so his warning was already far too late.

He put the phone back in the locker and leaned against the wall so as not to faint. His legs had turned to jelly and he felt dizzy. He was too old for this kind of stress. He should have thought things through more carefully before he had started off on this stupidity. He must have been out of his mind to have gone down this road.

87

The landing was an unusually bumpy one and the aircraft bounced on the runway a couple of times – so hard that the fittings rattled and Sonja was shaken about in her seat. The weather outside seemed to be fine and the blue spring light showed in merciless detail the bare landscape that still needed a few more warm days before it would take on a light-green hue.

She switched on her phone and it pinged at her twice. Maybe it was her imagination, but she felt there was a note of desperation in those sharp pings. Her heart sank as soon as she saw the exclamation mark, and it lurched as she saw the second message, with a row of the punctuation marks. This had to be something serious.

The aircraft taxied slowly up to the terminal. As usual the passengers were on their feet the instant the seat belt light had been switched off, pulling bags from the overhead lockers. There was little that Sonja could do. Maybe the exclamation marks meant there were dogs carrying out spot checks in the terminal. Maybe they would be waiting for her at the end of the jetway. The shipment was in the laptop case that was at her feet. She had taken no special measures this time to hide it other than to place the vacuum packs into empty coffee packs that she had then wrapped up in clingfilm. This had made a single flat package that fitted comfortably in the bag next to her laptop. The packages themselves were airtight in many layers of plastic and carefully sealed. She had refused to drop her standards, even when Nati had stood over her and laughed at her precautions.

It was impossible to be sure if the packages were dog-proof, as they had been packed so recently that it was not certain that the smell of cocaine had yet made its way through the three layers. But as she had no idea what the exclamation marks meant, she could hardly leave the aircraft with the shipment. The couple next to her were already on their feet and pushing their way into the gangway between the rows of seats to search for their bags. Sonja took an instant decision: she dropped to her knees, took the life vest from under the middle seat, took the flat package from her laptop bag and slipped it into the life-vest compartment.

Sonja felt the fresh air flood into the aircraft as the doors opened. A moment later the throng of passengers began to move, so she stood up in front of the aisle seat and pretended to be looking for something in the overhead locker. She quickly glanced around to check if anyone might be watching her, and when she was sure nobody was taking any notice, she put the life vest in the locker. Then she picked up her laptop case, waited her turn and joined the queue leaving the aircraft cabin. The drugs would be found before long, and the passenger list would show that this had been her seat, so this last-minute effort would probably not do much good. But it would at least buy her time – a little head space in which to think.

88

'I know her by sight. It's best if I go with you to pick her up at the jetway,' Bragi said to the younger of the two Reykjavík customs officers. 'You two go through the baggage with the dog. I don't want to hold passengers up longer than necessary, so it's best to check the bags quickly, but do it well.'

The drug-squad guy shrugged his shoulders, as if he was someone who only turned up at work so as to get paid and had little interest in what happened. The older of the customs officers looked at Bragi curiously.

'How come you know this Sonja Gunnarsdóttir by sight?' he asked.

Bragi leaned back in his chair until it was balanced on its two back legs, a ploy to make himself appear relaxed. 'That's the strange thing about this,' he said. 'I've picked her out of the line before now. She had nothing on her, but there was something suspicious about her.'

'Suspicious? How so?'

'Well, I'm not sure I know myself. There was just something about her that didn't ring true.' He smiled apologetically, and one of the young customs officers came to his rescue.

'We reckon that Bragi has a sixth sense. It's uncanny how he manages to pick out the smugglers just by staring at them.'

There was pride in the young man's voice and for some reason, it grated with Bragi. These youngsters who looked up to him would be in for a disappointing surprise were they to discover the truth.

'I don't know if it's anything as dramatic as a sixth sense,' he said with a laugh. 'More likely it's just years of experience.'

'Fair enough,' the older customs officer said, jerking his head to tell the drug-squad guy with the dog to come with him. 'Landing in five minutes. Let's get things going.'

Bragi felt how feeble his legs were as he got to his feet and set off with the younger customs officer, who chattered without a break about how he had always dreamed of a posting to Keflavík airport and how he was going to apply for a transfer as soon as he had more experience. When they were in the passage, the youngster slowed down – apparently out of consideration for Bragi – and they arrived at the top of the jetway just as the aircraft's engines stopped. Bragi wondered if Sonja had switched on the phone straightaway and had seen his warning, or if she was leaving the aircraft without any idea of what was waiting for her.

He saw from the look on her face as she emerged from the jetway that she had seen his warning.

'Could I ask you to accompany us?' Bragi suggested and lightly took her arm, indicating to the young customs officer that he should lead the way. He had already told him that they would use the staff corridor so as to not arouse the interest of other passengers by going through the arrivals hall. They were approaching the door when Sonja stopped and crouched down to adjust her shoe.

'Are you all right?' Bragi asked in a tone of forced concern as he looked down at her.

'Under seat 19E,' Sonja whispered as she rose to her feet.

89

'Take her in,' Bragi told the young customs officer. 'And ask the boys to meet me on the plane with the dog. We ought to search it before it gets cleaned.'

He was taking a chance, gambling on the possibility that the young man wasn't familiar with the airport's routines. He watched the two of them as they made their way along the staff corridor, and as soon as the door had closed behind them he hurried as fast as his sore knee would take him along the passage. He walked by the wall, against the flow of passengers heading cheerfully for the duty-free store. These had to be the people from the Oslo flight that had been scheduled to land ten minutes behind the London one.

He was out of breath and felt that his head was about to burst from the pressure building up inside it when he reached the jetway – just in time to stop the new crew from going on board. The pilot looked concerned and he checked his watch, and Bragi could tell what he was thinking.

'There shouldn't be any delay,' he said reassuringly as he stepped inside. 'There's a dog on the way and he'll be no time going through the cabin.'

The cleaning crew were already on board and they always started at the far end of the cabin and worked forwards, so there was a clear way to get to row nineteen. E was a middle seat and he leaned forwards to look underneath it. There was nothing to be seen on the floor, so he put a hand underneath and felt that there was something else where the life vest should have been. He lifted out the package and was surprised at how heavy it was. This was no small shipment.

Two of the cleaning crew were in the toilets aft and one was busily picking up rubbish from between the seats. Bragi waited until the man bent down, turned quickly and dropped the package carefully into a rubbish sack that was held open on a metal frame on wheels. He was just in time, because the man straightened up and dropped a handful of litter into the bag, immediately hiding the package inside.

'Everyone out!' Bragi called, loud enough for the people cleaning the toilets to hear him.

'Sorry, what?' the cleaner with the bag in its metal frame asked. He was a gaunt Pole, or so Bragi assumed – the badge pinned to his creased shirt told him the man's name was Pavel.

'Everyone out of the aircraft, please,' Bragi called. 'We have a sniffer dog coming. The dog's on the way.'

He clapped his hands to tell them to be quick. They responded instantly: the man and woman who had been cleaning the toilets dropped everything to the floor as they hurried out. Pavel was clearly about to do as he had been trained, leaving the metal frame with the bag behind, but Bragi snapped at him to take the damned thing out with him and get it out of the way.

Although the man looked at Bragi as if he was insane, he did as he was told, leaving the aircraft with the bin trundling ahead of him.

Bragi sat in the front row of seats to catch his breath. It would do Valdís no good if the stress were to kill him with a heart attack at this moment. He took deep breaths, counting to five with each one in order to slow his heartbeat. He had only done this a few times when the older of the two Reykjavík customs officers and the drug squad guy appeared with the dog.

'Nothing in the baggage,' the drug squad guy said, placing the dog in the gangway to search.

'Has anyone been on board?' the customs officer asked.

'The crew hadn't boarded, and the cleaners had just started when I sent them out,' he said. 'I'll go and have a word with them while you check the cabin.' He got to his feet and set off up the gangway, nodding to the pilot, who smiled with feigned patience.

The cleaning crew were waiting in a group at the top of the jetway. Bragi snatched the bag from its metal frame, to Pavel's astonishment, and snapped, 'Customs!' Now he would have to think fast.

He marched with the bag straight to a toilet off the corridor. He took the packet from the bag, stood on the toilet seat and tried with difficulty to push aside one of the ceiling tiles, but it was glued in place and he had to punch it. It shifted, but a crack had appeared in it, not that there was anything he could do about that. He shoved the package up into the suspended ceiling and hoped that nobody would notice the crack in the tile. Then he carefully got down from the toilet, picked up the bag and went back to the passage, into the staff corridor and downstairs.

'My bladder's killing me,' he quickly said to Vilhelmina, who had been monitoring the CCTV and who now came to meet him. 'I seem to have to take a leak every five minutes all day long.'

That was enough to forestall whatever she had been about to say. He emptied the bag onto one of the steel-topped tables, snapped on a pair of latex gloves and began searching through the garbage. There wasn't much there, just a few sandwich wrappers, two water bottles, an empty jar, one ripped magazine, a couple of chewing gum wrappers and some smaller rubbish.

'Nothing here,' he sighed. 'Not a damned thing.'

His walkie-talkie burst into life, telling them that the aircraft had been cleared.

Vilhelmina shrugged her shoulders. 'Do you think she's carrying it internally?' she asked.

'That wouldn't be a surprise,' Bragi said, sitting down and rubbing his knee.

90

It wasn't the first time that Sonja had waited at the clinic in Keflavík for the radiographer to arrive to X-ray her. The unfortunate woman had only just gone home when she had been called back.

When she saw Sonja, she gave her a tired smile. 'Hello, again,' she said.

'Hello,' Sonja said apologetically. 'I'm sorry to interrupt your dinner, but customs seem to like me.'

Since the exclamation mark had appeared on the screen, it had been all she could do to remain calm. Bragi had explained to her when they had started their cooperation how to behave if she were to be arrested; and that the best approach was to stay calm, but to ask at intervals why she had been picked, and when she would be able to go home. This gave an impression of innocence, he said. She had followed his instructions, and asked a couple of times while the customs officers interrogated her and reduced her luggage almost to tiny particles. Then they had brought in a man with a dog that had sniffed her, apparently without detecting anything suspicious. Sonja was relieved that she had stuck with her careful precautions that Nati thought had been way over the top. The tiniest grain clinging to someone's clothes would be enough to alert the dog, but she seemed to have got away with it. And if they were searching her and her luggage, they couldn't have found the package in the aircraft's cabin.

'Why did you pick me out?' she asked yet again while she sat and waited with the young customs officer for the doctor to finish examining the X-rays of her stomach.

'We had a tip-off,' he said. 'An anonymous tip-off.'

'That's really weird,' she said, but she knew there was nothing weird about it.

Adam had tipped them off: no doubt an anonymous call to the dope hotline or straight to the customs service. That meant that he must have worked out that she had been behind the arrests of his two couriers, and his conversation with Nati must have pushed him over the edge. She would have loved to have seen the look on his face as Nati had informed him that Sonja was taking over his role, and that must be the explanation for why he had been so amiable when he had allowed her to visit Tómas. He had already decided that he was going to inform on her and the visit had been an opportunity for Tómas to say farewell to her.

She closed her eyes, leaned back and rested her head against the wall. The mist of surrender that had wrapped itself around her since the flight to Mexico made way for a new emotion, which generated so much heat within her that for a moment she felt the blood boil in her veins. She was angry. She was livid, and the desire to fight back was rekindled in her.

'I think I know who's behind all this,' she said to the customs officer. 'Maybe you should have a word with Adam Tómasson and suggest that he shouldn't be making anonymous allegations about his ex-wife.'

'What?'

'I'm afraid you've got yourself caught up in a rather bitter custody dispute,' she said as the doctor appeared in the corridor.

'Nothing internal,' she told the customs officer.

Sonja leaned forwards and pulled the tape from around her ankles.

91

María parked in a space at the filling station on Sæbraut and left the car running while she went inside. It wasn't something she normally did, being generally a tireless proponent of green values, but she had felt such a chill since getting out of bed that she decided to keep the car warm. The outside temperature was only eight degrees and although the sun shone practically around the clock, there was still a long way to go before summer arrived.

She bought a SIM card, paid for it in cash and hurried back out to the car. She ripped open the packaging and inserted the card into her phone, replacing the usual one. Then she drove the remaining few metres to the special prosecutor's office, but before she got out of the car she punched in the Luxembourg number that she hadn't been able to identify. This was the only remaining unidentified number on the spreadsheet of Agla's calls. She listened to the high tone, the short pause and then a lower tone – usual when calling an overseas mobile number. There was no reply and María dropped her phone into her pocket in disappointment.

Her chagrin was lifted as she went into the office and saw the statement she had requested from the central bank. She ripped open the envelope and took an extra little tour out of the office again, in order to throw the envelope in the paper-recycling bin, inspecting the document as she went. It was a record of payments of more than half a billion krónur made by Icelandic companies to overseas entities over the preceding months. She placed a ruler over the first page of the statement and slid it slowly downwards. There was nothing remarkable to be seen on the first page, and nothing on the second. It was on the third page that she found what she had been looking for. This was a large payment made at the end of April – by the aluminium company in Iceland to its parent company overseas, and tagged in the central bank's system as a repayment on the loan made for start-up costs. She marked the line with a highlighter and continued down the page, then the next, and the next, until she had gone back eight months. There was no other comparable payment to be seen. This had to be a new payment on a new loan.

María jumped as her mobile phone rang. The unregistered SIM card was still in place, and the number that appeared on the screen was the one she had been trying to call, registered in Luxembourg.

'Hello?' María said nervously.

'Hello. Who's that?' a man's voice asked in English, but with a strong Icelandic accent.

María ended the call, switched off the phone and took out the SIM card. Now she knew what she had needed to find out. There was no need to ask the person's name. She recognised the voice from the recordings Finnur had given her of Agla's calls.

It was Ingimar.

92

'Not the face,' Adam told Rikki. 'But you can kick her legs.'

Sonja's hands were tied behind her back and she crawled across the floor on her front, pushing herself with her feet, while the dog growled in the corner where it had been told to wait. They had searched everywhere, but with no luck. The dog had pawed at the fridge, but she knew that was because it could smell traces from when she had kept stuff in the freezer compartment a couple of times.

'Where's the fucking gear?' Rikki yelled, delivering one kick after another to her legs so that she rolled over onto her side. He kicked her back and belly until she again lay on her chest. Then he started again on her legs.

'Customs took it,' Sonja gasped, one more time.

It was true enough, although she wasn't going to tell them that it had been *her* customs officer who had taken the shipment and hidden it behind a false ceiling in one of the airport corridor toilets, where it was waiting for Sonja to pick it up on her next arrival in the country.

'It would have been all over the news if customs had it, and you'd be on remand. So where the fuck is the gear?'

'I had to leave it on the plane and customs must have picked it up,' she said, the last word turning into a howl of pain as Rikki let fly with his boot at her back and the pain went right through to her belly.

'What's the name of the customs guy you're paying off?' There was nothing abnormal about Rikki's voice, and there was no indication that he was out of breath after battering her with kicks like a footballer. They knew that she had her own contacts in customs, and had known it for a while, but she'd die before she would give them Bragi's name.

'What the fuck did you say to Nati about me?' Adam hissed like an angry cat.

'Nothing,' Sonja gasped.

'What's this bullshit that you're working direct with Nati and I'm out of the loop?'

'She doesn't trust you anymore because you lost two shipments.'

'That's your fault, you fucking bitch,' Adam roared. 'You were the one who put customs on to my guys!'

Sonja expected him to kick her himself, but he held back. He had never laid a finger on her. It was as if there was something inside him that always stopped him at the last moment. But he had no hesitation in letting Rikki do it for him. He nodded to Rikki, who kneeled down, gripped her chin and began stuffing a huge bath sponge into her mouth. She felt as if her jaw was about to be dislocated, but he continued forcing the sponge with his thumbs until the whole thing was in her mouth.

Gradually her whole body went numb and all her thoughts focused on drawing breath. Her nose was blocked up with tears and blood, and neither air nor sound could make their way past the sponge, so her cries ended up somewhere deep in her belly. She tried to push the sponge out with her tongue, but that made her retch, so she stopped, concentrating on breathing through her nose. A heavy kick caught her chin and turned her over onto one side and she instinctively tried to scream, but no sound left her. This violence had become uncannily quiet. Rikki's kicks became harder and rhythmic, as if he was keeping time with a metronome inside his head.

'Not the face,' she heard Adam repeat, and for some bizarre reason she felt a moment's gratitude, even though she knew that it wasn't for her benefit that he didn't want to leave too many obvious marks.

She again cursed herself for opening the door. There was little sense in having two chains and a locking bar across the door when she was fool enough to open it. It was because Adam had seemed so relaxed when she saw him through the spyhole – standing there, tapping at his phone, as he always did when he had to wait. She had genuinely thought that he was coming to her to negotiate in some way, to make some sort of offer; a suggestion of how they could make peace and work together. But she should have known that Adam would never admit defeat of his own accord.

The beating stopped for a moment, but she had hardly drawn breath before Rikki pulled her upright by her hair. Unable to steady herself with her hands, her hair took her entire weight. She was surprised it was still rooted in her scalp by the time she was finally on her feet. Behind her now, Rikki kicked her feet from under her so that she fell forwards, crouched on the floor and Adam stepped close to her.

'You think you're so smart,' he said in a low voice. 'You think you can take my guys out of the game, steal my shipment, strike a deal of your own with Nati and then have the nerve to send the cops to my house.'

If Sonja's mouth had not been stuffed full with the sponge, she would have roared back at him that he should have the sense not to be giving anonymous tip-offs to the drugs hotline. Of course the police had arrived to question him after she had told the customs officer about the custody dispute, and she had added a few tearful sobs into the bargain. So it served him right to get a visit from the law, if only to remind him not to make false accusations.

Adam reached out to her face, pinched her jaw hard and pulled out the sponge. This took her by surprise. She gulped down air, and immediately retched as it felt that she was dragging something deep from her throat.

'Fuck, but you're disgusting,' Adam whispered. 'I don't understand how I could have ever loved you.'

There was pain in his words, and the same strange logic returned to her. She pitied him; felt sorry for the depth of his rage, the painful anger that was all her fault when all was said and done – just the same as her anger was his fault.

Rikki loosened the straps around her arms and her fingers tingled as if they had been burned, as the blood returned to her veins.

'You're going to tell Nati that you got it all wrong. There's no question that you're able to run anything here. You can't cope with it. You have no people, no protection, nothing. You're an idiot if you think you can take over from me.'

Adam walked out of the living room with Rikki behind him.

'Come on, Teddy. Tómas is waiting for you at home,' Adam called to the dog, which obeyed and followed him out.

Sonja collapsed into a ball and tried to control her breathing as she felt with her tongue back and forth, trying to moisten her sore, bone-dry mouth. Adam had not reacted as she had expected he would. She had been sure he would have been more sly, that he would try to negotiate instead of using violence. She had felt that she had been in the stronger position, that Nati's friendship would protect her. But now she had learned that Nati's protection did not extend as far as Iceland.

And she had found out where Rikki's Sponge nickname came from.

93

Sonja didn't answer when Agla rang the bell downstairs, so she once again rang the top-floor bell and a moment later there was a hiss as the old man upstairs opened the door for her. He seemed to work as a door warden for the whole block. Sonja was more likely to open up if she knocked on the door of her apartment.

She desperately needed to talk to Sonja. She had lain awake every night, running through her mind everything that she wanted to say to her. She was going to tell her about trying to kiss María, and the strip club, and everything. She was going to tell her that over the last few weeks it was as if a blockage inside her had been loosened. It was if the determination not to shift her position on anything, which had long been to her advantage, had gradually softened and thinned, almost without her noticing, until, finally, a hole had been punched through what she now realised was her armour. That was the hole that had allowed Sonja in, all the way to her heart. This was what she wanted to explain in the sweetest tones she had at her command. So it would be as well for Sonja to open the door.

She had been prepared to stand and knock for a long time, as she had often had to do in the past, so she hesitated when she saw that the door was ajar.

'Sonja!' she called, rapping on the door frame, but heard no reply.

She stepped over the threshold and had an immediate intuition that something was wrong. The little chest of drawers in the hall was on its side, its top drawer pulled open and the contents spread across the floor.

'Sonja!'

Maybe someone had broken in, and for a moment it occurred to her that the housebreaker could still be inside. Perhaps it was better not to call too loudly.

There was nobody in the kitchen and nothing unusual to see there, so Agla went cautiously into the living room.

Sonja lay in a heap on the floor, her eyes closed.

Agla dropped to her knees at her side and shook her gently. 'What happened? Are you hurt? Did you fall? I'm calling an ambulance.'

She fished her Icelandic phone from her handbag and was about to call the emergency line when Sonja's hand reached gently for hers.

'Don't,' she said, opening her eyes. 'Don't call. It was Adam.'

An hour later Agla sat as still as stone on the sofa, stroking Sonja's head in her lap. She had given her heavy-duty painkillers, made her wash them down with beer, and now Sonja seemed to be about to fall asleep with an ice bag to her cheekbone. Agla watched as the bruises began to appear on her arms. How could a custody battle become so bitter? And why wasn't it enough for Adam to have custody of the boy; why constantly try to obstruct the little access Sonja had to him? And why on earth had he resorted to violence? She simply didn't understand it.

As the anger boiled inside her, she felt the guilt she had suffered from ever since Adam had walked in on her in bed with Sonja evaporate. There was no need for her to feel the slightest responsibility for destroying their marriage. Adam didn't deserve Sonja. A man who could stoop to this didn't deserve anything.

Sonja breathed deeply now and appeared finally to be asleep, so Agla lifted the ice bag from her cheekbone and pulled the blanket over her. She was so slight and tiny under the blanket that Agla felt a stab of compassion. How could the man have found it in him to beat her?

Agla was proud of being calm under pressure. When she was angriest was exactly when she was at her most thoughtful. Of course she would have liked to have called in a big, strong man and have him subject Adam to the same treatment he had given Sonja, but there was no sense in that. She had a much better plan in mind that would set Sonja free.

94

María looked startled as Agla stepped into her office.

'Who let you in?' she asked in surprise and Agla couldn't help laughing.

The young man whose desk was right by the door had got to his feet as soon as she appeared, and punched his code into the keypad by the lock, as he had done many times before, letting her in with a smile. Apparently he hadn't suspected a thing. It obviously wasn't yet common knowledge among the special prosecutor's staff that her case had been concluded and she no longer had any reason to be there.

'They know me well here,' she said, closing María's office door behind her and taking the chair facing María's desk.

María adjusted the collar of her blouse, shuffled papers on her desk into a neat pile and cleared her throat. 'What can I do for you?' she asked.

Agla grinned again. This was so much more formal than the last time they had met.

'I'd really like to have my phone back,' she said.

Without a word, María pulled open a desk drawer, took out the phone and passed it to her.

She was relieved that María hadn't tried to claim to have had nothing to do with her phone.

'I don't suppose you had a warrant for this?' Agla continued.

María shrugged. Of course she hadn't had a warrant. If there had been, then she would have arrived with the paperwork and taken the phone legally, without having to resort to play-acting. Agla felt a slight flush in her cheeks as she recalled the incident.

'I presume you took this because it's registered in Luxembourg and you weren't able to get a warrant to intercept calls or get a call list. I could get my lawyer to lodge a formal complaint,' she said. 'We could make no end of a song and dance about this. Or we could strike a deal. You forget that you ever saw my phone, and I give you Adam on a plate.' She watched as María stiffened in her chair and a questioning frown appeared on her face.

'You remember Davíð at the bank?' Agla continued, opening the phone's recorder app and tapping in the code. The fact that her phone had been taken brought home to her the importance of locking important files behind a password; you could never be sure whose hands they might fall into.

'Of course I remember Davíð,' María said, with a slight impatience in her voice. 'And I was fully aware that he was taking the rap on Adam's behalf.'

'Listen to this conversation between me and Davíð,' Agla said, tapping the play button.

First there was an indistinct buzz – the noise of a coffee shop: the loud hiss of an espresso machine could be heard in the background.

'We need to get Adam out of some difficulties. Are you in?' Agla's voice said, coming from the phone's speaker.

The clatter of a cup being dropped onto a saucer could be heard before a man's voice broke in. *'Absolutely. Like I told you. Just tell me what needs to be done.'*

'You could get two years inside,' Agla's voice said.

'It's an opportunity. Two years is nothing compared to the life sentence I'm under at the moment.'

'Okay,' Agla's voice replied. *'We'll find a way to transfer your debts over to a holding company overseas and they can sit there for good. You'd better go home and figure out what you need in cash. And don't be shy. We want you to know that we appreciate this.'*

'Agla ... You don't know what this means to me. You've no idea how important this is.'

'That's good,' Agla's curt voice could be heard saying, followed by a click as the recording ended.

Agla put down the phone and looked into María's eyes as she leaned eagerly forwards over the desk.

'Do you want it?'

'Do I want it?' María echoed. 'Of course I do! What kind of question is that?'

'In that case I'm clear of everything to do with this beyond what you already have on me. Davíð gets a slap on the wrist for making a false confession and you get Adam. And we both forget the incident with the phone.'

Agla sat motionless as she watched María's expression. She could almost read her thoughts: initially there was a doubtful smile on her face that changed to a look of disbelief before morphing into interest and finally resolve. She stood up and went to the door.

'Wait here,' she told Agla before disappearing through the door almost at a run.

She was back before Agla had completed a round of patience on the phone she had just retrieved.

'Agreed,' María said and Agla stood up.

'I'll email you the recording,' she said. 'And Davíð will be in touch with you to change his testimony.'

95

Davíð's hair had been cut short. Agla almost felt herself missing his fair, angelic curls. He had also grown a heavy beard, which made him look older. That was just as well, she thought, as she had always seen him as an overgrown child.

'There are a few changes currently taking place,' Agla said and Davíð stepped over the threshold, pulling the door to his house closed behind him, muffling the sound of children playing inside. 'You're to go to the special prosecutor today to change your testimony.'

'What?' Davíð frowned, obviously concerned.

'You're going to admit that you lied to protect Adam, but you've seen the error of your ways and you want to see the truth come out. So tell them everything you know.'

Davíð put out a hand and nervously clutched at the lapel of her jacket. 'But, Agla. I took another loan on the house. I was totally relying on our deal!' Red blotches were appearing on his pale skin and he was becoming increasingly agitated.

'The deal stands,' Agla said. 'Don't worry about that. I can even push the figure up if you need it.'

Davíð let go of her jacket and sat down on the half-built wall that separated the driveway from the steps leading up to the house.

'I don't understand this,' he said. 'I don't see why I should stab Adam in the back now?'

'There's really nothing you need to understand,' Agla told him. 'All you need to know is that if you do as I'm asking you, then you don't need to plead guilty – wrongly – which means you get away without a prison term and our deal remains in place. It's a better outcome for you.'

'And a much worse outcome for Adam,' Davíð said.

'Yes. That's what it's all about,' Agla replied.

'I thought you all stood together in this.'

'For a long time that was what I thought was well,' Agla said. 'But when times are hard, you find out who your friends really are. You know how it is.'

96

Tómas sat in the back of the police car and pretended to be enjoying listening to the kids' programme that the policewoman driving had decided was just right for him. She hadn't realised that he was too big now for *Pippi Longstocking*, and that he was certainly big enough to understand that something out of the ordinary was going on – to want to know what this trip was all about.

The police who had come to take his father away weren't in uniform, but the others who came afterwards did have uniforms and baseball caps, and they said they would take him to his mother's place. He had asked again and again why his father had been taken away, but the two police women took turns to say that his mother would explain it. For the moment he couldn't stay with his father.

Going to his mother was what Tómas desired above all else, but all the same, he felt uncomfortable. It was so weird to see strangers leading his father away in handcuffs while Dísa walked back and forth, crying. Now he regretted that he hadn't spoken to his father for such a long time. As they emerged from the Hvalfjörður tunnel he had begun to cry, but the police woman who was at the wheel had switched the siren on for a moment to cheer him up, and it had worked. A loud noise cheered everyone up. His mother knew that and that's why she pumped the salsa music's volume right up whenever he was feeling down.

The closer they got to the city, the more he looked forward to seeing his mother. She would explain what had happened, as the police woman had said, and then they'd go and do something fun together. And since the police had taken his father away, he might get to stay longer with Mum.

Teddy was sitting on the seat next to him. Tómas stroked his soft fur and twisted a lock of his coat around one finger. Teddy seemed perfectly calm and even the wail of the siren hadn't worried him. He could always trust Teddy; he was the best dog you could imagine. His mother would surely be delighted to see them both.

97

Sonja woke up with a smile on her face and Agla knew it was because her son was with her. He had kissed them both goodnight the previous evening and gone to his room with the dog, and when they had peered around the door an hour later he had been fast asleep with the dog curled up at his feet. Agla had suddenly realised that there could be a real possibility of things staying this way in the future, that life could be as it had been that evening. Now they were awake and everything was even sweeter than it had been the night before. She gently stroked a hand across Sonja's blue-black back.

'How are you feeling?' she asked, and Sonja replied that she felt fine. All the same, Agla reached for the painkillers on the bedside table and handed them to her. Going by the livid bruises, she still had to be in pain. Sonja dutifully swallowed the pills and curled up again, while Agla got up. She peered into the living room, where Tómas sat watching TV in his pyjamas, and asked him if he wanted coffee. He laughed at the joke but then his mind was back on the screen.

In the kitchen she made coffee, on the strong side. She would have to get a proper espresso machine that she could keep here, as this standard filter coffee didn't have enough of a kick to it. There were a few things she would have to buy for this place. *Like a new fridge*, she thought, as the current battered fridge's door squeaked open.

Her phone rang, the one she had fetched from María's office and had been assured was not being monitored. She answered it happily. William was calling from Paris.

'I've completed the transfer,' he said and Agla knew that he meant the transfer to Adam's Tortola account. This was a large amount, although they had always referred to it as 'the *small debt*'.

'Thanks,' Agla said and William gave her a cheerful *au revoir*.

Agla selected Jóhann's number, and he answered immediately.

'Can you let Adam know, when he's released, that I've made the transfer to him for the small debt?'

'You two don't talk much these days...' Jóhann said.

'No,' Agla said. 'But don't worry. I've cleared half of the big debt and I'm working on the rest of it. Just keep the prosecutor off my back while I finish the job.'

'You're...' Jóhann said and fell silent.

Agla wasn't sure if he was going to swear at her or congratulate her, so she ended the call before it went any further. There was every chance he didn't know himself which way to go. He should be satisfied that she was working towards freeing them all of the debt, but more than likely he was terrified after she had given them Adam on a silver platter. It was no bad thing to keep him in a state of moderate fear.

The coffee was ready, so she filled two cups, splashed a little milk into each and carried them to the bedroom.

'This is luxury, having room service,' Sonja said as she half sat up in bed. Agla sat on the edge and sipped her coffee.

'In all seriousness, which of us is the guy?' she said. 'Is this some kind of Sapphic secret? Something you know but don't want to tell?'

'I've already told you,' Sonja said. 'I'm the guy.' But Agla could see from Sonja's expression that she was teasing.

'But I reckon that I could be the guy,' she said, hesitating.

Sonja laughed. 'And I think I'm the guy too.' She took a gulp of coffee.

'Really?'

'Maybe we're both the guy. Maybe we're a pair of homos.'

98

Sonja stirred the onion slices in the pot. They were almost translucent, so she added the garlic and ginger she had already chopped and continued to stir gently as the aromas rose up and found their way to her taste buds. She had suddenly wanted spiced soup for lunch, and decided to give in to her desire. Cooking was always calming, especially making soup. But her thoughts built themselves up alongside the ingredients she added to the pot. She was black and blue all over and every movement was painful. Agla had made her take a couple of powerful painkillers that morning so her injuries weren't overwhelmingly sore. What also mitigated the pain was hearing Tómas in the living room, talking to himself as he played with his Lego bricks on the floor. This moment was precisely what she wanted from life: the fragrance from the cooking pot and the sound of her son playing happily in the other room.

If only there wasn't that constant danger hanging over them. She couldn't be sure how long Adam would be on remand for the bank business, but she hoped it would be for as long as possible. The timing had been unbelievably perfect. The day after he had made sure that she was beaten to a pulp, he had been arrested for involvement in the market-manipulation case in which Agla was also implicated. In fact, it was astonishing that he had not been caught up in the case before, as, according to Agla, the case had been closed, but his arrest now suited her perfectly. There was something elegant about the way life turned out this way. She could use a little more of this kind of luck.

She added curry powder and onion seeds, stirring everything together with the oil as it took on a yellow colour and the aroma changed. Her arm was so sore though, she struggled to open the can of coconut milk; she had to wield the tin opener slowly. Yes, today was a day for slow movements. She also needed the leisure to think, and to do so carefully. She needed to face the fact that there were two threats. On one side were Adam and his henchmen, and on the other was Nati. Both had their claws deep in her, so if she were to escape one, she would still have the other to deal with. And that brought her to Sebastian's proposal.

She added a stock cube to the pot and stirred so it dissolved into the coconut milk that was gradually absorbing the yellow of the curry. Searching in the fridge she found two elderly carrots, which she peeled and chopped into fine cubes for the soup, but there wasn't a single piece of protein to be seen in the freezer. Shrimps would have been perfect.

She turned down the heat under the pot so it was just simmering and put the lid on it, and sat at the kitchen table to stare for a moment out of the window. Maybe she had got to the point at which it was best to stop trying to swim up to the surface. Perhaps it was time to sink deeper into the depths, in the hope that down there she might find something solid, a foothold at the bottom from which she could push herself up back upwards.

She picked up her phone and found the number she had stored eight days before when she had been in the mausoleum in Mexico. She pressed call. It rang a few times in a variety of tones as the signal threaded its way between networks, and finally Sebastian's voice answered.

'I've been thinking it over,' Sonja said. 'And I'm in.'

'I'll send you help,' Sebastian said. '*Vaya con Dios.*' – Go with God.

There was a carton containing three eggs in the fridge. They had passed their sell-by date, but everyone knew that eggs could be kept long after the date on the carton, so she carefully broke all three into the soup.

99

María was fired up after her morning's work. She had started with two cups of coffee while she waited for Adam to be brought from remand for the initial interview, which had been, as usual with an opening encounter, short and difficult. Adam had been angry and confused, and his lawyer had found it difficult to explain the situation to him, so there was no point in digging deep into anything. After twenty-four hours in a cell in the old Skólavörðustígur jail downtown, he would have quietened down a bit, and he would be even quieter after forty-eight hours. Although there was really no reason for him to be held on remand, as all of the case files were in the special prosecutor's keeping, and there was nothing he could do to damage their case by being at large, it didn't do these white-collar types any harm to be locked up for a few days. That was enough to knock most of the arrogance out of them and the usual result was that they were keen to spend as long as possible being interviewed, if only because it gave them some company – and that was ideal as the aim was to get them to talk. Considering she had been granted an arrest warrant in Adam's case, it was as well to make full use of it.

Now she was waiting for the special prosecutor to return from lunch. This was his first day back following leave and he had been besieged from the moment he had walked through the door. He generally never went far from the office to get a bite to eat, so he would be back before one o'clock. She had all of the documentation prepared to show him and was looking forward to hearing his opinion and what he thought would be the best move. She pressed the coffee machine's cappuccino button. She would be wired after all this coffee, but that was fine. This was an action day, not a desk day.

'You wanted a word with me?' the special prosecutor said as he came in, and María followed him to his office.

She took the first document from the stack she was carrying, the statement from the central bank, and placed it on the desk in front of him, pointing a finger at the transaction she had already highlighted.

'You can see here the massive payment from the smelter to the overseas parent company,' she said. 'The payment is logged with the foreign exchange register as a payment towards a start-up costs loan.'

'Really?' the special prosecutor put on his reading glasses.

'This payment is new, but it's tagged as a quarterly payment from now on.' The prosecutor hummed to himself as he peered at the statement. María continued: 'This is so large a payment that, over the year, the smelter will show a loss as long as this is being paid, and according to the agreement with the Icelandic state, they pay no tax while start-up costs are being paid off.'

The special prosecutor nodded. 'The smelter companies have always played these games,' he said. '"Lifting the value of goods in transit" is what it was called in the old days, when the parent companies sold raw material to the smelter at astronomical prices so they could create higher costs and lose any profits here.'

'That's right,' María said. 'But this is a brand-new debt and no start-up investment has been made by the smelter that would justify these figures. I've already checked.'

'And?' The special prosecutor looked at her curiously.

'I have reason to believe that a certain Agla Margeirsdóttir is behind the creation of this so-called loan, in collaboration with Ingimar Magnússon.'

María placed Agla's phone-call list on the desk in front of the special prosecutor.

He cleared his throat. 'Weren't you interviewing someone this morning who's potentially involved in the market-manipulation case? How's that connected with this smelter business?'

'It doesn't link to it; or rather, it does, but indirectly. Agla Margeirs-dóttir is connected to both cases. We need to keep her separate from all this for the moment, but we should have enough to justify taking a close look at Ingimar Magnússon.'

'Hold on a second,' he said. 'I'm losing track of this. Precisely what are you checking up on in connection with the smelter?'

'Whether or not Agla is helping the smelter's parent company to swindle the Icelandic State by inventing costs that don't exist.'

'And exactly which investigation does this come under?' The special prosecutor squared up the papers on his desk and handed them to María.

She stared back at him in surprise. 'Well ... Nothing that's formally in progress. Finnur had asked me to look into this to see if it would be substantial enough for an investigation, and that's what needs to happen now.'

'Finnur?' the special prosecutor said, taking off his reading glasses. 'What did Finnur mean by that? He has no authority to commission new investigations.'

'But I thought this had been done with your knowledge, looking into the intercepted phone calls.' María felt her smile stiffen on her face.

The special prosecutor lifted an eyebrow and shrugged. 'I don't have a clue what you're talking about, María,' he said. 'I just don't have a clue.'

100

María was just leaving the district court when her phone rang in her pocket.

She was buttoning her coat up against the bitter cold that was usual out of the sunlight in Reykjavík's early summer, and, without answering the call, she went over to the clock in the middle of the square to warm herself in the sunshine.

She had walked to the court from the office to give herself time to think and to work off her annoyance after the conversation with the special prosecutor. She couldn't understand it. She had worked with Finnur since her first day at the special prosecutor's office and had never been aware that his methods were anything less than completely above board. But just now, when the prosecutor had called Finnur, putting the phone on speaker so they could both talk to him, he had pretended to have no knowledge of the matter; and neither did the special prosecutor. All the same, right at the outset, Finnur had told her that this was with the special prosecutor's knowledge.

Or had he? Suddenly María was unnerved to realise that her memory of the conversation with Finnur was not entirely clear. She was sure he had said *we*. *We* can't justify how we received these recordings, and so on. She had assumed that *we* had meant himself and the special prosecutor. Now, it seemed more than likely that Finnur had never stated clearly that this oddly unconventional investigation was being carried out with their superior's knowledge.

Her phone rang again in her pocket.

'Did you just apply for a warrant to intercept Ingimar Magnússon's phone?' Finnur's deep voice demanded as soon as she answered.

She leaned against the clock tower's sunny side. There were so many questions she wanted to ask him. 'Good to hear from you, Finnur,' she said. 'There's a lot that we need to discuss. And, yes, I've just left the district court. I decided to act on my own initiative on this case, considering you stabbed me in the back just now by pretending to know nothing about it.'

'Please tell me you're joking,' he said, his voice low, almost a whisper.

'I know we generally never get much out of monitoring a landline, but—'

Finnur interrupted her and she could hear his voice tremble. 'You don't apply for a warrant to tap Ingimar's calls. You just don't do that. Go and cancel the application, right now, before all hell breaks loose! Shit, shit, shit!' He put the phone down.

101

The summer sunshine greeted them as they went out through the back door with the bicycles. Tómas looked so adorable in his mush-room-shaped cycle helmet that Sonja couldn't stop smiling. She loved this time of year – the still evenings, the midnight sunshine and the smell of new grass in the air. Her whole body was sore from the beating she had received, but she would be able to manage a short bike ride.

Agla was at the stove inside, cooking up something or other. She had said that she needed an hour's peace and quiet to finish cooking. Sonja had explained that she was still full after the lunchtime soup, and Tómas would be happier with boiled pasta and a squirt of tomato sauce than anything more complex. But Agla had been adamant, so they decided to cycle down to the playground.

Tómas took a few alarming swerves before he mastered the steering well enough to keep his balance, and Sonja wheeled her bike behind him and around the corner of the building. There stood a large, black jeep with darkened windows.

'I'm inviting you for a drive,' Rikki the Sponge said as he opened the back door, just as if he were a taxi driver.

'Sponge!' Tómas yelled happily, dropping his bike, running to Rikki and throwing his arms around him.

Sonja felt a sudden surge of nausea, so strong that she felt she was about to faint. There was something about seeing this man lifting up her son and spinning him around that revolted her. Tómas was already clambering into the back of the jeep.

'I won't get in a car with you, you bastard,' she hissed at Rikki, loud enough that she didn't have to get too close, but not so Tómas overheard. 'Tómas, come on, we're going for a bike ride, aren't we?' she called to him, and Tómas peered out of the car with his eyes flashing in confusion from Sonja and back to Rikki.

'You're going to a meeting,' Rikki said and gestured for her to sit in the back.

Sonja shook her head.

'Sebastian sends his regards,' Rikki said and stared at her with determination.

'Sebastian?' Sonja stood for a second and stared at Rikki in amazement. 'Sebastian sent you?'

'Sebastian sends his regards,' Rikki repeated, and glanced over at Tómas. 'And we'll grab ourselves an ice cream while your mum's having a meeting.'

Tómas whooped in excitement and was already announcing the combination of chocolate and vanilla ice cream he had in mind as Sonja took a seat next to him.

102

Húni Thór Gunnarsson, read the engraved script on the gilded plate on the letterbox. Sonja read the lettering twice to be sure she had not misread it, and paused on the steps while she made up her mind whether or not to knock. The shiny nameplate, the patterned flowerpots on the steps and the net curtains in the windows gave the impression that an elderly lady lived in this house, and not the man the gutter press liked to refer to as a political star. She had no idea what Húni Thór might want with her, or how he could be linked to Sebastian. Húni had been at school with Adam, and they had met a few times at parties and reunions, but she had clearly made little impression on him as he hadn't recognised her when they had met outside Thorgeir's office one time.

Sonja's heart sank. Thorgeir. He had to be the link. She had once asked Thorgeir how he knew Húni Thór, and his answer had been that he managed his election funds. But maybe the connection went deeper than that. Could Húni Thór be the connection between them all?

Sonja knocked lightly, then saw the doorbell and rang that as well. She heard the echo of a series of sentimental notes inside the house – it was as if they came from far-off church bells. They were still echoing when Húni Thór appeared at the door.

'Hi,' he said. 'Come on in.' It was a dispassionate but informal greeting, as if they had been acquaintances for a long time, but weren't close friends.

She followed him through the hall and wondered for a moment if she should take her shoes off, but decided against it as they were clean and dry, and she wanted to be able to beat a rapid retreat if she needed to. Her body was beaten and bruised, but was still ready to react fast, should the situation require it.

'Sebastian said that you're up for it,' Húni Thór said as soon as they reached the living room. Sonja quickly scanned the room around her and could hardly believe the motley array of furniture. The heavily upholstered brown leather sofa, which looked to be a few years old, clashed badly with the antique gold-and-white coffee table and the bright-red retro Westinghouse fridge at one end of the living room clashed jarringly with everything else. Húni Thór looked the type who would want to have everything around him white and minimal. He was a slim man with well-cut hair and a short, neat beard, wearing a suit that looked to be from the more expensive end of the range.

'What the hell do you have to do with Sebastian?' Sonja asked, genuinely surprised.

Húni Thór stood in silence and looked at her, as if he was trying to work out if she knew more than she was prepared to admit. He went over to the red fridge, opened the door and took out two beers. Sonja took the beer he handed to her and reflected that she would have to practise drinking beer more often. Everyone seemed to want her to drink it these days.

'It's best if you know as little as possible.' He spoke in a low voice, but with a weight to his words that had Sonja's belly tensing up. 'All you need to know is that, if you do this, then we're right behind you.'

'And who is *we*?' she asked quietly. The fear that had been her almost constant companion was back, returning so strongly that her voice was reduced to a whisper. A frightened soul in a battered body was how she thought of herself at that moment. It didn't matter how hard she struggled, the net she was caught in would always close in on her.

'Sebastian in America and me on the Europe side,' Húni Thór said and lifted his beer.

Sonja lifted hers as well, raised the bottle to her lips but didn't drink from it. 'Sebastian said that if I do it, then I'll be free. Completely.' Sonja could hear the suspicion in her own words.

'Your games have caused us so much trouble that personally I'd be delighted to be free of you. Adam said it was your pal in customs who pulled his guys at Keflavík. And on top of that, you got your girlfriend to have Adam locked up. It's actually brilliant on your part, I have to admit.'

Sonja wondered which question to start with. What was Húni Thór's real part in all this? What did he mean that Agla had got them to lock Adam up? And how did they know about Bragi?

'Can you guarantee that Adam will leave me in peace?' she said. This was the most pressing matter: Tómas's safety – and hers. 'And can you make sure he lets me have custody of Tómas?'

'No problem,' Húni Thór said, finishing his beer. 'Just let us know if you need anything else.'

Sonja felt faint and her knees became weak. She sat heavily on the leather sofa. This could be the solution. If this man genuinely had the power he hinted at, and could keep his promises, then she could have the solution to all her problems in her hands. Achieving her own freedom was down to her, and her alone. That was a terrifying idea.

'Why do you think I'm capable of doing this?' she asked, the question for herself as much as for Húni Thór.

'You're as hard as nails,' he answered. 'I know you were the one who killed Mr José. I've seen the video. You don't seem to be frightened of anything.'

If only you knew, Sonja thought, trying to stop herself trembling as an image flashed before her eyes: Mr José in a pool of blood while the hungry beast roared in the basement.

'I'm not on the video killing him, just helping Nati clear up after someone else did.'

'That's what you say,' Húni Thór said with a roguish smile and a wink.

103

Tómas felt his cheeks flush as their neighbour pinched one and told him what a sweet little boy he was. He and his mother had knocked on her door to show her Teddy and to make sure it was all right to keep him. Mum had said that it was a rule that you had to ask the neighbours if they minded you keeping an animal in the building.

'Tell me about it,' the neighbour had told his mother. 'These beasts become part of the family.'

Tómas wanted to contribute to the conversation. He wanted to explain that Teddy was practically his brother, so that she wouldn't be able not to keep him. But there was no need for him to say anything.

'He's more than welcome as far as I'm concerned,' she said, so she had to be a good person. She always had something pleasant to say to Tómas whenever they met on the stairs, and sometimes when he was staying she had knocked on the door to bring him something she had baked. Tómas smiled at her as Mum thanked her, and it was as if Teddy was smiling as well, with his tongue lolling out of one side of his mouth. He was such a well-mannered dog that he sat as quietly as a stuffed animal whenever he was told to sit.

'Is he with you permanently now?' the neighbour whispered to Mum, and Tómas knew that he wasn't supposed to hear, as they were talking about him and not the dog.

'It looks like it's going that way,' Mum said in a low voice. 'My ex is on remand right now.'

There had been no need to whisper, as Tómas knew all about it. His mother had explained that Dad had messed up some of the bank's affairs, so things would be difficult for a while.

'There's no question about it,' the neighbour said. 'Men like him always come unstuck. Tell me about it.'

Tómas had no idea what he was supposed to tell her about, but he was fully aware that his father had come out of this badly. It wasn't good to wind up in prison. He felt sympathy deep inside him as he thought of his father locked away in a little room with bars over the windows, but he did what his mother had told him to do when he was sad; quickly think about something else. It was as well not to think too much about it. It was a lot more fun to think about Teddy, who was now trotting up the stairs to the next neighbour's door. Tómas was so glad to be here, with his dog, and his mother.

104

María marched up the steps outside Finnur's house. She had tried to call a couple of times, after she had gone in confusion into the district court building to withdraw the warrant application to intercept Ingmar's calls, but he wasn't picking up. Several times the previous evening she had got up from her seat in front of the television to try to call him, but with no success. The only thing for it was to curl up at Maggi's side and to try to forget what a lousy day it had been.

It had actually been the lousiest of all lousy days, and today hadn't started well either. Finnur hadn't turned up at work and the special prosecutor looked at her strangely when she had gone to him that morning and asked again and again if he was sure he didn't recall discussing her investigation with Finnur. 'Are you all right, María?' he had asked, but she didn't reply as she was far from certain herself that everything was all right.

She didn't wait for Finnur to answer, but took hold of the handle and opened the door halfway.

'Hello?' she called, and at the same moment Finnur appeared in the hallway. He was dressed in an overcoat, with a scarf around his neck and wearing white trainers with his suit, making him a strange spectacle. A suitcase stood by the door.

'Have you been abroad?' María asked, relieved that there might be a simple explanation for why he had not answered her calls.

'No, I'm *going* abroad,' Finnur replied shortly. 'A long-overdue break. A very long-overdue break.'

'We need to talk,' María said.

Finnur groaned. 'No. What we do not need to do is talk,' he said. 'In fact, it's extremely inconvenient that you're here.'

María looked him up and down. He showed no signs of irritation, or that he was playing some kind of game with her. Her impression was that he was terrified.

'What's going on?' she asked.

'Nothing,' he said and plucked a set of car keys from a hook.

María stepped over the doorstep and shut the door behind her. 'I feel that I have a right to know what's going on,' she said.

Finnur sighed deeply, loosening the scarf around his neck. 'I thought it was clear that this was just between you and me, and you wouldn't discuss it with anyone but me,' he said. 'So you get the special prosecutor mixed up in this, and then go to the district court to get an intercept warrant?'

'My understanding was that you gave me this job so I could develop it into a formal investigation. And that was the step I was taking,' María insisted.

'Those of us who work on criminal investigations start with suspicions or clues and go on from there,' Finnur said. 'And the aim is always to get your suspicions confirmed or disproved. We all admit that most of the time we want the investigation to confirm what we suspect. That's what makes it fun, gives us a buzz; it's the driving force behind what we do. But sometimes, my dear María, just occasionally, it's a very, very bad thing when what you suspect turns out to be right. And this is one of those occasions.'

'I don't understand what this is all about, Finnur.' María was fighting to keep her voice under control, preventing it from rising or cracking under the stress. 'Why did you give me this assignment if this was something I actually wasn't supposed to investigate?'

'Because you always hope to stumble across something that will hold water, something that can't be doubted. But it has to be done secretly, without anyone finding out. That's because the only people you can lay a finger on in this country are losers wearing leather – typical crooks. The real criminals, the big wheels, are protected. And that's something you should be starting to figure out.'

Finnur picked up his suitcase, squeezed past María, and opened the door. María stepped outside and Finnur came after her. He shut the door so the lock clicked and set off quickly down the steps.

'Who is this Ingimar Magnússon, and what's he up to?' she called after him.

Finnur turned and pointed an index finger at her, like a strict teacher. 'You need to forget all this and give your attention to something else. Forget it all. Immediately.'

105

Agla was already at the restaurant by the Nauthólsvík thermal beach and had ordered a chicken salad and made a start on it when María arrived, somewhat later than she had said she would.

'No,' she said brusquely as Agla was about to hand her a menu as she took a seat. 'I'm not here to eat with you.'

'Really?' Agla wiped her mouth with a napkin and looked over at María.

She wasn't as smart and immaculate as usual. Her blouse was creased, she looked as if she had tied her hair back without thinking about it, and had completely forgotten any kind of make-up.

'You're the worst kind of bankster,' María hissed, so furious that she was hardly able to catch her breath.

Agla put down her fork and sipped from her glass of water. 'Is this something new?' she said calmly. 'I seem to recall hearing it from you before, when I was being interrogated.'

'I have the answer to the question I've been asking for a long time,' María said. 'The question of where the money came from to begin with.'

Agla picked up her fork, dug it into the salad and took a mouthful. It was better if she ate while María talked. That would stop her from saying anything.

'I have a theory about all this,' María continued. 'My theory is that you, the chief executive, Jóhann, and Adam conspired to set up a way of sending money out of the country for a certain aluminium company, so it could send the profits abroad and get away without paying tax in Iceland.'

And to get lower power costs, Agla thought, taking another mouthful of salad. Cut-down energy prices were part of the contract with the government, as long as the smelter was run at a loss. But María naturally didn't know that, as the contracts were secret.

'So I reckon that you three, the top guns at the bank, conspired to take the smelter's secret pile of cash and send it around the world, letting it reappear here as foreign investment in the bank, so it would lift the share price.'

Right enough, except that we didn't take the money. We borrowed it, with Ingimar's permission, Agla thought as she chewed. She said nothing out loud.

'Then everything crashed and the money disappeared,' María said and squeezed out a rictus grin that was probably supposed to be a sarcastic smile. 'And that made Ingimar the aluminium king an unhappy man.'

You're smarter than I thought you were, Agla thought as she took another mouthful and chewed patiently while waiting for María to continue.

'But now, after the financial crash, and with no way to launder cash out of the country by the usual methods as you did before, you did Ingimar a favour by inventing a debt for a loan that was never taken.'

Agla flinched. She coughed and took a gulp of water. She hadn't suspected that María had been snapping so close at her heels.

'Pepper, caught in my throat,' she apologised.

But María snorted with derision. 'And now all of the smelter's profits go straight into the overseas parent company's coffers, and that giant company pays no tax in Iceland, because our sweet little smelter that eats up almost all of the country's emissions quota is run at an artificial loss. You must be so proud of yourself, Agla. You really are a national treasure.'

María stood up and was about to march away when she caught her foot against the chair. It clattered to the floor. There was a moment's silence as the diners in the restaurant stopped talking and looked up. María bent over, righted the chair and walked out. Agla felt sorry for her. She had put all her cards on the table but there had been no trump card at the end. She had no evidence, no witnesses, no case to investigate.

Agla pushed the remains of her salad together on her plate and finished it. Her cheeks were glowing, and the shame now always made itself felt in a stinging rash on one cheek, as if she had been just been slapped. But she shook off the feeling. There was no reason to be ashamed; this was how business was done these days, and plenty of theorists had struggled to understand it. The country was wide open – all of its resources were for sale at knock-down prices, and if she hadn't taken advantage of the situation, then someone else would have. That's the way life worked. There was no cause for regret, and she wasn't doing anything that others hadn't done as well.

If María had known that they had also owed a hard-as-nails crime syndicate a few hundred million right after the financial crash, and that only yesterday she had paid off the debt via Adam's account in Tortola, then, maybe, she would have had something to be ashamed of.

106

At Sonja's request, they met at the city library, as she hadn't wanted him to come to her home while Tómas was there. Now that she saw him, she knew that she had made the right decision. He had arrived straight from prison. He was wearing creased tracksuit bottoms, his hair was uncombed and he had stubble on his face. He didn't come across as the man she knew. He even stooped as he walked over to where she sat in the library's reading room by the main door.

'You brought the paperwork?' he asked, sitting down opposite her.

She nodded, handing him the documents. He glanced at them, took the pen she offered and signed.

'Will there be dad's weekends?' he asked.

Sonja nodded again. 'Of course there are dad's weekends. I'm not the arsehole you are.'

She regretted being so crude the moment the words had passed her lips, and unusually, there was no vociferous retort from Adam. He merely grunted quietly, as if he agreed with her.

'Maybe we can start after a month or so, once the statements and all that stuff are done, and I'm not likely to be locked up again.'

'Okay,' Sonja said. 'I'll tell Tómas.'

'How did you explain it to him?' Adam asked, looking up for the first time to meet her gaze.

'I told him that you had made a mistake at the bank.'

'A mistake?' Adam looked relieved.

Maybe he had expected that she would have told Tómas some horror story about him, but that hadn't even occurred to her. While Tómas was angry with his father, she had no desire to feed the fire of his anger, knowing that this would only hurt Tómas even more.

'That's right. A mistake,' Sonja said, half expecting him to thank her.

But he shook off his dejection and gave her a teasing smile. 'How's it going with the dog?' he asked.

Sonja couldn't help returning the smile. 'It doesn't do any harm to have a coke-sniffing dog about the place,' she said, although if everything were to work out, it was unlikely that the dog's talents would be required; Teddy's role would be simply as a household pet. If the plans were to pan out and she could live up to Sebastian and Húni Thór's expectations, then there would be no more coke business or anything linked to it in her home.

Sonja took the papers and stood up. 'Goodbye, Adam,' she said.

'Bye,' Adam responded, and she had the feeling that for the first time she was genuinely saying her goodbyes to him, and that once she had walked out of the library, Adam would really belong to her past.

On the street outside she tapped Thorgeir's number into her phone, and listened to him answer sleepily. She could visualise him still wearing the same grubby dressing gown.

'Can you get me some Rohypnol?' she asked, then repeated the question when he sounded puzzled. 'Can you get me a dose of Rohypnol that's enough to put an elephant out of action, and drop it into my postbox?'

'Yeah, no problem,' Thorgeir said. 'When do you need it?'

'As soon as possible,' Sonja replied.

'I didn't think you lesbians went in for that sort of thing,' he said, then he put the phone down.

107

The Voice of Truth was nowhere to be seen. Instead, a couple of broad-shouldered men in blue overalls and dust masks were carrying everything out of his apartment on Grettisgata.

María approached the entrance, but didn't go too close as the foul smell that had previously hung around the door seemed to have been magnified as the stuff that was now filling up a skip of the largest size available was shifted.

'Is Marteinn here anywhere?' she asked one of the men in blue.

He put down the black bag in his hands and lifted the mask from his face. 'No. He's in the psychiatric ward, yet again. So we're taking the opportunity to get rid of all his crap.'

María winced. He had told her that if he were to be locked up in a psychiatric ward again, it would be her fault. But she could hardly be held responsible. Judging by the junk that was being carried out, the man was completely mad.

'Are there any of his relatives or friends here?'

'We're just contractors. But I could try and call the city offices for you and try to find a contact, if it's important.'

'No,' María said. 'I was just going to give him back something that he lent me.' She held up the folder containing his information about the smelter.

'I reckon you can just sling it into the skip. We're clearing everything out,' the man in blue said.

'Everything?'

'Yep. There's mould growing on everything, or so I'm told, and there are silverfish everywhere. The whole place needs to be fumigated, so we were told to get rid of the lot. Environmental health.'

'I understand,' María said and smiled as the man nodded and replaced his mask before returning to his task.

She stood in confusion on the pavement, unable to decide whether or not to take the folder away with her, when her phone rang.

'Hello,' she said.

'Hello,' the special prosecutor replied and then began to cough. 'It all seems to be coming to a head,' he announced at last.

He sounded uncomfortable and María could almost see him in her mind, pacing the floor as he always did when he needed to concentrate.

'All what?'

'Let's not play games, María. You know what I'm talking about. This solo effort of yours.'

'There was nothing solo about it,' María said. 'I was carrying out an assignment in good faith, something that Finnur asked me to work on, and as far as I was aware, it was with your knowledge.' She didn't say she had always harboured her own doubts about it. There had been an uncomfortable feeling inside her the whole time, but she had suppressed it because she wanted the assignment. She had given in to the wayward side of herself that she always fought so hard to tame. She had let her old self take control.

'That's a ridiculous thing to say and we won't go into that any further. I'm just calling now to tell you that you're on leave.'

'On leave?'

'Yes. On full pay, of course.'

'For how long?'

'Well, let's say it's indefinite. Other people will take over the tax-evasion case you were working on, and also the market-manipulation case of yours that came up, involving Adam. We'll see if this becomes clearer in the next weeks and months, but I'll naturally understand if you decide to look around for another job.'

'So what this comes down to is that you're firing me? Is that what you're saying?'

'It's not worth taking this personally. This can happen to people in this line of work – that they lose direction.'

María ended the call. It went without saying that he would never fire her; that was more dramatic and would attract attention. Sacking someone had to be justified. But placing someone on indefinite leave pending an investigation was more dubious and more of a problem for her.

Lose direction was what he had said, and maybe that was the problem. It could well be that she had lost her bearings and wandered into making a mistake; a mistake from which there could be no escape.

She walked over to the skip and hurled the Voice of Truth's folder into it. One of the men in blue appeared right behind her with a plastic bin full of paper that he emptied into the skip, burying the folder. This insignificant event suddenly seemed symbolic. The folder disappeared into the rest of the junk, becoming one with it all, so it was impossible to make it out in the pile.

María felt a sudden exhaustion, as if she had just got off a bicycle at the end of a long trip. She sat down on the pavement. There was a crack where the tarmac met the kerb, where one of spring's heralds – a small dandelion – had forced its way through: it had two leaves and she could see that it was about to open; there was the slight glitter of the yellow flower head. She reached out and was about to pull it up, but decided against it. The weeds would always grow back. Their roots ran so deep.

108

Bragi sat for a little while in the car outside the house, taking in the sight of the ambulance and the police car parked in the driveway. There were no blue lights and nobody was in a hurry, as there was no reason to hurry when a sick and elderly woman had parted company with life.

He had been driving along Reykjanesbraut on his way home when Amy had called in tears, saying she had been unable to wake Valdís after her afternoon nap. He had remained calm, had called for an ambulance, and it was only then that he realised that he had long been ready for this moment.

Now that he sat outside the house it was a relief that it had happened as it should have, as he had wanted it to. Valdís's life had ended in a secure and loving environment, in their home, in the house where they had lived for a quarter of a century, and in the best possible way. It was every elderly person's wish that death would come quickly and in their sleep. He hadn't expected this right away. He had imagined that it wouldn't happen for a few months, even a year, and he had always imagined that he would be at her side.

His knees almost gave way as he walked the short distance to the front door. The pain had somehow been magnified, as if Valdís's existence had been a panacea, which was now gone.

'Would you like to sit with her for a while before the undertakers get here?' the amiable police officer asked Bragi once he had hugged Amy, who was still weeping silently, and had accepted a cup of the coffee that the policeman had been thoughtful enough to make.

'Yes,' he said. 'I should say goodbye.'

He went into the living room and lowered Valdís's hospital bed down to its lowest setting so he could sit on the bed beside her. There was nothing to tell him that she wasn't just sleeping deeply, other than a blue tinge to her lips and the fact that her slim frame seemed to have wasted away to something even thinner. He reached for the hairbrush on the bedside table, unpicked her braids and gently brushed her hair. This silver hair had once glowed golden in the sun of their honeymoon in Italy and he had delighted in holding handfuls of it as they had romped on the hotel bed, making what would be their first child. His heart lurched. He would have to call the children sooner or later. They would have a long journey ahead of them from Australia.

For a moment it occurred to him to be sorrowful over how long it had been since they had come to see their mother, but he shook off the thought. It had been a long time since she had last recognised anyone, and they were busy with their own lives. They had their own children and loved ones in another country.

Bragi brushed her hair until the silver waves flooded over the pillow. Then he stood up and kissed her; first on the forehead, then each cheek and finally her blue lips.

'Goodbye, my Valdís,' he whispered and wiped a tear from his eye. 'Thank you for everything. I'll see you again on the other side.'

At least, so he hoped. If the afterlife in which Valdís had believed so firmly was a reality, then his lifelong record of trying to be a decent man might be enough to make up for his short and late-in-life criminal career. He was at least certain that Valdís would put in a good word for him with the Almighty.

109

'I want pizza,' Tómas said and pointed at a line on the kids' menu. 'Margarine pizza.'

Sonja smiled. She didn't correct him as she always felt it was so sweet when he said margarine instead of *margarita*. When he had announced his choice, he stood up and headed for the toilet. He had already drunk a large glass of pop, so there would be a few visits to the toilet over the next hour. Agla gazed at Sonja with a dreamy look on her face, as she had done over the last few days since she had found her beaten and helpless on the floor. It seemed that she had finally decided how she could be around her – what her role in her life was: her protector. Considering the condition Sonja had been in when she had found her on the floor, it was as well for her to be spoiled a little.

'Shall I get anything more for you?' Agla asked, pointing at the salad bar from which Sonja had already helped herself generously.

'No, thanks. I'll wait for the steak,' she said and sent Agla a smile, which she returned.

She had only recently started smiling; it was something Sonja would have to get used to. They gazed into each other's eyes for a while, and Agla pinched her leg under the table.

'Which of us is the guy?' she giggled. This was clearly set to become a standing joke between them. Agla always brought this up when she was in a good mood, in a mood good enough to let herself be teased.

'You're the guy,' Sonja said firmly.

'Really?'

It never made a difference what answer Sonja gave to the question, Agla never seemed to be satisfied.

'Yes,' Sonja said and leaned close to her to whisper. 'You're normally on top, you know, when we finish. So you're the guy.'

'But when I think about it, then I don't reckon I am the guy,' Agla said.

'You realise this is like asking a pair of chopsticks which one's the fork?'

'What?' Agla stared at her with a look of confusion on her face, but there was no opportunity to take it further as Tómas came back from the toilet and sat at the table.

The next time Agla asked the question, Sonja would claim to be the guy, and the next time after that she'd change her mind again, and so it would go on until Agla would be exasperated, and might even realise that stupid questions invite stupid answers.

'I've decided to pack in my work.'

'The computer work?'

'That's it. I've had enough of computers. I can't be doing these endless foreign trips now that Tómas is living with me.'

In her mind Sonja had prepared a speech about network servers and content management systems and software services. She always did this whenever Agla asked her exactly what it was she did, and then Agla would give up; just as she always gave up as soon as Agla started talking about bank stuff. But this time the speech wasn't needed, as an eager look appeared on Agla's face.

'I think...' Agla said. 'I think that's sensible. Like I've told you often enough before, it's ridiculous that you're working so hard when I'm in ... yes, well, what shall I say? The position I'm in.'

Sonja knew that this was what Agla had dreamed of, to keep her, to own her.

'I might need to accept some help from you,' Sonja said, 'if I drop this work.'

'You know that I'd be delighted to, Sonja. As I've told you before.' It was obvious that Agla was choking back her excitement, while her thoughts were in overdrive. 'Would you like it if I bought a house?' She hesitated. 'For ... us?'

'Maybe,' Sonja said. 'Let's think it over.'

Agla's smile stretched from ear to ear.

'But that doesn't mean you own me,' Sonja added, and Agla shook her head and raised her hands in front of her. 'I know. I know.'

'Can I have more Sprite?' Tómas asked and before Sonja could reply, Agla had already called the waiter and ordered it.

Sonja smiled to see Tómas looking so happy with his fizzy drink, and no less to see Agla's look of contentment. She tried to hide it, but could feel her heart soften for a moment, not with the passion of love or with any kind of anticipation, but more with a slow, sweet happiness that seeped through her veins gradually, like the melting ice in spring, searching the land for a channel.

She felt her phone vibrate in her pocket. The gentle happiness gave way to a jolt of fear and tension that gripped at her heart like an ice-cold fist as she looked at the screen and saw the message was from Nati.

London. Saturday. Limpet ready.

'Can you look after Tómas for me over the weekend?' Sonja asked.

'What?' The question clearly took Agla more by surprise than the answer to the *who's the guy?* question.

'I have to travel for a couple of days. It's my last trip abroad now that I'm packing it in.'

'I don't know how to look after kids,' Agla said.

'I'll show you how to look after me,' Tómas said, with an expression of expectation on his face. He undoubtedly saw a luxurious weekend ahead with sweets and endless games.

'All right, then,' Agla said. 'We should be fine.'

110

The first time Sonja had stood in front of this dark, heavy wooden door, the house had made her shudder. Once she had become acquainted with the people who lived there and the vicious animal they kept in the cellar, she had been afraid to venture inside, but now terror had rendered her virtually immobile. The things she had done in this house – cleaning up what seemed like an ocean of blood, stuffing a body into a freezer, arranging for it to be sawn into pieces and fed to a tiger – all that now seemed like child's play compared to what she was here to do. Whatever happened today, this would be the last time she would go through this door. This day would decide her fate.

Amadou opened the door and the hinges squealed piercingly as Sonja wondered once again when Mr José and Nati had deliberately neglected oiling them to make entering this place an even more spooky experience. She said nothing to Amadou, but their eyes met for a second as they shook hands and as she relaxed her grip. The package of Rohypnol remained in Amadou's grasp.

'Sonja! *Mi amor!* Welcome!' Nati whooped as she entered the living room.

She stood up and embraced Sonja, kissing her on the mouth, her lips wet. Sonja smiled awkwardly and turned her face away, while Nati refused to take no for an answer, taking her face in both hands and holding it while she kissed her several times more. Sonja had discovered the last time, when there had been no choice but to spend the night there, that Nati had no objection to overcoming a little resistance. On the contrary, she found it exciting.

The room had been redecorated yet again; now there was a thick white carpet on the floor, and the room had been scattered with heavy, blocky furniture with a retro seventies feel.

'Very smart,' Sonja said, looking around.

Her judgement clearly delighted Nati. 'I always wanted to be an interior designer,' she said. 'Maybe I should take a few courses. It's never too late to get some education.'

She dropped back into a deep sofa and Sonja took a seat on a chair facing her. It was higher than the sofa and the tension in her was such that she couldn't let herself sink into such soft comfort.

'It's never too late,' Sonja agreed, squeezing out a smile.

If Sebastian's plan, which was now also her plan, was to work out, then it was definitely too late. The echo of the tiger's growls down in the cellar added emphasis to her thoughts.

Amadou brought coffee and placed it on the table between them. Nati poured and Sonja took her cup, lifting it to her lips without drinking.

Nati took a long drink from her cup and cleared her throat. 'The limpet is here, but the rubber leaks and it'll take two days to fix,' she said and laughed out loud. 'I'd like to see the legs of the guy who made it now!' Her laughter felt as if it cut through flesh and bone.

Sonja's body reacted with a flush of heat and she felt the sweat breaking out on her upper lip, as if she sensed that this laughter was the precursor to something much worse to come. Nati had laughed a lot the night that Sonja had stayed with her. 'And I have a diving teacher for you. You'll meet him tomorrow at the aquatic centre.'

Sonja looked around the living room as if she was checking out the new decoration, giving Nati an occasional glance. She seemed to have drunk half of her coffee now.

Amadou put his head discreetly around the door, the second time that he had taken a look, and Sonja hoped that Nati hadn't noticed. As Sebastian had said, he was too nervous to take on anything major by himself, plus he only had one hand.

Nati finished her cup and put it down. Sonja saw her look at her own cup, notice that it was untouched, and for a moment there was a questioning look in her eyes. Sonja decided to take her attention in another direction.

'Do you know a guy called Húni Thór?' she asked, and saw that her aim had been achieved. There was no doubt that Nati knew Húni Thór and she didn't like the subject.

'Why do you ask?' she asked sharply.

Sonja shrugged. 'I was just wondering what his connection is to all this,' she said. 'He was at school with Adam.'

'Húni Thór is one of those men who finds it difficult to have a woman as his boss,' Nati said, her lip curling in disgust.

'Really?'

'Yes. He never had a problem doing what José told him to do, but since I took over, he has been taking too many liberties.'

Sonja smiled. It confirmed what she had suspected: a power struggle.

'Excuse me for a moment,' Sonja said, getting to her feet and going out into the hall, where she locked herself in the guest bathroom.

Her heart was hammering in her chest, so she sat on the toilet and took a series of fast breaths to drive the oxygen up to her brain.

Now she would have to wait for a quarter of an hour. In her mind, she counted up the profit side, all the things she would gain by carrying out this assignment: *Security, freedom, peace of mind, Tómas. Security, freedom, peace of mind, Tómas.*

After flushing the toilet and letting water run into the basin for a good while, she hyperventilated a few more times, and then jumped on the spot, both feet together, as she counted up to a hundred to warm herself up for the coming exertions. Then she opened the door and went out into the hall.

Amadou was nowhere to be seen and there was no sound from the living room. She tiptoed to the door and peered in, ready for action, almost as if she were expecting the tiger to be roaming around. But another growl from down below conformed that the beast was still in its place, locked away in its cage in the cellar. She had nothing but her own weakness to fear.

'It's a question of whether you're a wolf or a rabbit,' Sebastian had said when he had outlined the plan for her. 'And rabbits don't live long in this business.'

Sonja stealthily made her way into the living room, every fibre in her taut and her senses more aware than ever before. She was no rabbit. She was a bigger animal, ready to rip its enemies apart to protect its young. She was more powerful than a wolf and more fearsome than the tiger.

She was an ice bear.

111

Nati was still on the sofa, but had slid to one side and a trickle of clear saliva had leaked from the corner of her mouth into her glistening black hair.

Sonja approached her cautiously, and Nati's eyes followed her. Sonja was surprised at how clear her eyes were, that Nati was obviously wide awake; fully conscious, even though her body had been paralysed.

Sonja took the nylon cord from her pocket, tied it into a loop and placed it around Nati's neck. Nati's eyes widened and Sonja felt an urge to say something, to explain to Nati exactly why she was about to take her life, but there were no words that could justify this. This was just what it was: murder.

She sat on the sofa at Nati's side and tightened the cord around her neck. Nati muttered something unintelligible, but made no movement until Sonja hauled on the cord with all her strength. A series of powerful tremors passed through Nati's body. Sonja fixed her eyes on the ceiling and pulled as hard as she could.

Security, freedom, peace of mind, Tómas, she thought, avoiding looking at Nati's eyes or the paralysed hands that occasionally clenched as if they were vainly trying to catch hold of some lifeline, some hope; these hands that had in their own sly and soft way done Sonja more harm than bunched fists ever could.

A wave of hatred snatched at her heart, and it was followed by exhaustion. The power of a polar bear she had felt before had evaporated, her strength was gone and her eyes filled with tears. She let go of the cord and as she did so, Nati coughed and her lungs fought for air. Sonja could not kill another person. The life in this paralysed body was stronger than all her own accumulated fear; stronger than all the hatred.

'I can't do it. I can't make myself finish this,' she sniffed as Amadou came into the living room and stared at Nati taking eager breaths, and his dark face filled with desperation.

112

No words passed between them. It was as if their eyes spoke. Sonja rolled herself into a ball on the floor, unable to remain close to Nati as she lay, paralysed and coughing, half on and half hanging off the sofa. Somehow she pushed herself backwards with her feet, further and further from Nati and the clear eyes that watched her, neither accusing nor frightened, but beseeching. With her back to the wall at the far end of the living room, she finally lost control and screamed with all the energy left in her. She had no control over her voice, the fear and pain inside bursting out of her. There was a release in her scream, a physical relief, and her screams continued as Amadou crouched over Nati on the sofa, took hold of the cord with his one hand and pulled it tight.

Long after Nati had stopped jerking and her eyes stared lifelessly upwards, they sat in silence in the living room – Sonja still on the floor, while Amadou straddled Nati's corpse, the cord still looped over his hand. The sweat had dried on his face, rendering his dark skin matt as the yellow street light outside came to life and its brightness illuminated him.

'I'm free,' he whispered cautiously, as if he dared not believe it himself. 'And so are my children.'

'She had her claws in your children as well?'

'Her claws were in everyone's children. I tried to find *her* children for Sebastian, but she keeps them in a boarding school and moves them regularly to keep them safe. But she always knows where everyone else's children are, and she always said she could have my children snatched.'

Sonja closed her eyes. Now she was also free. She had finally been let go. The moment she walked out of this house, the last two years would be behind her and she could go back to being an ordinary person leading an ordinary life, with Tómas and maybe with Agla. And now she could even give Agla a proper chance.

'The freezer and the tiger?' Amadou asked.

'Yes,' Sonja said. 'And don't be tempted to keep the head.'

Amadou giggled, and glanced at Sonja, and their laughter overflowed. They looked into each other's eyes and roared with laughter. There was madness in their mirth, and Sonja still felt that there was a cloud hanging over her that prevented her from putting her thoughts in order. She looked from Amadou to Nati's corpse and back, laughing as the tears rolled down her cheeks. It wasn't exactly Nati or her fate that she cried for, but regret for a part of herself that had been lost forever.

113

'Parmesan or ordinary cheese?' Agla asked.

'Ordinary. Kids like ordinary cheese,' Tómas replied in the mature, pedagogic tone he had used all weekend whenever she had found herself at a loss.

She had never babysat as a teenager, as her friends had done, but instead had spent her hours outside school over the photocopier of a large accountancy firm. That was where she had learned a great deal – from reading the annual reports of a variety of large companies. But she had never picked up any of the finer points of handling small children that many people imagined were something that women were born knowing.

She put Parmesan on her own slice of bread and ordinary cheese on Tómas's.

The weekend had worked out well. She knew all about boys and easily worked out what he enjoyed doing, so they had watched football on TV, taken the dog out for a walk a couple of times, and played first snap, then rummy and snap again. He had spent hours on end on the floor with his Lego bricks, so she had peace and quiet to deal with the overseas accounts and check out property websites. She had found a few houses that she thought Sonja ought to take a look at.

Now they were sitting opposite each other at the little table under the kitchen window when the doorbell rang and the dog set off barking for the door.

Tómas stopped chewing and a look of fear appeared on his face. 'Who's that?' he asked, staring at Agla, his mouth open and still full of sandwich.

'I don't know,' Agla replied, getting up to answer the door.

An older woman wearing a beige coat and a silk scarf over her hair-do, as if she had been sent from the seventies, stood in the hallway. Teddy ran in circles around her and sniffed urgently at her shoes.

'I'm Sonja's mother,' the woman said. 'I'm here to collect Tómas.'

Agla stood for a moment and stared at the woman, who glared back at her. There was a clear likeness to Sonja: she was a handsome woman, but her lips were tightly pursed and deeply lined, which her lipstick served only to highlight.

'Can I offer you some coffee?' Agla said. 'I've just made some.'

The woman hesitated, clearly unsure of what to do next, but finally shook her head. 'No,' she said. 'I'm just here to collect the boy.'

Agla looked her up and down. There was no way she was going to hand the child over to this woman. Sonja would never forgive her that. But neither could she slam the door in her face, as she had no wish to make relations even worse between mother and daughter. The last thing she wanted to do was to make darker the painful shadow that passed across Sonja's face when she mentioned her mother. So Agla decided to fall back on the negotiation tactics that had always served her so well at the bank: a mixture of firmness and flexibility that would give her the final victory in the matter without the other party realising quite what had happened.

'Sonja hasn't said anything to me about anyone taking over, so I'll have to call her. But come in and say hello to Tómas.'

'Hi, Granny,' Tómas said from behind Agla so that the woman's face softened and the pursed lips curled into a smile. 'There's coffee here,' he said taking his grandmother's hand and pulling her inside.

Agla poured a cup for her and placed it on the kitchen table alongside the carton of milk. 'Please help yourself,' she said, gesturing for the woman to take a seat.

She seemed to hesitate, glancing suspiciously around. Agla sat down with a feigned calmness, and picked up her phone to select Sonja's number, knowing that it would go straight to voicemail.

'Sonja's not answering,' she said. 'She's flying home. Tómas and I are going to the airport later to pick her up.'

'It's best if I don't stop,' the woman said, without sitting down. 'Tómas, you're to come with your grandmother.'

Tómas looked at the two of them in confusion and unconsciously sidled behind Agla, where she could feel that he took a handful of her blouse and held on tight. Her heart swelled for a second. That tiny movement on his part was so important – that he should seek safety behind her lit a fire in her heart.

'Tómas, won't you go to your room and get the Lego monster you made, so you can show it to your grandmother?' Agla said, and he raced out of the room to escape the situation. Agla got to her feet and took one step closer to the woman, who instinctively stepped back. 'Tómas isn't going anywhere without Sonja's permission,' she said in a low voice. 'Now that she has custody, you need to negotiate with her if you want to see Tómas.'

'You can't negotiate with someone who leaves their child with a person of your type,' the woman snarled.

It would pay to accept the other party's point of view as valid, for the moment. 'I can understand that you might have concerns,' Agla said. 'Of course, my face has been all over the newspapers, and the coverage has been less than pleasant. In fact, the same applies to your son-in-law, Tómas's father. I take it you've heard all about that?'

'That's why I'm here!' the woman spat. 'Tómas needs a capable person to bring him up, considering his father has given him up because of his problems.'

Now it was time for a gentle approach to sway the other party's opinion. 'Sonja loves her son more than anything, and that works both ways. Tómas loves his mother, as all children do, and children should be with their parents.'

'With their parents, yes! And what does this so-called parent do? Leaves him behind with an immoral financial criminal!'

'I've managed to look after him pretty well,' Agla said. 'He goes to sleep early and I put ordinary cheese in his sandwiches.'

Now Tómas was standing in the doorway with a Lego edifice in his hands that he had been thoroughly proud of that morning, deciding that it was a monster.

'Take a seat, please, and let Tómas show you what he made with his Lego bricks this morning.'

Tómas went to his grandmother and handed her the mass of bricks as she sank onto a chair.

'Drink your coffee while it's hot,' Agla said.

There was nothing more she needed to do. She had won. Defeat could be seen in the woman's body language. Now she would leave peacefully and maybe even feel that she had achieved something. It could well be that the cup of coffee here at the kitchen table could be a step towards mother and daughter becoming reconciled.

'The way you live...' the woman muttered, glancing sideways at Agla, not quite ready to admit defeat, but Agla decided to take her comment as an observation on Sonja's sparse apartment.

'I'm working on buying a house,' Agla said, giving her a warm smile.

114

Reykjanes was mostly grey and yellow, even though spring had certainly arrived, with pale-green patches of pasture to be seen down by the sea. The lava fields that filled the peninsula, covered in a thin layer of moss, seemed hardly to change from one season to the next.

Sonja sat in the window seat as the aircraft approached to land, her head against the glass, enjoying swooping over the landscape; and for the first time in almost longer than she could remember, with nothing to deliver. She was free.

But freedom had a different feel to it than what she had expected. There was a strange lethargy inside her, along with the delight, as if these two emotions were oil and vinegar in a bottle that could only be mixed with a great deal of effort – and even then, there was no guarantee which taste would be the stronger. That was what Sebastian had told her in that little ante-chamber in the mausoleum in Mexico.

'You'll never be the same person again,' he had said. 'Everything changes when you kill someone. And that's the price of freedom.'

At the time she hadn't paid attention to what he had said as she was too occupied with the technical side of his proposal.

'You're the only one she lets come close without a bodyguard,' he had continued.

'Except Amadou. You could get Amadou to do it,' she had said.

'Amadou is useless. He'll be so stressed out he'll get drunk and blab the whole story. And he only has one hand.'

Sebastian had undoubtedly underestimated Amadou. There had been an unbelievable strength in that one arm as he had tightened the noose around Nati's neck. Sonja shook off the thought. Nati's face in the throes of death had come back again and again to haunt her, and it had been all she could do to turn her thoughts elsewhere to something joyful before the gloom took too strong a hold of her. Now she was safe and she was free, and she would constantly remind herself of that. She hoped that time would work in her favour. She would think of it in such a way that, when Agla had to go to prison, she would be sitting out a sentence for both of them. She herself had already served a long enough sentence, even though it hadn't been a formal one, surrounded by prison walls.

From now on she would pay her taxes on time, never park in front of a hydrant and never give in to the temptation to cross a junction with the lights on amber. And then, gradually, life would hopefully forgive her.

'This is about business interests,' Sebastian had said. 'There's a deal between me and the Icelander to split things between us once Nati is out of the game. He looks after business in Europe and I handle America. Mr José had promised me America and I had my own routes, and then Nati persuaded him to start this Iceland connection, and my business became chaos. Then she murdered the old man and was going to start using limpets and all kinds of things!'

'Killed the old man? It was Nati herself who murdered Mr José?'

This took Sonja so completely by surprise that she didn't wonder who the Icelander he had mentioned might be, simply assuming him to be Adam, not Húni Thór. She had not even thought about what he had meant by the limpet until a few hours later.

The jet's wheels touched down on the runway and Sonja switched on her phone. It pinged an alert to tell her there was a message. Although she knew immediately it could not be from Bragi, now that he was on compassionate leave following the death of his wife, she still started in alarm. But her heart softened with fondness as she read the message.

Agla and Tómas had come to fetch her. In a few minutes she would walk through the terminal without feeling the slightest apprehension over customs, and wouldn't even think of the shipment of coke that was still somewhere above the false ceiling in the corridor toilet at the airport. It would be an insurance if she were ever to need it.

Outside the terminal Agla and Tómas would be singing along to an ABBA CD in the car. She would plant a kiss on each of them – maybe even a couple of hefty ones, and driving along the long Reykjanesbraut road into town they would all sing along.

She would choose the first song, as she was the one who was coming home from abroad.

She didn't have to think hard what it would. She'd choose the same one as always:

'What's the Name of the Game?'

Acknowledgements

Iceland, being an island far up in the North Atlantic, sometimes feels further away from the rest of the world than it actually is. The Icelandic language, while ancient and beautiful, is spoken by very few people, so writing in it means writing for a small readership. For Icelandic writers therefore, getting their books translated into a big language like English is very important, because it offers them a precious opportunity to present their work to more people.

My acknowledgements go to my publisher, wonder woman Karen Sullivan, and her extraordinary team, who have made the publication of *Snare* and now *Trap* an adventure. Editor West Camel has been my rock in the editing process, and I am very grateful for his help, always put forward with care and insight. My translator, Quentin Bates, one of the very rare Icelandic speakers in the world and a skilful crime writer himself, has of course been the key to getting this novel into English. Our collaboration has been inspiring, fun and without a single stormy moment.

Once a novel has finally been published in English, the process of marketing it begins, so I am very grateful to all the people who take an interest in and promote translated crime fiction.

I want to thank all the crime writers, Icelandic, Scottish and English, who have been so wonderfully welcoming and supportive, giving me encouragement, quotes and help. I am in awe of your generosity. In particular I want to name my sister – in crime only – Yrsa Sigurðardóttir, whose support has meant so much to me.

Last but not least I want to thank the readers who have read *Snare* and who will now read *Trap* in English. Thank you for taking the chance on a new author – at least, one who is new in your language. I hope you enjoy this book.